JERUSALEM SYNDROME

RICHARD MARSDEN

The right of Richard Marsden to be identified as the author of this work has been asserted in accordance with the Copyright, Designs and Patents Act 1988.

All rights reserved. No reproduction, copy or transmission of this publication may be made without written permission. No paragraph of this publication may be reproduced, copied or transmitted save with the written permission or in accordance with the provisions of the Copyright Act 1956 (as amended). Any person who does any unauthorised act in relation to this publication may be liable to criminal prosecution and civil claims for damage.

First published in 2001

Paragon Press-Publishing, Suite 676, 37 Store Street, Bloomsbury, London WC1E 7QF
ENGLAND

E-Mail: info@paragonpress-publishing.com

Paperback ISBN 1-84199-031-0

To Kinsy

JERUSALEM

"I was glad when they said unto me,
Let us go into the house of the Lord,
Our feet shall stand within thy gates,
Oh Jerusalem"

Psalm 122

CHAPTER 1
The Beginning (February 1999)
Flight LY 318

Christ, I'm bored.

The flight to Tel Aviv had been uneventful - no turbulence - and the in-flight meal of goulash and zucchini with its accompanying wine and a cup of coffee had been and gone for some time. I was feeling very tired and dry, feelings I suspected that were shared by the others in my row of the Boeing 737; Robin, the tour organiser, Barbara his wife and the Minster priest, Derek who also happened to be my father. I picked up the complimentary copy of *Jerusalem Today* given out by the stewardess at embarkation and started leafing through the pages. It was the previous day, Friday's edition and I briefly wondered if it wasn't printed on the Jewish Sabbath, Saturday. The headlines were dominated by the anguish in Kosovo and the Kurdish backlash against Israel following the death of three Kurdish rioters after they failed to storm the Israeli embassy in Berlin. Then at the bottom of page 3 a headline caught my eye, which read:

"*Members of the Philadelphia Doomsday Cult are in Israel*".
I began to read the article:

> "*Ten members of the missing Philadelphia Doomsday cult are in Israel where the cult's leader has predicted he will die in December of this year. Joshua Fisher III, leader of the Caring Christians, expects to be resurrected three days later as he allegedly considers himself to be one of the witnesses of the Christian book of Revelation, that gives the biblical account of the end of the world. However, the Jerusalem police, who have established a special taskforce to prepare for the influx of pilgrims during the millennium estimated at millions, said the group does not yet pose a threat to themselves or others but were continuing to monitor the situation. As many as 65 of Fisher's followers sold their belongings and left their homes in the US prior to October 20, of last year, the day the leader predicted Philadelphia would be wiped out by an earthquake marking the beginning of the Apocalypse, as described in the book of Revelation.*"

"What do you think of that, dad?" I asked, passing him the paper.

"Not a lot," he replied, having read it briefly. *Typical dad answer.*

"What is it?" enquired Barbara.

"I'm not sure but it seems that some fanatical bunch are in Israel from the States ready to getting the old millennium party off with a bang."

"What do you mean?"

"Well according to this," I said pointing at the article, "the leader of this Christian group is going to induce the Apocalypse."

"And what are they called, this group of Christians, if that's what they are?"

"Hold on, I just read it, oh yes the Caring Christians. Well he's predicting that he's going to die in December in Jerusalem and so provoke the Apocalypse." I read out the article.

"Oh, I wouldn't worry about that," Robin joined in the conversation, "people have been predicting the end of the world for well, probably since the beginning of the world." *Ah, a Genesis believer.* "They crop up now and again," Robin continued. "Remember David Koresh and the Branch Davidian at Waco. His name wasn't David Koresh, it was Vernon Howe and he was little more than a mouthy handy man who managed to take control of the Branch Davidian when his predecessor went crazy."

"I didn't realise you know about these things," said Barbara, turning to him.

"No I don't, not really, not a lot anyway."

"What else do you know of David Koresh?" Robin was more interesting than I had originally thought.

"Well the Branch Davidians broke away from the Seventh-Day Adventists in the 20s which was all related to the Second Coming, I think. Seventh-Day Adventists believe in the imminence of the coming of Christ. David Koresh was a Seventh-Day Adventist but nobody seemed to like him apparently because he was so mouthy. The name David, he took from the Kingdom of David, Koresh is something to do with a King of Babylon. I'm not sure. Anyway when the Waco thing happened, the FBI and that customs firearm enforcement agency, or whatever they were, listened to a bunch of psychiatrists who said that the likelihood of self-harm was minimal as opposed to the cult experts who said the chances of self-harm were high." I was amazed that the tour organiser was into Christian cults and his wife didn't know. "When the FBI went in, Koresh was writing a sermon on behalf of God which, supposedly, when it was complete and listened to he was going to give the game up. But the FBI thought that they had waited long enough and that probably provided the catalyst of destruction that took place. No one really knows. Well somebody does but nobody's telling. The Branch Davidians believed Koresh to be the Lamb of God, not just Jesus Christ and those few that survived either think he's on the way back or are otherwise attempting to sue the authorities for trauma." Robin sat back in his seat.

"Well really, Robin," commented an amazed Barbara, "you really come out..." she never finished her sentence. Dad had his middle fingers on his lip, a sign he was deep in thought.

"What about that bunch who tried to hitch a lift on the comet?" I asked eagerly leaning toward Robin. He leant forward,

"Oh yes, they were from Heaven's Gate an off-shooter of previous cults. I'm not quite sure what happened here but it is something like this. There are two witnesses in the Revelation, like it said in the newspaper article, you know, what's his name, Joshua something, believed himself to be a witness. Well Heaven's Gate had two spiritual leaders called Ti and Do or something like that. Ironically they believed themselves to be the two witnesses of the Revelation which means, if you include that chap in the paper, we now have three witnesses. One too many. Anyway Do happened to be a bloke called Marshall Applewhite and his partner was Ti and I think she died in the 80s from cancer. But that wouldn't have bothered them anyway, as the Heaven's Gate belief is that the human body is a temporary container of one sort or another and between containers you zip around the universe on a UFO, or something like that." Barbara was tutting and Robin looked embarrassed. "After the woman died," Robin continued, "Applewhite became more severe and demanded the same of his followers. Allegedly he become kind of wrapped up," and he stole a glance at Barbara, "in his alleged homosexuality. Unlike the Branch Davidian the culture of the cult was suppressed in gender and sexual activity." He clearly had made this speech before. "Anyway," he went on, "eventually the decision was made that they no longer needed their containers and decided to jump ship, so to speak, on the orbit of a comet which they believed to have a UFO in its tail ready to pick them up, or something like that. I think the UFO was supposed to depict a higher level of heaven for those of course who believed in it."

"Hale Bopp," said dad, lowering his fingers from his lip.

"Sorry dad, what did you say?"

"The comet," he replied "the comet was called Hale Bopp."

"Then of course, there was Jim Jones...." Robin began.

"Well, Robin, I really think that that's enough Christian cults for one flight thanks," Barbara interrupted and he settled back again into his seat, satisfied with the opportunity. I also settled back into mine and considered what kind of person it is that can enable a group of people to commit mass suicide; charismatic, dominating, as in the case of Applewhite, sexually extreme, (either suppressed or promiscuous), grandiose and undoubtedly sick. And then I considered what I was doing here myself, an agnostic, with 49 middle England Christians heading for a whirlwind pilgrimage around the Holy Land with a personal agenda to find psychosis; and psychosis, in its extreme, was exactly what I found.

My name is Sebastian, Seb to my friends and this is my tale of religion and pilgrimage and perception and psychosis.

"Ladies and gentlemen, this is Captain Zelkine again. We will be making our final descent into Ben Gurion airport shortly. Temperature Tel Aviv is a modest 17 degrees and the local time is now 5.10. On behalf of all the crew I would like to take the opportunity of thanking you for choosing El Al and trust you will have enjoyable and interesting visit to the State of Israel. Goodbye." The seatbelt and no smoking sign flicked on and the aircraft descended into the early morning blueness that was Israel.

II
Derek phones Seb at work

Christ, somebody must be dead. Dad seldom phoned me at home, let alone at work.

"Hi Dad" I replied, unable to hide my surprise to both my father and the other people in the conference room grouped around the magnificent mahogany table for the 10.15 meeting.

"Is somebody dead?"

"No, what makes you think that?"

"I'm not sure really, just surprised to hear your voice I guess. Is everything ok?"

"Yes everything is fine. Are you able to talk?" he continued.

"No, not really, I've got people here you see. I'll phone you back in half an hour or so. Is that ok?"

"That's fine but can you make it this morning."

"Yea sure, I'll speak with you soon." Dad hung up.

"That was my dad", I announced rather foolishly to the rest of the group as I turned towards the table. No one showed the slightest bit of interest. "Somebody must be dead," I continued to which one of the group, a man from Sierra Leone (who was worried about his family at home) answered unemotionally, "I doubt it," and so the meeting continued.

An hour later I phoned back.

"Hi Dad, it's Seb. Is there a problem?"

"No, there's no problem, Seb, I'm actually phoning to enquire whether you would like to accompany me to Israel in February. We could go on pilgrimage together."

I briefly paused, taken back by the question.

"I don't know, dad, you've caught me off guard. I'll need to talk with Laura first, but you know if she's ok and the hospital's ok, then maybe this would be fine."

"When do you think you'll know?"

"I guess tonight. I can clear things with the hospital today and talk to Laura later on. Remind me when it would be?"

"February," he answered. "February, 1999"

"I'll phone tonight, ok."

"Ok, but make sure you do. I spoke to Robin and he says there aren't many places left so the quicker the better."

"Don't worry," I answered, "I'll phone."

I hung up and briefly thought of the events of the previous month. Dad was a priest at Stowton Minster in the heart of rural

Warwickshire. He had not always been a priest, it came to him late in life after years in insurance, but eventually he managed to manoeuvre the dogma and doctrine of the Church of England to become a respected member of the clergy in the Minster with a particular leaning towards the pastoral needs of those about to die. A year before he, with my mother, Mary, had undertaken a pilgrimage to the Holy Land with 50 other worshippers from the Diocese that the Minster was the spiritual heart of and took in a manic, whirlwind tour that covered Jerusalem, Galilee and the Judean desert, returning with such enthusiasm that he recommended, with huge support from Mary that myself and Laura should go on the next one.

The prospect of going on such an event, whatever the conflict and history, to myself, an agnostic, was daunting. Laura much bolder in her religious outlook through her passive support of Western Atheism was horrified.

"We're not going. We can't possibly. How can we sit on a coach for ten days with fifty religious crazed semi geriatrics? I just can't do it," she barked in the car back to London from Stowton. "Who'll look after Jack anyway. Mary? My mother? We can't do it, Seb."

"Don't worry, don't worry. We won't go. You're right we've got other commitments. I've got this South London thing taking off, haven't I?" I reassured her formulating my excuses at the same time. "I don't think they'll give me the time off work anyway. I'll phone him in a day or two and knock it on the head."

A couple of days later, however, through the letterbox dropped the itinerary for the pilgrimage sent to us from Robin, the tour organiser and his wife, Barbara who I had met at the previous week's service at the Minster.

"They're pretty serious," I mentioned to Laura over breakfast. "I must say it looks interesting, Jerusalem, Galilee, Nazareth." Laura took the itinerary off me and briefly browsed the pages.

"Look, Seb, it does look interesting, I agree. But it's the sort of thing we could do together when we are older, when Jack's left or something. You know my feelings at the moment. Ring Derek will you. Let's just get it sorted." So that night I rang him.

"Dad, thanks for the itinerary," I began.

"Don't thank me, thank Robin," he answered.

"Well I will next time I see him."

"Well?" Dad enquired "What do you think?"

"Look Dad, we would love to go but we just can't at the moment. I've checked things out at work and they're concerned about the South London project. Laura is worried about Jack. Really it looks fantastic, it's just the wrong time."

"Oh never mind, Seb, it doesn't matter. Another time." He sounded disappointed.

"Of course, another time. As I said it looked fantastic." We chatted on for a few more minutes and then hung up.

"How was he?" Laura asked

"He was fine about it," I replied. "Absolutely fine," and that we thought was that.

III
Seb makes a decision

High summer passed into autumn and we heard no more about it. Then with the country bracing itself for winter the phone call to work arrived.

"You have to let me know soon though Seb, because Robin says there are only four places left."

"Look dad, I'll phone you tonight. Let me check out a few things first," I replied stalling for time. The South London project had collapsed, Laura could look after Jack and I didn't have the bottle to turn round and say, "Look dad, this simply isn't my thing."

I decided to go and though I didn't realise it - how could I ever have predicted what was going to happen – I was soon to witness a tragedy, borne out of one tiny sentence to an Essene called John preaching at the Jaffa Gate, *"That's a lot of responsibility"*, that caused a man to lose his head.

When I told him that night he seemed pleased. For a moment I felt pleased with the opportunity to share some time with him.

"Right, I'll give Robin and Barbara a ring and get back to you when it's confirmed. By the way this is on mum so say something to her." I was genuinely touched and unfairly considered what was on her agenda. Laura was more concerned. In the seven years of our marriage we had spent very little time apart. My work takes me away for a couple of nights occasionally and Laura sometimes takes Jack to see his grandparents, Tom and Ingrid, in tranquil West bay when I am particularly busy. Once, at the beginning of the relationship, I toured France for 10 days on a railcard with a very unstable person, the sole memory of which I have is of him abusing nuns on a night train from Nice to Biarritz. We were headed for the world surfing championships. They were returning from the pilgrimage to Lourdes. We both had a miserable time. And now the prospect of us being separated for another 10 days filled us both with a degree of dread borne out by a love that is deep, excluding and at times selfish.

IV
War with Iraq

In December the allies started bombing Baghdad from its bases in Italy and Turkey. There were also reports of a deterioration in relationships between Israel and The Lebanon over, unsurprisingly, a border dispute and Tel Aviv was regularly on 'gas mask' alert. In other words the situation in the Near East and Middle East as 1998 became 1999 was destabilising and I flirted with the thought that, outnumbered 49 to 1, not only would I do well to psychologically survive but the prospect of getting there and back in one piece may actually be an achievement in itself. This is somewhat irrational, now I look back, now that the horror is over, for horror is what it was. Indeed it is disrespectful, but there is mitigation in understanding how these thoughts are provoked and that, in essence, is through my cosy suburban middle class Englishness. Dad did not share my concern. In a conversation with Laura one evening on the phone, Laura talked of her worries about the fast approaching trip. Dad remarked casually, "Well, you've got to lay your bones somewhere."

CHAPTER 2
Saturday (Winsmoor Hill – Wood Green – Heathrow – Tel Aviv)

I
Seb goes to the shop

I woke on the Saturday of departure with a headache. Laura and myself had followed our usual Friday routine of a disco with Jack, a romantic meal after he had gone to bed, and then a drunken game of chess which invariably Laura won despite my finely formulated and conceptualised drunken strategies. I lay in bed cursing my hangover particularly on a day when I had to fly. My brother-in-law, also called Jack, and myself share a common irrational fear of flying. Once in the 80's he managed to get himself to San Francisco but couldn't get home due to this fear. After being stranded for six weeks there was a massive earthquake, one of San Francisco's worst and it was only then that he could confront his fear and board a plane. Whilst my reasoning is slightly less damaged in this area I don't feel comfortable travelling at 35,000 feet in the hands of some stranger. Give me a train any day. This is of course about control or more essentially lack of it and the thought of nursing a sore head and nausea in some part of the stratosphere did little to help my confidence.

I was not due at Heathrow until 7 that evening. The pilgrims were to meet at the Minster at 1.30 for a blessing service and to celebrate communion prior to boarding their coach and driving south. I would link up with them at the airport so I had plenty of time to sort out my head. Jack was already up and playing 'The Legend of Zelda: Ocarina of Time' on his Nintendo 64 which Father Christmas had given him and which Jack had become unhealthily obsessed with. As usual we had no painkillers so I walked to the small, we sell everything shop, on our road and picked up a packet of Neurofen, some bacon and a copy of 'The Independent'. It was a beautifully cold, bright day and the inevitable queue of cars were beginning to assemble to dump their rubbish in the recycling centre across the road from our house. For those who are pre-occupied with social position, it could be argued that we might live at the wrong end of Winsmoor Hill. A cousin of mine, who, at some point in his youth, had lived in Ayr once described to me that in the West Coast town you either lived on the right side of the railway bridge or the wrong side of the railway bridge. However, the local population believed that the side they lived on was the right side to live on so both sides of the bridge were the right side and the wrong side at the same time.

"Looking back," he reflected to me on a recent trip to London for a football match between Tottenham Hotspur and Nottingham Forest, "I suppose I was on the wrong side of the bridge but there again I can't be sure. A lot of old nonsense", and, of course, it was nonsense.

II

Winsmoor Hill

Winsmoor Hill lies nestled between Enfield in the north and Wood Green to the south. Locally it is thought that the name derives from the moor at the top of the hill on which the whin (gorse or furze) grew, thus Winsmoor Hill. It is an affluent part of London and the population gets a certain materialistic satisfaction out of demonstrating this affluence to the poorer communities on the other side of the Great Cambridge Road and the North Circular. It is a smug, pseudo, toffee-nosed community that both physically and psychologically looks down on its neighbours. The journalist, Will Self took the piss out of it in one of his early short stories for its smugness and deservedly so. There is a reasonable cultural mix, particularly Greek, Italian and Turkish and this is reflected in its restaurants and shops. Up on the green are the biggest properties with their swimming pools, tennis courts and mock Gothic colonnades, rumoured to be homes or the second homes of reclusive stars. They must be reclusive because you never see anyone famous in Winsmoor Hill, but as you fan out down the hill from the green, the housing becomes more modest urban spillage until if you travel south you reach our cottage style (estate agents lingo for small) home, built at the turn of the century to house nursery workers whose nurseries have long since vanished. In the 50s they, whoever they were, decided to close down the outdoor swimming pool opposite our home, developing it into a badly managed rubbish incinerator, before environmentalists, on the wave of the green explosion, succeeded in having the incinerator knocked down and the site developed into a much better managed recycling centre.

III
Downloading

When I arrived back at the house I took a couple of Neurofen and made bacon sandwiches for the three of us. I also took a couple of Neurofen, a poorly made cup of coffee, (for some reason Laura thinks I make crap coffee), and a sandwich up to Laura in bed and turned on my computer.

"Lousy coffee," she moaned, "I'm going downstairs to make another one. I'm going to get myself ready." This meant that Laura wanted to make love and when she came back upstairs with the fresh coffee (it looked just the same as the cup I had made), I was already erect at the prospect. We fucked each other unusually hard, I suppose in recognition of our fast approaching separation and comfortable in the fact that Jack was completely absorbed in Zelda downstairs. When we had finished our lovemaking I returned to my computer. I had been monitoring the political situation in Israel though the Foreign Offices' 'advice to travel' website. It hadn't changed over the past months reflecting that things had generally settled down, though it did however advise UK citizens travelling independently to the country to report their presence to the British Embassy. Following that I downloaded from the Encyclopaedia Britannica information on the sites indicated on the itinerary sent to the pilgrims by Robin and Barbara. I decided that, unlike dad on his first trip, I did not want to go completely ignorant and chose to make up a file which I felt with my Rough Guide would probably be enough. So I downloaded information on Tel Aviv-Yafa, Jerusalem, Bethlehem, Bethany, The Mount of Olives, Mount Zion, Gethsemane, The West Wall, Masada, The Dead Sea, Qumran, Jericho, Nazareth, Mount Tabor, Beatitudes, Capernaum, The Sea of Galilee, Tiberius, Mount Carmel and Caesarea.

IV
Jerusalem Syndrome

There is a psychotic phenomena as old and holy as Jerusalem itself which is characterised by people, during the course of a pilgrimage to the Holy City, believing that they had become biblical figures and often predicting, to whoever would listen, the second coming of Christ. The condition is generally temporary though occasionally fixed affecting mainly Christians and, once it has passed, often causes severe embarrassment to the sufferer. This phenomena, called Jerusalem Syndrome, is thought to be caused in those who have had no remarkable past psychiatric or social experiences by some sort of cognitive crisis rising out of the conflict between the mental image of ancient Jerusalem and the chaotic realities of the modern city.

In the build up to the trip there had been a noticeable increase in the reporting of Jerusalem Syndrome in the western press. This was linked to the end of the Millennium and the Israeli government's concern of the rise of sufferers with the syndrome reported by psychiatrists in Jerusalem, with millions of people being drawn to the city to celebrate what they consider to be the 2000th anniversary of Christ's birth. However, many sufferers of Jerusalem Syndrome also believe that the millennium will be the time of Christ's return to earth, which they generally agree will be somewhere on the Mount of Olives. The problem with the Second Coming of Christ is also, of course, that it may be considered by some as representative of the end of the world and so the authorities were increasingly concerned with a small group of sufferers who were prepared to assist the apocalyptic process, that group of people, psychiatrists would say, who act on their delusions to the detriment of themselves and others around them. The press had reported an increase of threats of violence at the point of the millennium from numerous unstable and diverse individuals and more alarmingly, group threats, such as the one from an ultra Christian band operating out of the bible belt of North America, whose primary objective was to convert all Jewish people to Christianity through whatever means they could. A kind of modern day Inquisition, I suppose.

For many weeks I had been struggling how I would survive my time away from Laura. Initially I followed dad's idea of going completely ignorant allowing myself to deal with the conflicts as they cropped up then I moved to the other extreme wanting to know all and everything but quickly realised that was impossible. It was a case of balancing knowledge with mystique, so compromise was needed and Jerusalem Syndrome became my angle.

V
Seb gets a lift to Wood Green

After lunch I started packing Mary's sturdy suitcase that she had insisted I use. I wasn't quite sure what to pack. Israel's weather in February can be as diverse as its cultures and whilst it may be burning hot 400m beneath sea level at the Dead Sea, 30 miles to the west on the higher grounds that Jerusalem proudly sits on, snowflakes may be falling. I decided chinos were the best option with t-shirts providing layers as needed, no jeans or shorts, not flexible enough. In my new, blue Christian Loving Dove bag, provided by the tour operator with the words emblazoned on one side and the logo, a white loving dove, on the other, I packed my money belt with the usual travel documents, traveller's cheques, credit cards, some shekels, a pair of binoculars, my camera, the 'Rough Guide to Israel', a black file containing the information I had downloaded earlier on, a packet of biscuits, (McVities digestives), a small bottle of water, a can of Kronenberg 1664 and 'The Last King of Scotland', a novel about Idi Amin that I had already read but decided to read again. I planned to pick up a sturdy notebook and a couple of ball pentels at Heathrow but forgot and in the end salvaged a flimsy, loose leaf and Bic off dad on which I kept my record of the trip.

As the afternoon wore on I found myself becoming more anxious. I took a Stella from the fridge and went out into our small garden. The day was still glorious and the garden shared its glory. My brother-in-law, he who can't fly, had spent the previous summer recycling the garden from a monotonous concrete slab into a spectacular cacophony of colour. We now had rockeries, flower beds, herb gardens and vegetable patches. In the flowerbed, 100s of spring bulbs shoots of Crocus and Daffodil were testing their environment. One, deciding that the time was right, had blossomed into a small yellow and golden flower; it looked really vulnerable.

"When I get back you'll have a few more mates," I said to the flower and immediately felt a bit foolish. I turned around, went inside and took some Valium that Laura had stolen from work.

At precisely 4.30 Forest went 2-0 down and I said to Laura that I felt it was time to leave. We had had some thought about Laura and Jack dropping me at Heathrow but decided against it. Instead they would drop me at Wood Green where the Piccadilly line runs south from Cockfosters into Central London before heading west and onto Heathrow. I sat in the back of our Rover with my sturdy suitcase and my Loving Dove bag and we chugged along Green Lanes and its plethora of Turkish, Greek, Jewish and Muslim shops through Palmers Green and into Wood Green. Wood Green was heaving with early evening shoppers. Looking at the shoppers it struck me people seem to go to Wood Green for one primary reason, to pick up a bargain. This seemed to be reinforced by the number of bags that weighed down the shoppers, generally not bags of large chain stores but those of individual cheap and glitzy boutiques who are supplied by the equally cheap and glitzy suppliers that line both pavements of Fonthill Road in Finsbury Park. Laura eventually drew to a stop at the tube.

"Well baby like I said, when I get myself sorted out I'll give you a ring in a couple of days or so." Laura was struggling, I was struggling. I quickly unloaded the case onto the pavement careful not to bang into the shoppers, their frayed tempers and then the obligatory curses. I leant through Jack's window, gave Laura a kiss and then Jack.

"Take care of Jack," stupid thing to say, "and you, you take care of mummy and I'll see you in 10 days." I stood up and Laura drove away. I watched the car disappear slowly into the distance along with the rest of the shoppers, picked up the case and entered the station.

VI

A strange affair on the Piccadilly Line

I expected the tube to be busy but it wasn't. Arsenal were playing a cup game against Sheffield United and I expected it to be swamped at the old Gillespie Road station by Gooners, but Arsenal station was empty. I eventually learnt that extra time was being played so they were all still in the ground awaiting an outcome. I took my Rough Guide out of the Christian Loving Dove bag and turned to the chapter on drugs, not that I do drugs anymore, well not illicit ones anyway. But I guess it acts as a poor indicator about tolerance within a society, if there is such a thing. The guide told me that mainstream Israeli and Palestinian society was extremely conservative in their attitude towards illicit drugs and should the urge take me and I wanted to start peddling over the next 10 days then I would be sent to prison if caught. It then went on to advise me that if I did want to take on board some narcotic I should stick to yat, a mild stimulant brought to Israel by Yemeni Jews and quite legal. I rested the guide on my knees, gradually felt my eyes grow heavy, toyed briefly with the thought that maybe the Stella and Valium hadn't been such a good idea and drifted into sleep assisted by the gentle, rolling movements of the train.

"Sebastian, Sebastian, walk to the Green Hill. It's easy, through this Gate of Judgement and follow the path."

"Why do you want me to do that?" There was no answer so I walked out the gate and followed the path to the Green Hill where a man was being crucified.

"Why are you here Sebastian?" a voice says behind me, "Why are you here?"

I turned around and saw a woman dressed in blue robes and behind her another woman.

"I don't know why I'm here, I was told to."

"By who Sebastian?"

"I don't know."

"Who told you to come to Christ's crucifixion?"

"I don't know."

"Well now you're here you better stay."

"Who are you?"

"Who do you think I am, Sebastian?"

"I don't know."

"Haven't you been reading your bible?"

"No."

"Why not?"

"I'm an agnostic."

"Oh, you're an agnostic, did you hear that Mary, he's an agnostic."

"I heard it."

"Well who are you?"

"Have a guess."

"You're his mother."

"Yes that's right."

"His Virgin mother."

"On no Sebastian, that's not right at all."

"Virgin mother!" the other woman screeches.

"What do you mean 'that's not right at all?'"

"*Exactly that, I'm not the Virgin Mary.*"

"*But the Bible says.....*"

"*Oh you shouldn't worry about the Bible too much. It's not as it is written.*"

"*So you're not the Virgin?*"

"*No, I haven't been a virgin for a long time.*"

"*But the Immaculate Conception?*"

"*It's impossible, Sebastian. You just can't do it, believe me I've tried. I have lots of children, not just this one dying on the cross.*"

"*So if God's not the father, who is?*"

"*Who do you think?*"

"*Joseph?*"

"*That's right Sebastian, Joseph.*"

"*Is that why Joseph accepted it – you know I never heard him show any jealousy or anything like that.*"

"*Of course.*"

"*And that's why he must have gone to Bethlehem with you, because he loved you.*"

"*Wrong this time, Sebastian.*"

"*What, he didn't love you?*"

"*No, he did love me, it's just we never went to Bethlehem.*"

"*You never went to Bethlehem?*"

"*No, that's made up. Jesus was born in Nazareth.*"

"*But, everybody thinks he was born in Bethlehem.*"

"*I know they do.*"

"*Then, why?*"

"*I don't know Seb, you'll have to find that out for yourself.*"

"*Is that Mary Magdalene?*"

"*Yes, it is.*"

"*Why is she here. Is it because she is a disciple of Christ?*"

"*No.*"

"*Well why then?*"

"*Why don't you ask her yourself?*"

"*Why are you here Mary?*"

"*Why am I here? Let me tell you why I'm here. I'm here because Jesus, up there on the cross,*" and she looked affectionately towards the dying man and whispered, "*he's my husband.*"

"*Your husband, how can that be? I thought you were a whore.*"

"No, I'm not a whore," she smiled," I may have been once but I'm his wife now. I'm getting ready for him...."

"Are you ok, mate". I felt a tapping on my shoulder.

"Sorry," I said startled and turned in the direction of the tapping. I was looking at a man with a stubbly ginger beard and dressed in khaki combat overalls sat next to me.

"I fell asleep. I'm sorry," I repeated.

"You fell asleep alright. Your head was on my shoulder. I think you just asked me if I was your wife," he laughed. "Here, is that your book?" and he pointed to the Rough Guide that had fallen to the floor of the train.

"Yes, thanks," I answered and leant over and picked it up.

"Israel," he said.

"Yeah, Israel. I'm off tonight. A pilgrimage."

"Pilgrimage. Heavy duty. I've been, kibbutz and all that."

"What was it like?"

"Great, great. A place called Ein Gev on Galilee. The Golan Heights right behind it. We used to think the Arabs were coming any moment. Where are you going?"

"Galilee but first a few days in Jerusalem."

The train pulled into Hounslow West and the man got up to leave.

"Jerusalem, heh. You're going to love that. Keep your wits about you."

"What do you mean?" I shouted after him, but he had gone, vanished into the chill of the February night.

VII

Seb arrives at Heathrow

The now near empty train pulled into Heathrow and the station for Terminals 1, 2 and 3. I was early, it was only 6.30. I was due to meet the rest of the party at the El Al (God Air) reception desk at the rear of desk 76, isle N. But Terminal 1 seemed to end at 75 so I sat and waited. Heathrow, like Wood Green was heaving. I took out my Rough Guide and arbitrarily opened it. The author was describing the Mount of Beatitudes where Jesus preached the Sermon on the Mount. He described it as a truly wonderful speech and one that even the 'staunchest atheist would be hard put to read a modern version of the sermon and remain unmoved by its genius even if not accepting its divinity'. I took out the black file from my Christian Loving Dove bag and found the information I had downloaded on the Beatitudes and read the 9 Beatitudes in Matthew.

> *"Blessed are the poor in spirit for theirs is the kingdom of heaven.*
> *Blessed are those who mourn for they shall be comforted.*
> *Blessed are the meek for they shall inherit the earth.*
> *Blessed are those who hunger and thirst for righteousness for they shall be satisfied.*
> *Blessed are the merciful for they shall obtain mercy.*
> *Blessed are the pure in heart for they shall see God.*
> *Blessed are the peacemakers for they shall be called sons of God.*
> *Blessed are those who are persecuted for righteousness sake for theirs is the kingdom of heaven, blessed are you when men revile you and persecute you and utter all kinds of evil against you falsely on my account rejoice and be glad for your reward is great in heaven for so men persecuted the prophets who were before you."*

It struck me immediately that this was beautiful and meaningful. The author of the Rough Guide, who referred to it as a Christian manifesto because the second part of each beatitude contextualises the kingdom of God. However if you consider only the first part of each Beatitude you are left with a manifesto of simply how to behave. The final Beatitude was particularly absorbing and I found myself trying to interpret it. All religions talk of prophets and false prophets and there have been, during the course of history, considerably more of the latter. Until fairly recently society killed their false prophets as heretics, witches, the devil whatever. Jesus was killed as a heretic by his own people. The Romans only ensured the sentence of the guilty verdict was carried out. At least that is what I thought. It is also likely that a number of these false prophets were psychotic or, in biblical times, filled with demons. *Did Jesus' society think he was filled demons? Did Jesus' society think he was psychotic?*

I looked up and saw Robin, the pilgrimage organiser stood in front of me.

"Robin," I said getting up from my seat. He looked at me blankly; he didn't recognise me. "It's Sebastian, Sebastian Carrington," I said holding out my hand. He blinked his remembrance.

"Oh Sebastian hi, hi, you got here okay?"

"Yeah, no problem. I came on the tube along the Piccadilly line. I slept most of the way. I couldn't find point 76 so I just hung around here at 75. Presumably dad's with you?"

"Yes he is, last time I saw him he was over there somewhere," and he waved vaguely in the direction of a car hire company and a Bureau de Change.

VIII
Seb and Derek are interviewed

I walked off in that general direction with my two pieces of luggage and joined dad chatting away to one of the group, a pleasant middle aged woman desperately attempting to cling on to her youth but failing. She was called Jan, she told me, something that I had already worked out from her name badge that all the members of the group were wearing. I fumbled in my pocket for mine and pinned it onto my jumper. It said 'Loving Dove Christian Travel' and then, in my father's best handwriting underneath, 'Sebastian Carrington'. For some reason dad had filled my name badge in and posted it to me, but I couldn't remember how that came about. I guess it isn't that important.

"You got here OK then?"

"No problem, I fell asleep. I had a strange dream about Mary Magdalene. At least I think I did. Do I know anyone dad?"

"No, not a soul."

"Do you know anyone?"

"Oh, one or two," he replied and turned to resume his conversation with Jan. I looked around to the assembled group. They were not as old as I thought they were going to be. There were married couples, small groups of women friends accompanying each other, one family of four, a couple of widows and a father and son. Everyone in the group was white. This was, I thought, religious middle England where conservatism and the power of the church still reigned supreme.

"What would make you dream of Mary Magdalene?" Jan interrupted my thoughts. I briefly contemplated telling her a concoction of anxiety, agnosticism, lager and Valium could have provoked such a dream but quickly dismissed it.

"I don't know, Jan, I really don't know," I lied.

And then there was the Bishop and his wife. He was a slight man dressed in a purple frock with his obligatory dog collar, a crucifix around his neck, smart chinos and perched on top of his head a Trilby that gave him the look of the two tone mod era. He seemed also to be smoking a Café Crème, (wasn't Heathrow a non-smoking environment?) and between inhalations he coughed a deep rasping hack that suggested the Bishop was not a particularly well man. Attached to the Bishop was his wife, a squat woman with a round face and glasses. Every time the Bishop moved she moved with him like a magnet. Divine Siamese twins and almost immediately I said to myself "and everywhere the Bishop went his wife was sure to go." All the members of the group had their Christian Loving Dove bags strung over their shoulders.

At 7.30 Robin called the group together to check into the flight and we followed him to the first security check of the evening. A queue was forming as the pilgrims passed through the metal detectors and their cases were conveyed through the x-ray machines. At random the customs men stopped some people on the other side and the contents of the cases were inspected. The pilgrims collected their smaller belongings from the x-ray machines and cast nervous glances at the suitcases being searched. I felt a tap on my shoulder. It was a customs man.

"Can you come with me, sir. Let's see if we can speed this up a bit."

"Do you want me to bring my suitcase, it's on this trolley". Dad was pushing the trolley with our two sturdy cases.

"No, just bring yourself and your hand luggage," he answered and he led me through a door to my right. Once through the door was again a security channel but it was completely empty. The two of us weaved through the channel to the desk, I put my hand luggage through the x-ray machine and I walked through the detector. It didn't go off.

"That's fine, thank you, sir. You may go on," and I walked over to the other security desk where the pilgrims were continuing to be randomly checked. I could see dad some way down the queue and it was a good hour before he emerged with Jan with the suitcases.

"That was odd," I said to him.

"Yes it was odd," he replied and we carried on to the El Al check in desk. The check in desk was actually a room on its own halfway between security and the departure lounge. The pilgrims were queuing up in orderly fashion outside. Every so often a young Israeli would come out of the room and ask a pilgrim or a couple to come into the room with them.

"Part of their national service I expect," said dad. "They're going to ask us a few questions before we can hand our cases over." Eventually our turn came. A pretty blond woman, a little older than 20 with her hair tied back and clinically dressed in blue and grey came out of the room.

"Are you two together?" she enquired smiling,

"Yes we are," dad replied.

"Could you follow me then," and indicated for us to enter the room. The room, like its employees, was clinically dressed in blue and grey. It wasn't particularly large but packed with little podiums on one side of which would be a pilgrim and on the other side a smiling young Israeli offloading questions to the bemused recipient.

"Now let's see, uh there's a free one. Please come with me," and we marched across to the only free podium in the room. I felt like a quiz show contestant. I was once in a quiz show. I did it to see what it was like. In the rehearsal I couldn't get anything but in the actual contest I blew the other contestants away and only marginally failed to win a holiday to Malta because I couldn't remember the name of Edward VII's wife.

"Ok, let me explain this procedure," she continued still smiling. "This is all part of security. Security and your security are of a particular importance to the state of Israel. As part of ensuring your security I need to ask you some questions. Is that ok?"

"Fine," we answered in unison.

"Ok here we go. First of all your luggage, did you pack the bags yourself?"

"Yes," we both replied.

"Have you always been in attendance of your luggage?"

"Yes," again.

"Have you left your luggage at any point between packing it and now?"

"No."

"Have you opened your luggage up between packing it and now?"
"No."
"Are you aware of what is in your luggage?"
"Yes."
"Are you carrying any weapons either on you or in your luggage?"
She smiled at us. "No," we answered.

"Are you carrying anything that may be used as a weapon, a can opener for instance?" "No," said dad. I tried to think if I had anything that may be used as a weapon and then concluded "No."

"Are you sure?"
"I'm sure."
"Where do you live?" she said specifically smiling at me.
"North London," I said.
"Where in North London?"
"Winsmoor Hill."
"Oh near Enfield?"
"Yes that's right, near Enfield."
"Are you married?"
"Yes."
"Do you have children?"
"Yes, one."
"What is your relationship with this man?"
"He's my father."
"What do you do for a living?"
"I'm a Hospital Manager."
"What's the hospital called?"
"Grenton."
"What sort of hospital is it?"
"It's a forensic psychiatric hospital."
"What does that mean?"

"It means we look after people who have broken the law because they were mentally unwell when they committed the crime."

"What sort of crimes?"
"Well, a wide range I guess."
"Give me some examples."

"Burglary, theft, drug dealing, sexual assault, criminal assault, ABH, GBH," I paused and then added, "murder". She was quiet but still smiling. "Are you a doctor?"

"No, I'm a hospital manager. I do however have a clinical background. I trained as a nurse a decade or so ago." She turned to dad.

"And where do you live?"
"Warwickshire."
"What do you do?"
"I'm a priest."
"Why are you going to Israel?"
"Tourism."
"Have you been to Israel before?"
"Yes, once last September."
"Why are you returning so quickly?"
"My son wanted to go and asked me to accompany him." That's interesting I thought to myself making sure I didn't register my surprise to the woman.

"When you were last there, did you go on your own?"
"No. In a group much like this," dad answered waving his arms around the room at all the other pilgrims.
"Did you ever leave the group last time?"
"No."
"Did you meet and converse with others outside of the group?"
"No."
"Do either of you intend to leave the group at any point in this visit?"
"No," we answered.
"Where are you staying?"
"In the Knights Templar Hotel in the Old City in Jerusalem and then the Restile Hotel in Tiberias," dad informed her. I didn't have a clue where we were staying.
"Do you know anyone or of anyone in Israel?"
"No," dad answered. It occurred to me that I did know of someone who lived in Israel. His name was Jimmy and he was Laura's mother's cousin. During the second world war he had been a fighter pilot for the American airforce but after some kind of accident, maybe he was shot down, I'm not sure, and uncle Jimmy sustained some form of brain injury. After the war he lived in Minneapolis before moving to London where he had plenty of contact with Laura and the rest of her family and made a living out of wheeling and dealing on

the financial markets. Then in the mid 80s he packed his belongings and set up home in Tel Aviv and refused to leave for any reason including the illnesses and subsequent funerals of both his mother and father, his only son's wedding and the birth of a grandson. The family speculated that he probably couldn't leave for political reasons; he was a spy or something. However, Jimmy wrote a book about the end of the world due to a comet striking the earth and we should all shut shop and go to live on another planet, a bit like the American B movie 'When Worlds Collide'. The book was published and it struck Laura and myself that uncle Jimmy may be psychotic as opposed to the espionage theory that the rest of the family clung to.

This was reinforced when a few weeks before the pilgrimage Jimmy amazingly turned up in the United Kingdom with his fourth wife, fifty years his junior, for the first time in nearly two decades and he called on Tom and Ingrid in West Bay. At meal times Jimmy would only eat one item of food that was on offer so when they had Sunday lunch he ignored the roast beef, Yorkshire puddings, roast potatoes and carrots and opted only for the mange tout. At the following day's breakfast he had one slice of bread with no butter, margarine or other preserve. Jimmy said he did this because it improves digestion. This is of course not medically proven therefore the idea he holds is false, a false belief is a delusion and a delusion is a psychotic phenomenon. And thoughts about the end of the world. Could it be that Jerusalem Syndrome already existed in the family, perhaps?

"Do you know anyone or of anyone in Israel?" The woman repeated her question.

"No," I answered wondering how on earth I could explain away Jimmy, possible spy, probably psychotic with interesting thoughts on the alimentary canal and the digestive experiences of the human body.

"Ok this interview is nearly finished just two more things. We are very concerned about bombs. Israel and its people has been the target of many bombs. Remember the Olympics and the suicide squad at Ben Gurion?" She was still smiling. I certainly remembered the Munich Olympics but the suicide squad I couldn't. I later learnt she was referring to a Japanese red army suicide squad working with the PSLP who threw grenades into the custom hall at Ben Gurion airport killing 25 people, mostly Puerto Rican Christian pilgrims.

"We share your concern about bombs," dad responded thoughtfully. "Yes," was all I could think to say, "That's right."

"Are any of you carrying illicit drugs?" *Christ, this is like Knights Move thinking, were jumping all over the place.* "No." The prospect of dad as a drug dealing representative of the Church of England seemed remote.

"Ok that concludes the interview. I would like to thank you for your co-operation and I would like to wish you a good flight and an enjoyable stay in Israel." She positively beamed.

"Thank you," we both acknowledged. As we were about to pull away to the check-in desk I turned round, "Is this part of your national service or something?"

"No, it is not, I live in London, have done for the last four years."

IX

Pilgrims

After that it didn't take us long to check our bags in.

"Right, next stop duty free shop," dad remarked to no one in particular as we left the room. "One litre of Whisky and a litre of Gin I think will do. Take the Gin back for your mum." Dad always bought duty free on the way out with the intention of early evening liveners prior to supper. Robin and Barbara were in the shop and we started chatting to them.

"Tomorrow morning worship at the Holy Sepulchre, what's the state of play with that?" enquired dad of Robin.

"Three line whip I think but I'll check it out with the Bishop," answered Robin.

"Oh blast I hoped I could get a couple hours of shut eye before Bethlehem." I was also disappointed. I knew I would be unable to sleep on the plane and I had also planned to skip the service at the Holy Sepulchre in order to rest up for the rest of the day's itinerary. So much for toil and labour. We left the duty free shop and headed for the departure lounge.

"Do you want a drink dad?" I asked.

"Yes why not," he answered and I went to the bar and bought him a large Gin and Tonic and myself a pint of Kronenberg 1664. We sat at a table and quietly surveyed the scene. Prior to accessing the departure lounge there was a final security check and a large queue was forming in front of yet another x-ray machine and metal detector. There were other groups of pilgrims now all identifiable by their different coloured bags with the names of the tour operators proudly emblazoned across them, CL Bible Tours, (red) Inter-church Travel, (green) Jasmine, (purple), Loving Dove Christian Travel, (blue). None of the groups appeared to mix with each other; people just stuck with their own no doubt in preparation for sticking to the order of not straying once in the Holy Land. Sipping our drinks we let the queue thin out and then joined it and passed through the security check without any difficulty. Once inside the departure lounge dad asked if I wanted a roll. Mary had packed him off with enough rolls and crisps to feed 5,000. Cheese and tomato and tuna with mayonnaise. I took one from the Tupperware box she had packed them in and wondered how many of them we would throw away. The departure lounge was packed and for the first time I became aware of the large amount of Orthodox Jews taking the flight recognisable by their severe clothing, facial hair and the locks of hair that fell over their ears to their shoulder.

Feeling ignorant again I consulted my Rough Guide and learned that the principle tenant of Judaism is the belief in the five books of Moses, namely Genesis, Exodus, Leviticus, Numbers and Deuteronomy, otherwise known as the Torah. Three times a day practising Jews recite a prayer, The Shema. The Shema is made up of three biblical passages from the Torah, the first of which in Deuteronomy reads: *"Listen to Jehovah your God, Israel, Jehovah is one, Love Jehovah your God with all your soul and your might and take these words I'm commanding you today, to heart. Instil them in your children and talk about them when you are sitting at home and when you are walking down the street and when you go to bed and when you get up. Tie them as a sign on your arm and tie them round between your eyes, write them on the door posts of your house and on your gates"*.

"Flight El Al LY318 to Tel Aviv is now ready to board at gate 16," came the announcement over the intercom system. "The procedure for embarkation this evening will be by blocks of rows which will be announced. Can passengers holding boarding passes in rows 1-30 please board the plane." I checked my boarding pass, row 55.

The second great religion of Israel and the Palestinian territories is Islam. Muslims worship Allah through the Koran, the literal word of Allah dictated through the Archangel Gabriel to Mohammed, Allah's prophet. Followers of the faith are guided by the five pillars of Islam. Shahada (declaration of faith), Salah (prayer) observed five times daily facing Mecca, birthplace of Mohammed, Zakah (the giving of alms to the poor) and Haj (the pilgrimage to Mecca that should be undertaken at least once in every lifetime). The fifth pillar is that of Ramadan, the holy month when no food or drink must be taken between sunrise and sunset. "Air flight LY318 to Tel Aviv," the intercom clicked into action again, "passengers holding boarding passes rows 31-60 are requested to board the plane." So here we came, representatives of the third great religion, Christianity, believers in its law and teachings, believers in the trinity of God, the father, the son and holy ghost and the divine teachings of Jesus, God the Son and the prophesied Messiah of the Old Testament whose work is illustrated in the four gospels of the New Testament, Matthew, Mark, Luke and John.

X
Katapagea

East of Brussels the plane changed course south-east over Germany and Austria, followed the line of the Adriatic before changing course again across Greece and over the Islands of the Aegean. Myth has it that these islands were formed by the Gods of Olympus haphazardly throwing pebbles into the sea and so creating the Dodeconese on the fringes of Turkey and further to the north-west the group of islands known as the Cyclades.

"The island, two to the right to the one we're going over, kind of long and thin, that's Katapagea," I said casually to dad pointing to the flight path displayed on a monitor above us. Dad turned to Barbara and repeated what I had said. "His wife's aunty lives there" he continued. "Pretty difficult to get to by all accounts, or at least it used to be."

XI
Lavidea

Laura's aunty is called Katy. As the 60s drew to a close she left England and took up residence in a barn on the island of Mykonos and became, according to her passport, a peasant. But during the 70s and 80s beautiful Mykonos became a playground for the rich and then shortly afterwards the gay scene and whilst neither sets of people upset the peasant, the popularity for the island and subsequent shattering of her isolation did and she moved out of the barn for islands new. By the time she left the symbol of Mykonos, a pelican that could be found waddling around the port had been buggered by a drunk English tourist and not survived the ordeal, so story has it. So Katy headed nautically south-east around the Cycladian capital of Naxos and landed at the small port of Kamares at the northern end of Katapagea. Three small villages high in the mountains, Kastro, Lavidea and Potamos surround Kamares. Katy set up shop at the top of the mule track in Lavidea where she etched out a living teaching the local children English (and thereby opening up the world to them) and attending an olive grove that produced fine Olive oil. Lavidea is a beautiful white washed village with deep blue doorways and window frames that epitomise the Cycladic architecture, with their pretty window boxes and the piles of Donkey shit that sit steaming beneath them on the steep cobbled streets. My first visit to Lavidea was after I had completed my training in the early 90's and Laura and myself took off on a cheap flight for a couple of months in the sun. We took the boat from Piraeus to Sifnos for a wild week or so then a rest in quiet Folegandros, another wild week on Naxos and another recovering period on the tiny island of Schinnousa. On Schinnousa one evening, I got rip-roaringly drunk with an ex-Irish rugby international called Tommy and to the amusement of the locals we re-enacted great and sad moments from his career with a watermelon. Three weeks after leaving London we arrived at Lavidea and took the island bus up the rough track that wound upwards along the contours of the mountains to Lavidea. Us moving in meant that Katy moved out to a house she was renovating in an abandoned village in the valley beneath called Strombo. We would however meet every evening in Lavidea at 6pm for Oozo and to watch the brilliant sunset, literally a mass of fire disappearing behind the mountains of Kastro and admire the view west and the other visible islands of the Cycladese, Ios, Iraklia and Naxos, jutting out of deep blue horizon.

We quickly settled in to a routine of getting up late, walking to the beach at Aiegili, swimming, reading and stealing a shower from the local hotel (Katy had no running water). In the evenings we would meet up with Katy, eat grilled chicken and zucchini at the local taverna, and then sit in the village square, the platia, playing backgammon and drinking retsina and oozo until we could play backgammon no more. Occasionally we would muster the energy to go on a trip, once to the magnificent monastery that seems to be part of the rugged cliff that it is built into and where the monks supply visitors with Turkish delight and rakki. Another time we conned an old fisherman to drive us to the south of the island along the sheer cliffside track that dissects the island to its capital, Hora and the main island port of Katapola. This part of the island was busy with French tourists, who, on the back of a successful French film which was filmed on the island, had come to experience Katapagea for themselves.

One evening, Katy said over oozo, "I think it's time you were off." So the next day we packed up our backpacks, said goodbye to Evangelia, who had kept us supplied with feta, tomatoes and oozo from her kaffanian in the Platia, with a slice of sickly cake from the cake shop in Kamares and took the overnight ferry to Syros.

Here I am then set on a plane with 49 pilgrims going psychosis hunting in the Holy Land. Things are looking up since we flew over Katapagea; the tour guides given us a lecture on Doomsday Christian Cults, there's one in Jerusalem at the moment, though it doesn't seem to be a problem. What a very strange situation I find myself in.

"You'll be pleased to know we've got Rachel," dad interrupted my thoughts and so brought myself out of my predicament as the plane taxied at Tel Aviv.

"Who's Rachel?" I replied

"She was the guide we had when we came last time. Very knowledgeable. She's a French Jew but lives in Jerusalem now. We couldn't wish for better. You'll learn a lot from her"

CHAPTER 3
Sunday (Tel Aviv – Jerusalem - Bethlehem)

I

Derek introduces Seb to Rachel

The queues at immigration were reasonable but slow. Ahead of us, in our queue, there was a problem as a man struggled to convince the young severe official that he was who he said he was and in fact he was no threat to the State. She remained unconvinced and eventually her supervisor appeared and escorted him off behind closed doors. At this point the official decided not to deal with anyone else until the problem of the man's identity and his agenda was resolved so we waited and we waited for him to return. We, that is dad and myself, could have joined another queue but decided against that as we were next up and rationalised that the guy would be back soon. It was a mistake and as the other pilgrims passed through their examination and onto the luggage carousels we were left in an immigration hinterland, wondering what had happened to the vanished man. At this point a fleet of airport buses spewed a group of tourists from Beijing into the hall, swelling the queues dramatically so that our other option of changing was now a non-starter. Robin paced up and down the immigration booth, looking at us and pointing to his watch. His meticulously planned 10 day itinerary was off to a bad start and he was getting upset. All we could do was shrug our shoulders and avoid his eye contact. Eventually the vanishing man reappeared from stage right and returned to the booth. After a brief interchange with the official he picked up his bags and headed off to collect his luggage.

"Next," the official barked and obediently we shuffled up to her desk. Again she fired questions at us, pumping information into her computer and after what felt was an eternity, we were issued with visas, our passports stamped and we were allowed to pass.

"Quick, quick," hissed Robin "your last. Go and get your luggage. Quick, quick." So we quickly walked to the carousel to retrieve our big sturdy suitcases, only dad's wasn't there.

"Dad's doesn't seem to be here," I said to Robin.

"Oh bloody hell Derek, how can that be?" Dad looked blankly and grinned. The carousel was empty apart from my case.

"Have you tried the far end, there's a blind spot," went on Robin and he trotted to that end of the carousel. We saw him disappear briefly from view and reappear with dad's large case and we both felt a bit foolish.

"Well done Robin," said dad as he handed it over.

"Right let's catch up with the others," and he jogged through the departure lounge to the group of blue bagged pilgrims congregated on the airport concourse. The Bishop was talking with a woman all dressed in black, with long dark hair.

"That's Rachel," said dad. She saw dad and came over.

"Hello, hello welcome back, how are you?" she said kissing him on the cheek.

"I'm fine," he said.

"And where is your wife? Gosh this is terrible I can't remember her name."

"Mary, oh I left her at home and brought him instead. This is my son, Sebastian."

"Hello Sebastian, welcome," she turned towards me and we shook hands.

"Hi Rachel, how are you doing?"

"Fine," she answered and turned to the pilgrims. "Right everybody, we need to load the coach up ok so our driver here, Ahmet, will give you a hand." Ahmet was a Palestinian and with a big smile and with a wave he indicated for the pilgrims to put their cases onto the coach.

"Look, dad, this may take a little while. I'm just nipping over there to get a paper." I pointed to a small kiosk not far away near the taxi rank. The papers were neatly piled up and offered a range of publications from the local dailies Ma'ariv, Yediot Ahronot, Ha'Aretz to the English language newspapers, the Israeli *Jerusalem Post* and the paper I had read during the course of the flight, *Jerusalem Today*. There were also recently out of date foreign publications such as *The Times, The Sunday Correspondent, The Herald Times, The New York Times* and the *Wall Street Journal* as well as a number of magazines; *Newsweek, The Economist, Time and The New Statesman*. I picked up a copy of Jerusalem Today and Time magazine, paid for them and returned to the group. Things had thinned down somewhat and I managed to get our cases loaded and find a seat on the coach. It was nearly 7 by the time we left Ben Gurion and we started our ascent west towards Jerusalem. Rachel spoke to us, French style, for the first time over the microphone

"Ok, ok, well welcome to you all. Welcome to Israel. How are you all? Sorry to say this but you all look and sound a bit tired. I had a word with the Bishop and he feels if you want, oh how do you say it, oh yes, you can knock the Sepulchre service on the head if you want." Dad and I sighed with most of the coach as one. As pilgrims go, we were clearly not into the suffering side of things and the opportunity to crash out for a few hours was clearly a relief to everyone. "Ok," Rachel continued, "what we are going to do today is, we'll arrive at the hotel," she checked her watch "in about an hour maybe, A little bit more perhaps because we will hit the Jerusalem rush hour, which is no fun but can't be helped. Once there you will have breakfast and then pick up your things at reception and take them to your room at the Knights Templar hotel. Then we'll meet again at 12 at reception, we'll take the coach south of Jerusalem for a panoramic view of the Old City, have lunch at a kibbutz called Ramat Rachel and then we'll head off to Bethlehem, and the Church of Nativity. How does that sound?" There was a murmured acknowledgement. "Ok, ok I understand you're tired. You'll be fine soon. In terms of our journey to Jerusalem, well today we are not going the usual route which will be directly from the west, instead we are going to a place called Ramallah and then head south into the north of the city. The reason we are doing that is because there is a big protest today in the Jewish community. The ultra Orthodox are protesting over the secular ways of the non-Orthodox. It probably is very busy now, so we are coming through the north." She switched off the microphone and sat down.

II

Joshua Fisher III

I was struck as we drove, by the amount of activity on the roadsides, construction work, soldiers hitch hiking, people selling fruit.

"They're strengthening the infrastructure, building bigger more efficient roads. Helps to move tanks and troops around better," dad informed me. After 30 minutes or so Rachel picked up the microphone.

"Ok we're going to go through a checkpoint. When we pass through it we will cross what is called the Green Line out of Israel into the West Bank which is Palestinian controlled. The West Bank refers to the West Bank of the River Jordan but you'll learn about these things during the course of the week. At Ramallah you remember we will turn south and cross the Green Line back into Israel. We will cross a lot of checkpoints over the next few days. There probably shouldn't be any problems because there is no trouble but you never know." She sat down. The check point, which looked like a concrete bunker, was deserted except for one Israeli soldier at one end who waved us through with a smile and an equally happy looking Palestinian who welcomed us into the West Bank with another hearty wave and we sped of west towards Ramallah. Tired, I picked up my recently purchased copy of Jerusalem Today, started flicking through it and stopped at the headline;

'Apocalyptic Christians detained in Israel for alleged violence plot.'

I turned to dad. "I don't think I should show this to Robin at the moment," he smiled and I started reading the article. It read:

"Crack Israeli police units swooped down on a pair of homes in a quiet Jerusalem suburb yesterday and arrested 14 members of the US based religions group The Caring Christians. The Caring Christians vanished in October from their Philadelphia homes having sold their property and possessions. The police forces said the arrest might have foiled a plot by the group to see in the new millennium by inciting a blood bath in the Old City, which they considered to be a catalyst for the Second Coming of Christ.

'They planned to carry out violent exchanges in the streets of Jerusalem at the end of 1999 to start a process of bringing Jesus back to life, General Ali Her, national police spokesman informed Jerusalem Today. Another senior police source, speaking on condition of anonymity said that members of the group believed that being killed by the police would lead them to heaven. He also confirmed that the violent acts would be carried out in the Old City including on Temple Mount, traditionally a flash point for religious

> *tensions between the Jewish and Muslim communities. The police said they planned to ask the interior ministry to deport 3 adults and 6 children who were detained. They would not release the names of any of the suspects arrested. However a senior police spokes person said that the children were not in jail but were being held in an institutional office with their mothers. The men, he reported, were in custody. Apparently the leader of the group, Joshua Fisher III, was not among those arrested."*

"This seems to be getting a bit heavy," I said.

"What do you mean?" said dad.

"Well, on the plane the article said this Caring Christian bunch were not a problem but now they're saying that all hell is going to break loose in December."

"Oh I wouldn't worry about it," dad said smiling, "it's only February."

III

Jerusalem

Jerusalem, like Wood Green and Heathrow, was heaving and the Sunday morning rush hour was bumper to bumper. It took a good hour for us to pass through the city's northern Jewish suburbs of brilliant white tenements along the Road of Prophets and find ourselves at the magnificent Damascus Gate, the jaws of the Old Walled City. Here the coach turned right and following the course of the Old City, headed slowly up Solomon Road.

"Ok, this is what we are going to do folks. The coach will park at New Gate shortly. New Gate is another entrance to the Old City. At New Gate we will get off and we will then walk to our hotel which is not far to have breakfast. Your luggage will be taken care of, then we will meet back at New Gate at midday and head off towards Bethlehem." The coach came to a halt by New Gate which was considerably smaller than its neighbour the Damascus Gate but still impressive. Leaving the coach we walked through the gate along cobbled streets just wide enough for a single small car to pass through and flanked by small, dower shops opening up for the day's business.

At the hotel we were greeted by its proprietor and other male members of his family and entered through a large stone floored corridor with ornamental suits of armour and a huge painting of the dragon getting its comeuppance from a heroic St George, into a dining room with long wooden tables, much like an old fashioned school hall. The proprietor, Mohammed, led us to the table at the end of the hall and invited us to queue up and help ourselves to breakfast of scrambled eggs, fresh fruit, orange juice and very dry bread.

"Charming place this, quite charming," muttered dad to no one in particular as he tried to provoke some life into a particularly lifeless slice of bread with a large dollop of strawberry jam.

"It's like they've kind of gone for the crusades look. You know, the armour and all that, strange thing for non-Christians to do," I commented.

"Business, Seb, business," dad replied and attacked his bread with another dollop of jam.

IV
Water causes war

A couple of hours later we were back at the New Gate boarding the coach. We had managed to grab a couple hours of sleep in our dreary hotel bedroom and now the Christian party were headed off to start re-living the journeys and footsteps of Jesus and I was off to spot psychotics re-living the lives of people long gone.

"Ok, here we are. First stop," said Rachel, "will be a panoramic of Jerusalem and I'll give you a little bit of history. Listen, when we get to the panorama there no doubt will be people trying to sell you their goods. In Israel these people are all over the place trying to sell you goods. Most of them are fine if you just are firm with them and they won't hassle you. Some however are a little bit more over zealous so keep your cash and stuff close to you. The best place for shopping is in the shops. I'll take you to a decent shop tonight when we leave Bethlehem." Ahmet opened the door of the coach and we descended out into what was initially a blanket of heat and a scrum of hawkers thrusting their wooden camels and panoramic photographs into our faces.

"2 for the price of 1!"

"No, no thanks," I said and briefly wondered how the man had set his prices and his mark up and then, suddenly I emerged through the mass to one of the most spectacular sites to be witnessed. Jerusalem in the blueness of the day looked amazing. We gathered round Rachel but it was not her who spoke, it was the Bishop.

"In Jeremiah it says: '*stand at the crossroads and look and ask for the ancient paths. What the good way lies and walk in it and find rest for your souls*". He waited a moment. "Over to you Rachel."

"Thank you, Bishop" she replied turning to us and then stretching out her arm towards the Old City in front of us she said, "This is Jerusalem." We looked, we admired, took photographs and then she began. "I brought you here because this is not only the best view but it is also a picture of history. Water causes war," she paused. "If you look out right that is west and you see those mountains, those mountains are the mountains of Jordan, and what you see if you come in towards us from Jordan towards Jerusalem, it is yellow and that yellow area then is desert. If you now look out left or east, you can see it is greener and this area is fertile, things will grow of course. Jerusalem is a crossroads between fertile and unfertile from which the great western religions Islam, Judaism and Christianity emerged. This is where Abraham offered his own son Isaac to God, which all three religions acknowledge as the event that was catalytic to their evolution." She paused whilst we took in what she was saying. "The Old City," she continued pointing to the scene in front us, "you can see is surrounded by two valleys, the Kidron Valley to the east as we look and the Hinnom Valley along the west. These were natural defences and of course a source of water in a very dry land. If you look at the Kidron Valley and the slope on the far side at the bottom is Gethsemane where Christ was betrayed and above it is the Mount of Olives. On the far side of the Mount is Bethany, which is where Christ ascended into heaven 40 days after his resurrection. Here would have been your first stop on the way to Galilee. We will be exploring this area tomorrow." Again Rachel paused whilst we absorbed this information. "This church here, in front us, and outside the wall, is called St Peter in Gallicantu where Jesus was taken after his arrest. The house of Caiaphas who was the High Priest stood here and where allegedly Jesus was kept overnight before his judgement and execution. This is where, of course, Peter denied him three times allegedly and the church is also known as the church of 'St Peter of the Crowing of the Cock'. Anyway don't worry about that you will see it all up close tomorrow. Any questions?"

"Yes, when was Jerusalem built?" somebody behind me enquired.

"Gosh that is a difficult question and that's because Jerusalem has been built and rebuilt approximately 18 times and it's changed its position. The walls you see in front of you were built in the 16th century by Suleyman the Magnificent but look at the left part of the Old City some way back and you can see a large grey citadel. That is the church of the Holy Sepulchre, the site of Christ's crucifixion and entombment. And we know Christ passed throughout the city wall when he went for execution somewhere round the eighth station of the Via Dolorosa. So that means the city was different in shape and we can prove that through excavations that show that the city was generally further south towards us. There has been a city here though since before 10,000 BC. The original city Ophel was a city of a tribe called the Jeducites. Probably down in the valley there," she said pointing, "and this is where it would have been in the time of David. But we are going do all of this and much, much more over the next few days. Are there any more questions because we have to get on?"

"Yes," I said, "I have a question Rachel. What do you mean by 'water causes war'?"

"I'm not going to answer that question now, you'll discover what I mean during the course of the week and by the time you leave, next Sunday you'll understand why water causes war. Ok, I'm just worried, it's nearly lunchtime and I'm just going to briefly point out a few more sites and then we'll move on." She turned back towards the Old City, "The fantastic golden dome, that is the Dome of the Rock." We all looked at the brilliant golden dome that dominated the view glinting in the sunshine. "The Rock," she went on "is a sacred rock, allegedly this is where Mohammed was brought by the Angel Gabriel and where he ascended into and descended from heaven. It is built on the site of Solomon's temple and the Second Temple. The only wall remaining of the Temple, you really can't see it now but you will see it during the course of the week and this is to the left of the Dome and is more famously known as the Wailing Wall, the spiritual centre for Judaism. In front of the Dome is the very famous Al-Aqsa Mosque. Unfortunately it is difficult for us to visit the Dome or the Mosque, but we'll see. Now if you look out of the Old City, look at the architecture of the new city to the east and the architecture is flat. There are no real tower blocks so this is the Arabic part. The other western side is more traditional, perhaps it reminds you of home. This is western architecture and looks more European and this is the Jewish area. Ok that's all I'm going to say for now. Back on the coach in five minutes and we'll go for lunch." The group fanned out along the width of the viewing point. I took my binoculars and surveyed the scene in front of me and agreed that spectacular it was indeed. I then saw Keith. Like the rest of the group, he was looking out intensely over the Kidron Valley to the Old City flanked on each side by people who I was later to learn were his parents and sisters. I watched him for a minute or two. Keith didn't flinch, just stared at the glorious scene in front him so that the only thing that told me Keith was blind was the thin white stick that he clutched in his left hand.

V

Salad and Carlsberg

We had lunch at the kibbutz called Ramat Rachel. It wasn't how I had pictured a kibbutz to be: big, hotel like and swarming with groups of pilgrims identifiable by their coloured coded sun hats and bags. The group with the blue bags swarmed over the self-service cafeteria. I chose a salad and a Carlsberg and settled down to eat. I sat with Jan and she recounted stories of when she hitched around Europe in the 60s. I looked at her and realised the 60s for Jan, the decade I was born, was a long time ago. After lunch we headed south towards Bethlehem.

"Ok folks, we're going to cross a checkpoint shortly because Bethlehem is in the Palestinian territory. This village we're going through now is called Hal Homa. Even though there are not many buildings, the Jewish authority is going to build houses here. This has really annoyed the Palestinians because it means that Jerusalem would almost be entirely circled by Jewish settlements so they feel threatened. Anyway, like everything in Israel, we'll just have to wait and see. If you look around you this is the sort of land Jesus would have walked in, fairly green with large rocks exposed which had been shaped by the weather."

"Denudation," I said to dad.

"Sorry?"

"Denudation, that's what it's called when wind and rain erode rock formation."

"Really."

"'A' level Geography and all that."

"I seem to recall you didn't do very well at 'A' Level Geography and shoosh, I'm listening to Rachel."

"Before we arrive at Bethlehem, we will stop at a place called Shepherds' Fields. This is a great example of the weather eroding the limestone rock and allegedly where Gabriel appeared to the shepherds to tell them of Christ's birth. This is where St Helena, wife of the Roman Emperor, Constantine, founded a monastery in the 4th century, the foundations of which are still very evident." Rachel sat down.

"Much messier this side of the Green Line," said dad staring out through the window at a village we just entered.

"What do you mean?"

"I mean that this side of the Green Line is not as well kept," he continued, "much messier. That struck me last time out."

"That's a bit sweeping, isn't it dad?"

"No, not really," and he folded his arms and closed his eyes.

VI

At Shepherds Field

At Shepherds Fields we again tumbled off the coach through the hawkers and walked up the long avenue of lime trees pleased for the shade in the heat of the mid afternoon sun to the small church that marked the spot, or close to the spot where Gabriel appeared. The foundations of Helena's monastery were away to the left and protected by spiked iron bars that smoke screened both the layers and the depths of the excavations. Inside the church the roof was painted in a deep night blue with stars shining, one particularly brightly, above a fresco of Gabriel bringing the message of birth to overawed shepherds sheltering in a cave of weathered limestone rock. The shepherds looked terrified staring up at the glorious seraphim as their dogs hunched on their back legs and growled towards the angel with saliva dripping from their bared teeth. The sheep, however, were completely unconcerned by this extraordinary sight and continued unperturbed to sleep the night away. Back outside we congregated around the Bishop underneath a shading lemon tree.

"Gabriel showed himself to the men on the night shift," and proceeded to read from Luke Chapter 2. I looked around at the pilgrims, they stood motionless, hanging on to every word with their

heads bowed and their eyes closed. Behind the pilgrims were another group decked out in bright yellow shirts with the name of a church from Hamburg emblazoned across their chest. Their guide was talking passionately, his body movements reflecting the arrival of Gabriel and the fear of the shepherds. For a moment I found it strange that there would be this Christian group from Germany here in the Holy Land but quickly dispelled this as ridiculous because when the genocide started, German, driven by the mythological core beliefs of the Nazi leadership, killed German. The reading finished and after a silence for reflection Rachel announced,

"Ok, time is moving on. We must head back to the coach."

"Where exactly is Bethlehem from here, I mean which way did the shepherds go," asked a woman who I later learnt was called Sally and during the course of the trip I became friends with.

"That way," replied Rachel pointing out over Queen Helena's monastic ruins.

"Isn't it that way to Bethlehem, Rachel?" said the Bishop pointing 90 degrees west.

"Bishop, now I have to think," and her face broke into a wide attractive smile and fleetingly her authority seemed to ebb. "No Bishop, it is definitely that way," and again she pointed across the 4th century ruins.

"I stand corrected," responded the Bishop also smiling who then took out a café crème, lit it up and proceeded back along the avenue of limes to the coach.

VII

Word made flesh

"Ok, here we are in Bethlehem," announced Rachel, "but we have a problem and this is what it is. We cannot take the coach up into Manger Square because of the building work going on in preparation for the millennium celebrations, so we need to leave the coach here and walk up the road about 200m or so and then we'll arrive at Manger Square. On the far side of the square is the Church of Nativity where Jesus is believed to have been born. We will park near that taxi rank." As we left the coach, two of the taxi drivers who had been idling next to their yellow vehicles started arguing with each other. The argument became more heated whilst the other drivers looked on.

Then one of them picked up a rock at which point the other taxi drivers jumped between the two of them.

"Did you see that?" I said, turning to Barbara.

"That's nothing," she replied. "When we came out last time planning the itinerary things were a little bit tense you could say. I think it was over the land at Hal Homa. When we left a couple of kids started throwing rocks at the coach."

"That's scary. Why did they do that?" I was genuinely shocked.

"Well, I'm not actually sure Sebastian but I saw a film crew filming the whole thing. I think they needed a bit of newsreel so bought the boys to provide it. CNN or something, can't think of any other reason why they would want to stone us." I pondered on this as we walked up the hill to Manger Square. The gorgeous smell of spicy chicken kebabs filled the air from the cafes that lined the narrow roads. Manger Square itself however, was a building site. There were bulldozers, construction equipment, with piles of sand and rocks everywhere. In between groups of pilgrims squeezed through the chaos sporting their identity and following dutifully their guides who held multicoloured umbrellas high into the sky so that stragglers would not get lost. We too, weaved through, following Rachel and avoiding the vendors shouting out their humorous English one liners of "buy now, pay later" or "cheap, very cheap, Asda price" and eventually arrived at the entrance of the Church of the Nativity.

"So," said Rachel, "this is the entrance to the church. As you see it is very low. The reason is not a military thing about protection no, it was built in Turkish times to keep out camels. Once through you will pass through the Justinian porch through a huge wooden door and into the back of the church. We will meet there." One by one the pilgrims passed through the narrow gate into the gloom of the church. It was dark and the atmosphere heavy with incense and the smell of time.

Was this really where Christ was born? It doesn't feel like it. The Bishop preached to the group.

"At the end of the 3rd century Eusebius, Bishop of Caesarea wrote, *'The inhabitants of Bethlehem bear witness of the story that has come down to them from their fathers and they confirm the truth of it and point out the cave in which the virgin brought forth and laid her child.'* Let us pray." The pilgrims obeyed, closed their eyes and bowed their heads. "Almighty God who wonderfully created us in your own image and yet more wonderfully..." my mind began to wonder.

This would be a great place to spot some Jerusalem Syndrome, the birthplace of Christ, a certainty for the Virgin Mar, surely.

The church was busy but the light made it shadowy and the only people who were clear in the eerie gloom were the scattered Greek Orthodox monks splendid in their attire of robes, vertical hats and flowing grey beards. They were guarding their scene jealously.

"Amen," the group echoed.

"Over to you Rachel."

"Ok this is the Church of Nativity. At the back there are steps down to the cave where Jesus is believed to have been born at least by the Christian world. The Empress Helena again built the first church here in about 325. Over the cave was built an octagonal shrine with a conical roof. The top of the cave was removed and worshippers would look down into the place of the birth. This Basilica stood for about 200 years when it was demolished by the Saracens but was replaced by the Emperor Justinian at the plea of the wilderness hermit, St Saber. What happened then is that the octagon was replaced by the existing choir, you see over there and two entrances were dug into each side of the cave so that pilgrims could now descend into the place. The Persians spared the church when they took control of the region in the 7th century as did Muslim Arabic invaders out of respect of Jesus who they believed to be a great prophet and also their own belief in the Virgin birth. It also survived the crusades, Saladin and of course interdenominational rivalry. So you see the Greek Orthodox monks here, well there are also chapels attached to the church belonging to the Franciscans, the Armenians as well and also next door is the very impressive Roman Catholic Church, St Catherine's. These denominations all Christian, all worshipping the same God, they just don't seem to get on. Rumour has it that in the 80s they had paid, how do you say it, heavies, yes heavies to protect their rights in controlling these sites and sometimes violence would erupt. You'll see it also at the Sepulchre church back in Jerusalem when we visit. Anyway, walk around, visit the cave and we'll meet in that door way leading through to St Catherine's in half an hour." The pilgrims dispersed uneasily, unnerved by the fact that the denominations did not get on and recognising their faith was one of those included and headed towards the entrance of the cave. Nearer the Justinian choir, the light from candles helped to cut away the gloom to reveal large and faded mosaics and frescoes around the walls of the church which in their day, in their century, must have shouted and echoed the glory of God. Instinctively we joined the single file queue that slowly etched nearer and nearer to the cave. Pilgrims from numerous countries and Christian denominations were preparing themselves for a massive spiritual experience, some through prayer, some through meditation and some by crying. I followed my father through the cave entrance, ducking so as not to hit my head and started down the steep flight of steps cut into the stone to a small vestibule in which a blue star embedded in the stone floor, presumably marked the spot of the birth with a small shrine positioned around it. Briefly my father now confronted the shrine and then pressed his eyes, lips and forehead onto the star, kissed it and said something that I couldn't hear. He then stood up and touched the limestone ceiling of this, the Manger and whispered, *"word made flesh"* before heading up the stairs which again were cut into the rock that led to the exit back into the Church of the Nativity. Neither feeling inclined to pray, kiss or quote I retreated to the back of the cave, approximately 3 metres or so, and watched the next pilgrim come through. A severe looking monk, positioned also at the back to stop photographs being taken, stared at me. I smiled at him but he didn't smile back and for a second and for no reason I was reminded of the priest on Katapagea who demanded a friend of Laura's to hand over some clothes of her newly born baby that he had worn at his christening and had been blessed with Holy Water. The priest took the clothes and buried them but Laura's friend discovered where they were buried and dug them up. Briefly I remembered the dream I had on the train less than 24 hours before, which again provoked the thought *could Christ have been born here*. Eventually I could only conclude, as I marched up the steps, not being able to bear the stare of the monk any longer, that if he had been born, he had been born somewhere and so why not here, *though of course Mary in the dream had insisted that he was born in Nazareth.*

VIII
A ginger cat

Back inside the church I noticed dad and Rachel talking to each other in the front pew and went over and joined them. Dad was asking Rachel, who sat with her legs crossed, about her 9 year old daughter when out of the gloom a Palestinian policeman dressed in a dark navy uniform and with a submachine gun dangling casually over his shoulder, marched up to the guide and said something to her. Rachel immediately uncrossed her legs and the policeman retreated back into the shadows. She didn't seem flustered by what had happened but simply carried on talking to dad about her daughter. I turned around and noticed the group congregating next to the door into St Catherine's and as I turned back to advise Rachel on this I noticed a ginger cat had jumped up onto the seat next to mine and stared at me with deep yellow eyes.

"Look," I said rather dumbly, "a cat."

"There are cats everywhere," responded Rachel and then added. "Perhaps the Turks didn't build the church entrance gate low enough." Joining the rest of the party we moved into St Catherine's which in contrast was bright and fresh. A service was underway and we quickly exited back into the building site that was Manger Square.

IX

Evening

Back at our hotel room I mixed dad a Gin and Tonic and poured myself the Kronenberg 1664 I had packed only 24 hours before and then a slightly cooler Maccabi that I had picked up from a small shop just inside the New Gate.

"Seen anybody who's crackers as yet?" dad enquired.

"No, not really, I don't think so," and decided not to add unless all the pilgrims have it in a mild kind of way. "That was a bit strange dad though wasn't it, that shopping trip on the way back, you know being locked in the shop." We had stopped in a tourist shop on the outskirts of Bethlehem and been ushered into it and the pilgrims had bought all those sort of things that you wonder when you get home, why on earth you bought them including panoramas and wooden camels.

"Yes," dad agreed, "yes it was strange. Come on, drink up or we'll be late for dinner."

Supper was uneventful. We sat with an elderly man called David Brown, a widower, whose father had been shot dead at the carnage of the Somme, his first action.

"Of course I never knew him," he mumbled to me sadly, "my mother was expecting me at the time." During the course of the meal he became cross at my surprise that he lived in Oxford and worshipped in Stowton, was mortified at the demise of the football club he supported, Portsmouth, and continued to mumble in great depth of the Trans-Australian railway adventure he had undertaken when he was a younger man. By 9 lack of sleep, wine and the ranting and bitterness of this sad old man left me ready for bed and when I awoke ten hours later, Sunday had become Monday.

CHAPTER 4
Monday (Bethany – Mount of Olives – Mount Zion – Yad Vashem)

I
Breakfast

I left dad asleep in bed and went for a brief walk that took in St Francis Road, David Street and the Latin Patriarchate. Again I bought a copy of *Jerusalem Today* and returned to the hotel. I went straight to the dining room, loaded a plate with scrambled eggs and fruit and found myself a quiet table, slightly away from the hushed tones of the breakfasting tourists. I opened the paper and found what I was looking for on page 5. The headline read:

"Cult Members want to go to Greece"

"Members of an American Doomsday Cult awaiting deportation after allegedly plotting violent acts in Jerusalem want to go to Greece rather than return to the United States, their lawyer said yesterday.

Ben Sayed, a lawyer who represents three members of the religious group known as the Caring Christians arrested two days ago in a Jerusalem suburb said his clients also told him that their leader, Joshua Fisher III, was in London and not in Jerusalem. Mr Sayed said his clients preferred to go to Greece because other group members are also there and because they believed the United States would be destroyed soon. Fisher and several dozen followers have not been seen since selling their homes and belongings in the Philadelphia area last October. Fisher predicts his own death in the streets of the Old City of Jerusalem in December 1999 followed by his resurrection three days later.

14 cult members, including 6 children, came to Israel in September of last year and rented two homes in the Jerusalem suburbs of Nedasseret Zion and Moza. Israel police have said that the cult members plan to provoke bloodshed by attacking policemen in Jerusalem.

Deportation orders were issued against 11 members including 3 women and 6 children. 3 others were being investigated a senior police source confirmed, on grounds of plotting violent acts near Jerusalem's Holy sites in the belief that this would trigger a bloody Armageddon and hasten the second coming of Christ. Though the men have denied this, the judge has ordered that Patrick Dunning, Paul Hart and Thomas Shern, all of Philadelphia, be deported.

Israeli special forces are expected to work up into the millennium with special agents from the Federal Bureau of Investigation who are trained to negotiate in hostage and armed stand off confrontations. A source for the FBI have stated that tactics following the 1993 debacle at the Branch Davidians cult's compound near Waco, Texas have been rethought. The compound was set fire to by the cult members when federal agents attempted to storm the compound following a 51 day siege. More than 80 people died, including David Koresh, leader of the Branch Davidian".

"Morning, Seb. Can I introduce you to Robert and Emily worshippers at the Minster. Mind if we join you?" I looked up and there was dad, flanked on one side by Robert in a red checked lumber shirt and shorts and on the other his wife, Emily.

"No, morning dad, hello Robert, Emily. Nice to meet you," and decided not to extend my hand as all three were carrying trays. "Please sit down, be my guest." Robert and Emily replied to my courteousness and all three sad down.

"Anything interesting in the paper?" asked dad as the group tucked in to their breakfast.

"No, nothing really." For some reason I was starting to feel uncomfortable talking about Christian cults, "though there is some talk of tension growing on the Lebanese border." We sat in silence for a period then Robert stated,

"Your dad says you use to be a bit of a rugby player. I use to be a bit of a rugby player, I loved it."

"Well, I didn't play much beyond university but got as far as a trial for North of England Colleges team. Didn't quite make it," I replied.

"I played for Birmingham briefly."

"That's a good standard," I acknowledged.

"Well I suppose it was 30 years ago or so, but we weren't really up to much compared with today."

"It's the internationals on Saturday, England versus Scotland. We'll be in Tiberias and it's the Sabbath so I doubt we'll find it," I said.

"I doubt it, but you never know. Who do you think will win the Scotland game?" he asked.

"At Twickenham, England without doubt."

"I wouldn't be so sure."

"Robert is a true Scot," chipped in dad.

"Oh dear, I'm afraid we're the anglicised version," I grinned apologetically at Robert.

There was a banging on the table behind and the Bishop stood up and immediately silence descended on the room.

"Morning folks," he began slowly and cheerfully, "trust you are all refreshed. Just thought I would outline the day for you. After breakfast go and get what you need and then meet at reception as soon as possible, then its onto the coach where we will drive to the top of the Mount of Olives. We'll then walk down the Mount of Olives, looking over the east wall of the Old City, down to Gethsemane. From Gethsemane we'll take the coach up to St Peter in Gallicantu, the church Rachel pointed out from the panorama yesterday. Then we're heading up to the holocaust memorial, Yad Vashem where we'll have lunch and we'll tour it in the afternoon before driving back past the Israeli parliament, the Knesset. Ok, see you in reception in five minutes." Breakfast, it would seem, was over.

II

Pater Noster

By the time we arrived at the top of the Mount of Olives the sun had burnt off the gloom of the early morning as it had been when I went out for my walk, and was shining brilliantly in the blue sky. We were looking out, collectively, over the eastern wall of the Old City from a point close to where Abraham had been prepared to sacrifice his son for the love of God and it was disturbing me. This ridiculous image of myself and Jack kept jumping into my head, him lying there staring at me, all six years of him. *"Christ, snap out of it,"* I murmured angrily under my breath. Who the comment was directed at, myself or God, I wasn't quite sure. Rachel was talking about the view in front of us.

"The Old City is split into four quarters," she said, "the Christian quarter where we are staying, the Jewish which is to your left at the back and then the Muslim and Armenian. Even from here you can see the architecture in the Jewish quarter is different. It is newer and that is because the quarter was destroyed in 1948. 1948 is of course the year that the British mandate in Palestine ends and the Jewish National Council and General Zionist Council in Tel Aviv proclaims the establishment of the Jewish State of which David Ben Gurion became the Prime Minister. But tomorrow, when we do the Via Dolorosa and the Wailing Wall you will see it all much better. Remember yesterday I said that the Old City has moved geographically quite a lot. Out to my left towards Peter in Gallicantu and Mount Zion, this would have been the wealthy part of Jerusalem in the time of Jesus, but as you move right along the Kidron valley and the terrain is lower the people are less wealthy. It's as if the higher you are geographically the higher you are in status and the more money you have." I thought of Winsmoor Hill and our cottage style home at the bottom of it and the mansions on the top and decided the next time I bought a property it should be informed by ordinance survey as opposed to creepy estate agents.

"Ok then," she continued, "first we'll go to The Pater Noster Church and then we'll head down the hill." Rachel finished and we followed along the road, now clogged with tourist coaches, spewing logoed pilgrims into the increasing heat of the day. The Pater Noster Church allegedly the scene of the ascension had the prayer 'Our Father' in the tongues of the world that were scattered far and wide after the Babel Tower fiasco. As we were leaving I noticed one in Doric and pointed it out to dad.

"Your mum would like that. 'Noo and forever.' Very witty," and he promptly took a picture. Outside the church an unkempt, hunched up old man with a long stick held out his hand stating continuously, "blind man, blind man." Nobody gave him any money and the party started down the twisting track towards the Kidron Valley to the echo of the desperate pleas of the man, who had by now changed his wail to "God bless you, God bless you, God bless you." Half way down Rachel stopped.

"We are at the entrance of the church Dominus Flevit. Before we go on look across there. That is the Jewish cemetery and this is where the wealthy Jewish population want to be buried as they believe the next coming of God will be here on the Mount of Olives." At this point and as if to confirm Rachel's comments a taxi appeared around the bend in the track and turned into the cemetery. An old ultra orthodox Jew appeared from the back seat and examined a plot of the land. Through my binoculars I could see a hole surrounded by thousands of large stone caskets. The man was inspecting his resting place and was nodding his agreement. "Beyond the cemetery," Rachel went on, "is the town of Bethany. This is where Jesus lived when he was in Jerusalem. Many people from Galilee lived here. This is also where Lazarus was raised from the dead."

"*I am the resurrection and the life. He that believeth in me though he died yet shall he live,*" exclaimed the Bishop in a loud voice.

"Amen," responded the pilgrims.

"Ok, we're going to go in now to the church gardens. Stick close to me. It will be busy," and busy it was.

III
A lump of wind

We congregated by an orange tree. It was getting warmer.

"This is where Jesus stood," said the Bishop, "and he looked over Jerusalem and wept because he could see what was to happen. Let us pray for our great redeemer."

"It's really hot," Jan whispered to me, "we could do with a breeze or something, some wind," and for a moment I found myself in the luscious pink heather of Exmoor trying to fly a red kite with Jack. Jack held the string and I the kite, about 10 yards away holding it up and waiting for the breeze.

"What we need dad," shouted Jack excitedly "what we need is a lump of wind."

A lump of win, ye, that's what we need. "You're right Jack, we need a lump of wind," and then I was back on the Mount of Olives overlooking the great city, the site of the temple where Jesus preached and where Jesus wept for the incompetence of man. I turned to Jan and whispered, " what we need is a lump of wind."

IV
Derek explains redemption

The prayer for the Great Redeemer came to an end and the group headed towards the church. I caught up with dad.

"What is all this redemption stuff?" I asked.

"Well Seb, this redemption stuff, as you put it, is really about doctrine," he answered. "The Christian view is that the universe, the cosmos if you like was created by God but things went a bit wrong you know. We couldn't behave ourselves, Seb and a fracture between God and man existed. In the bible this fracture is illustrated through the myth of Adam and Eve. Jesus was sent by God as the redeemer, the person to mend the fracture if you like and it was healed by his execution on the cross and where true sin was admonished. Maybe he taught God tolerance," he pondered.

"Who knows," I answered.

"Who knows indeed."

Outside the church Rachel again spoke to us.

"This is the Franciscan church of Dominos Flevit, which means the Lord wept. It was built in 1955 under the instruction of the Italian architect, Antonio Barluzzi and if you look you can see it in the shape of the tear. The tear wept by Jesus. It's built over a 5th century monastic chapel and inside you will see preserved mosaics from that time. Look out across the altar, through the window there, it will frame the Dome of the Rock for you."

Thirty minutes later we were walking back down the track towards Gethsemane the scene of Jesus' betrayal by Judas and soon entered the garden.

"These olive trees, they could have been here in biblical times. You can see they are very old, they were the witnesses to Jesus' suffering probably." For once Rachel was less than convincing though the trees, a myriad of weaving branches, certainly gave the impression of age. "Over there, is the Church of All Nations otherwise known as the Church of the Agony which we will visit first and then we will go over there to the tomb of Mary, allegedly where she was assumed into heaven three days after she was buried," and Rachel pointed to what looked like a crater in the distance.

The noise from the road that ran through the Kidron Valley was quite immense and distracted from the peace and quiet of the night of Jesus' arrest. Slowly, we marched towards the Church of All Nations, myself as usual at the back, when I caught notice of a man waving his arms through the metal fence that acted as a boundary between church and road. I went up to him.

"You want to change any money?" he asked "I'll give you a very good rate, a very good deal," and he produced a thick wad of shekels from his back pocket. "Traveller's cheques, dollars, I'll change anything."

"No, I'm ok I don't need to change any money."

"You want something else then?"

"What like?" I enquired

"You know, some dope or something. I've got some great dope at the moment and it's real cheap." There was some appeal about walking around Jerusalem's antiquities with 50 pilgrims stoned but the appeal was fleeting and I rejected his offer.

"You sure, you look like you could do with something. What are you doing with all that lot anyway?"

"I suppose I'm on holiday. Great city you've got here."

"Yeah, not bad, not bad. Anyway look I've got to go. See you around," and with that he was gone.

"What was that all about?" dad asked me, as I caught him up.

"He wanted me to change some money."

"And did you?"

"No," I answered. "He also wanted me to buy some dope from him."

"And did you?" dad repeated the question.

"Of course I didn't. Why should I want to do that?" I answered annoyed.

"I was only joking, Seb. You shouldn't be so sensitive," and we entered the chaos of the Church of the Agony.

V

Seb listens to Boomer

Inside the church the Bishop was giving a reading but the noise from the road and the thousand of tourists meant I only caught certain words. *Sweat...Blood of Jesus...agony of the cross...the agony of eternity.*

"I can't hear a thing. I'm off for a stroll round," I said to dad. It was so busy that people were clambering over the pews both to get in and out of the church. Eventually I tagged on to a group of Americans decked out in red and green t-shirts with a booming guide capable of matching the noise around us.

"The Church of the All Nations," he boomed, as they slowly meandered towards the altar, "is called so because 12 nations financed its construction back in 1924. Again Barluzzi designed it. It's other name is the Gethsemane Basilica of the Agony because it marks the spot where Jesus came to pray with his disciples whilst awaiting Judas and the deadly kiss of betrayal. According to Luke, Jesus was in a deep depression or 'being in an agony'. This floor we are walking on, these impressive mosaic depicting the betrayal are from the original 4th century church dating AD380." He stopped and turned to his people and I was struck by the view that there was no room for allegation here; this was for real. "Outside to your right is the beautiful garden of Gethsemane with its ancient Olive trees, the witnesses of this agony." He used the same phrase as Rachel without the probably. "And it is here that Judas hung himself." Briefly I pondered Hannibal Lecter's question of whether, as part of the act, Judas Iscariot disembowelled himself at the point of his neck breaking. Avarice and suffocation, suffocation and avarice. Boomer was glaring at me.

"Very interesting," I said and marched off. I sat down next to two Japanese women at the fringe of the church. One was deep in prayer, the other sat there crying, wiping away her tears every so often with a paper handkerchief. I decided to leave them to their ritual and feeling a draining sense of claustrophobia battled with the crowd and left the agony behind me. Back outside I met up with dad.

"This is all pretty heavy duty stuff," I said to him. "Tell me something. Did Judas Iscariot's bowels fall out when he hung himself?"

Dad turned to me thoughtfully, finger on lip. "Read the Acts of the Apostles and you'll find out."

The group walked back past the Olive trees. *There's not a big enough drop for your bowels to fall out, the American must be wrong*. Coming from the opposite direction, here in the place of a betraying kiss, a stunningly beautiful woman was approaching. She was young, in her 20s full in the face, slender and tall and she was dressed in the habit of a nun. Apart from being disturbed by this and not knowing why, I couldn't stop thinking about the sexual emancipation of Julie Andrews in the film 'The Sound of Music'.

VI

Monstro

To reach the Tomb of Mary you have to descend a long flight of steps into a gloom more intense than that of the Nativity Church. Whilst the others went to pay their spiritual respects to the Lord's mother, I stood at the bottom of the steps, looking upward at the entrance with the shapes of shadowy faces of pilgrims ascending and descending into the tomb itself under the watchful gaze of the Armenian monks who currently had control of the site. It reminded of the whale in Pinocchio called Monstro catching tuna in his massive jaws. In the background a choir was singing for Mary which pierced the gloom and added to the eerie atmosphere. From the roof hung thousands of ornate candleholders, their occupants inexplicably inefficient in providing any light. Outside in the intense light of the midday sun I sat on an elevated wall and watched Monstro suck in and spit out pilgrims at will. I counted our own group back into the courtyard below.

"Come round me now please, come round me," shouted Rachel. "Come round me. Ok we're going in the coach to Peter in Gallicantu now. It will take only 5 minutes and then to Yad Vashem for lunch."

"Jan's not here yet Rachel, I've been counting," I said to her.

"Oh bloody hell, I'll go and get her," muttered an irate Robin heading once more into the tomb with his itinerary again under threat.

"Well, while we wait, let me point out something," said Rachel, "over there behind the tomb is the grotto of Gethsemane. Some religions believe that this is where Judas betrayed Jesus, not at the site of the Church of the All Nations. Now this is the case in the Holy Land. There is a lot of argument and confusion exactly where things happened and I suppose we'll never really know now. I don't suppose it matters really." Boomer wouldn't like that I thought to myself and looked over to the grotto suddenly out of which emerged Jan. Casually she ambled up to the group rewinding a film that was now used up. Then Robin reappeared out of Monstro.

"I can't bloody find her, it's packed."

"It's ok Robin, she's here," said the Bishop. Robin turned to her.

"Where the bloody hell have you been? I told you we all need to stick together."

"No harm done Robin," intervened the Bishop. "Now come on, back to the coach." The group turned as one. The Bishop however, gently took hold of Robin's arm and in a hushed tone said, "A bit less of the bloodies, please, Robin."

VII
Seb hears a cock crow

At St Peter in Gallicantu, Jan discovered that her Barclaycard had been stolen. "It must have happened when I was changing the film," she muttered to a beleaguered Robin outside the church.

"Has anybody got a Barclaycard? It may have details of how to cancel it," he asked the congregated group. Not one person of the 50 owned up to having one.

"Ok," said Robin, taking charge of the situation. "The only thing to do is to report it lost to the police and get them to cancel. I'll go with Jan on the coach and we'll pick you all up as soon as we can."

"I'll think I'll come with you," said Barbara diplomatically, "just in case it gets to be a little distressing," and off the three of them went.

"This then is the site, or alleged site, of Caiaphas's home. Caiaphas was a High Priest and this is where Jesus was brought after his arrest in Gethsemane," began Rachel, "and where Peter denied him three times."

"*Before the cock crow thou shalt deny me thrice,*" interjected the Bishop.

"We are actually standing on the eastern slope of Mount Zion, the burial place of King David, and Oscar Schindler amongst others. The church was built in the early 30s but what I think is most remarkable is the cistern inside where Jesus may have been kept." Inside, one of the pilgrims, a priest called Peter, read the story of the denial. Peter's wife Helen began to cry and was comforted by the Bishop. I headed down into the cistern that Rachel had talked of. It was probably 15 feet high but only 4 feet wide.

"Do you see the 3 crosses?" Pam, mother of the blind man Keith said to her husband Gordon.

"Where?" he asked.

"There, there in front of you. 3 crosses probably scratched on by prisoners."

"Oh yes, I can see them now. Yes, you're probably right."

I looked where they were looking and saw nothing. Dad was just behind me in the cramped cubicle.

"Can you see them?" I asked.

"See what?"

"Three crosses scratched on the wall."

"Yes I can."

"Where are they?"

"There," he said pointing at the wall Gordon and Pam had been looking at.

"I can't see anything, nothing at all."

"You aren't looking at it correctly."

"What do you mean I'm not looking at it right? How should I look at it?"

"The correct way," he said, turned and ascended the steps back into the crypt. I looked at the wall and was reminded of those books that were briefly popular for spotting shapes in sequences of dots, again which I could never see, saw nothing on the wall in front me and followed him up the steps. I found him outside by a magnificent bronze statue of a woman pointing an accusing finger at Peter in front of a Roman Legionnaire, staring out over the Kidron Valley towards the Mount of Olives and Bethany.

"I couldn't see them, the crosses."

"Don't worry about it," he shrugged.

Behind me I heard the meow of a cat which confidently walked over and sat between us and started washing its tabby coat.

"Funny that," I said to myself.

"What's funny?"

"We keep seeing cats. At the Nativity Church we saw a cat. I also saw one at Mary's tomb and at Dominus Flevit. Just one cat but there's never any more than one cat. Always a cat but never more than one."

"Well it's like Rachel said yesterday Seb, Israel is full of cats."
Somewhere down in the Kidron Valley a cock crowed.

VIII
Holocaust

"Ok I know you haven't come to talk politics but in Israel it is hard to separate it from religion. Over to the right is the Knesset building, the Israeli parliament where all the big decisions are made. Currently we have a man called Bejamin Netanyahu in power but there'll be an election soon and I think a man called Barak will replace him. He's better for the peace process, at least I think he is." We were back on the coach and Rachel was struggling to condense 10 millenniums of conflict and history into the 20-minute trip from Mount Zion to Yad Vashem where we were headed for lunch. Jan, Robin and Barbara returned with the coach having reported and put a stop on the lost credit card. Unfortunately it had already been used.

Yad Vashem is the memorial that sweeps out over green hills to the victims of the holocaust. I didn't know what to expect, except that it would be something awful and something that had to be seen. As we entered the gates the Bishop read:

"Even unto them will I give in mine house and within my walls a place and a name better than of sons and of daughters I will give them an everlasting name that shall not be cut off". He paused briefly and looked up. "Yad Vashem: a place and a name, Rachel."

"Ok, first we will be having lunch. It's quite late so we will need to meet at 2.30. I'll then guide you around the children's memorial, then we'll walk in the Janusz Korczak Park and then we will go to the exhibition, so lunch first." Rachel was giving nothing away. It could have been an exhibition of cars or butterflies. Lunch was the usual scramble round a salad counter in a packed cafeteria before retreating to a nearby table with salad, pitta and a couple of Carlsberg. At 2.30 we had assembled outside. A number of the group decided not to go avoiding the pain as too upsetting and so displaying that uncanny attitude of denial that allows genocide to happen. Briefly I thought of confrontation but weakly chose not to. Rachel was then on her way, us following, and shortly we arrived at the entrance to the children's memorial.

"For me," she said, "this is the most moving and powerful place I think I know. It just evokes question after question but I can never find any of the answers." With that she turned around and went through a high door that seemed to be built into the greenness of the hill. Inside it was as if we had entered a great dome and reflected onto the dome were millions of pure light beams that twinkled in the darkness and gave the impression of universe and cosmos. Every few seconds a name was mentioned, the name of a defenceless child whom adults, with gas and guns in the name of racial purity, had murdered.

"Each light," Rachel whispered, "is the light of one of those children killed and the mentioning of names never stops." The group stood stagnant not saying anything, watching the beams fade then glow then jump. *This is real agony.* We stood there for what seemed like hours but was in fact only a couple of minutes listening to the names of slaughtered youth. This was the real slaughter of the innocents.

"Come on," Rachel whispered, "let's go."

Outside there was a silence. People were trying to find their own space, many were crying. Suddenly, out of the exit came another group. They too were reeling from the enormity of what they had just seen. They stopped nearby and their guide started to talk to them. They were German, and again I experienced the uncomfortable feeling first experienced at Shepherds Field the previous day.

"We need to move on," Rachel broke the silence and again we followed her along one of the woodland trails. We found ourselves in the field of statues depicting the horrors of the holocaust. She stopped at one of the statues, one of a man trying to protect children he was charged with.

"This is Janusz Korczak. He was a writer and teacher in Poland. He looked after orphans in the Warsaw ghetto. When the Nazis came for the orphans he could not be separated from them and died in the gas chambers with them. Have a wander round and then we'll go on to the exhibition."

I looked at Janusz and agreed with Rachel that this place provoked many questions and no answers. *How do you learn to be so brave? Where does it come from, however bad things are? What drives people to kill 6 million other people? Why does it still happen?* The exhibition entitled 'Warning and Witness' tracked the rise of Nazism and its final solution. Huge black and white pictures had been blown up sometimes as large as 8 feet depicting the misery, slaughter and the corpses. The one however that caught my attention the most was the one of the young boy holding up his arms in the Warsaw ghetto, - you know the one, - it was in your history books, the boy with the flat cap and in this massive blow up you can see into his eyes and touch his fear.

IX
The Lost

I walked with dad back to the coach along The Way of the Righteous and so passed the Hall of Remembrance. At that point a number of limousines pulled up outside the Hall. They had small stately flags flying from their bonnets. It was the flag of Croatia. Dad and I watched the dignitaries leave their cars and enter the Hall. A soldier then shut the entrance.

"I wonder what that's all about."

"Don't know," answered dad. "It might be helpful if they bring a few of their neighbours next time."

"You could be right about that."

The coach journey home back to the Knights Templar was a quiet and sombre affair. I stopped at the small shop next to the New Gate and bought a couple of beers and some Arabic tonic water to mix with dad's gin. For some reason he had decided to drink gin, not his usual whiskey. Once back at the hotel, I decided I needed to speak to Laura and rang her. She and Jack were both fine and she said she had arranged a small get together for some friends of hers on Thursday. Before supper we had our customary drink and discussed the events of the day. "It's all part of the whole," dad stated. "Have you ever read 'Birdsong' by Sebastian Faulk?"

"No."

"A woman goes to trace her grandfather who fought in the trenches and comes across a huge memorial as big as Marble Arch in a field. On the Arch were thousands and thousands of English names. She asks the caretaker if these are all the English killed in the war. He answers that the dead are in the cemeteries, these are the lost people who went over the top and vanished. Stunned she asks if this is all of the English lost. "No", he answers, "this is the lost from these few fields in front of you." Its all part of the whole," he repeated. I didn't know what he meant.

XI
Sudden Death at the Sin Bin

At supper I sat with two female priests Liz and Catherine. Catherine looked familiar, a face from the distant past. She asked where I lived.

"North London," I replied

"Oh North London, I use to live in North London 10 years ago or so," and then I knew who Catherine was. Catherine Kenton was a volunteer at Causton Hospital, helping entertain the elderly, the psycho-geriatrics as they were labelled. She was a frumpy devout woman who also helped the hospital Chaplain perform his duties. Just when I was leaving Causton I heard she had started her nurse training and fallen for a silver tongued charge nurse who, after getting his wicked way, unceremoniously dumped her. Now here she was 10 years later, sat opposite me in the Old City of Jerusalem eating Muttabal and pitta and now a woman of the cloth. Causton was like that though; it was the kind of place where devout virgins lost their virginity. It was pure asylum. I once tried to write about it but the best I could come up with was a short story called 'Sudden death at the Sin Bin' which went something like this:

Handover time. As I entered I immediately sensed there had been a change. Oh yes, the entrenched ambivalence continued to meander indifferently through the room like a giant atmospheric amoeba catching its dinner but for once there was also a definable edge of excitement trying to break through and announce at last something has happened. On first sight however the scene that greeted me gave little indication of anything irregular having taken place. All the characters were in their correct position. Olga was wedged between the television set, unfortunately stuck on BBC2 and the large bay window looking out across the walled garden below. As was usual, she was holding a loaf of white bread in her left hand, intermittently plucking a chunk from it with her right before lazily tossing the piece through the open window. She smiled at the screeches of delight that the lucky recipients made. A verbal acknowledgement of her kindness. To her left sat John in his old tatty armchair dreamily following the ark of the bread disappear beyond his view and waiting with some anticipation for the next piece to follow. John was unshaven, smoking and sweating beer. The other four students sat in a crescent in the centre of the room facing the manager. His name was Tony Campbell and it was his belief, if not shared by anybody else, that this was Campbell's kingdom. My accepted contribution to this routine was always to be five minutes late without fail and as was usual I duly offered my apologies before taking up my position with the other students. The frightening concept that this routine was under threat became apparent as I now faced the manager whose expression confirmed my initial reaction that indeed something had happened. For once he looked fulfilled, excited, God forbid, almost happy. He licked his lips, rubbed his hands together and every few seconds attempted with fluctuating fortune to flick the wedge of greasy hair from his left eye with quick and quite violent jerks of his head. The eye, an eye that I had hitherto never seen, positively gleamed against the intruding warm summer sun. Oddly it's companion remained dull and lifeless and par to the man himself seemed sadly pathetic and exceptionally lost. Like John he was sweating. Then after an uncanny length of flicking, jerking, rubbing and licking he eventually announced,

"Little Joe's dead." Immediately Campbell scanned his subjects for their reaction. There was however no reaction, well nothing significant bar a few unscripted gasps from certain members of the cast and a crescendo of squawking came from the garden as Olga received the news by pitching a more than generous chunk of bread out through the window. The manager looked disappointed, even hurt, and the horror of excitement that I had momentarily experienced was draining through me like sand through an egg timer to be methodically suppressed until the next time.

All that remained was a residue of discomfort. The discomfort was also glaringly obvious in the other students as we sat in our semi-circle, shuffling from side to side in our hardback chairs and pulling and picking at imaginary flakes of dead skin around our fingernails. You see it was time to talk about death.

"Ok so how did he die?" one of the famous five, an unoriginal label remorselessly christened on us by our manager, ventured. The jerking started up again.

"The cause of death," the manager stated in his most official medical manner and the only manner in which he was vaguely effective, "was by acute impactation." The famous five nodded as one. Ah yes, acute impactation.

"So what is acute impactation, eh?" he continued assertively, "come on let's have a quick rundown, symptoms, treatment...if any," he quickly added. The nodding heads gradually began to shake.

"I can't understand you. Why don't you ask if you don't know? You're here to learn you know." Campbell was trying to sound irritated. "Perhaps John, you can help out." John appeared to be in a trance as he continued to stare at Olga and her projection of missiles. The rolled up cigarette, which he held between his teeth, had died and a trail of ash wound in an uneven fashion down his shirtfront to his groin.

"He was full of shit," he eventually pronounced without looking away from his distraction.

"Oh come now, John can't we try to be a little bit more clinical, they're here to learn you know." Campbell smiled nervously. John turned in his chair and with the same intensity he had stared through the window he now stared at us.

"What I mean," he began slowly and precisely, "is that poor Little Joe was so impacted with faeces that it created a toxicity in his system with which his body could no longer tolerate. It poisoned him."

"No wonder the little fucker didn't speak," Olga stated dryly without looking away from the scene beneath her.

"Shut up Olga, not in front of the students," Campbell immediately retorted. The five of us however were not listening. We were just sat staring back at John boggle eyed, shocked and fascinated. This wasn't in the script. The first death was suppose to be natural, a heart attack or stroke maybe. Call the resus. team, ensure that the last rites were administered (as according to policy of course), keep his mouth moist and then lay him out angelically in his virgin white shroud: TLC. To be poisoned by your own faeces was neither natural nor, from Joe's point of view, a satisfactory way to *die. The girl next to me let out a long deliberate stream of petuli breath.*

"Stop the earth I want to get off," she cornily cliched her favourite phrase in an even longer drawn out drawl more in tune with a psychedelic solstice than a psychiatric ward. As an after thought she added,

"Heavy shit," and realising her slip, if it was one, she covered her mouth with her hand and studied the intrinsic system of cigarette burns in the carpet around her feet. John meanwhile was glorifying in the effect that the cause of little Joe's death was having upon us.

"Apparently turds the size of footballs, up to his stomach." John's clinical expression, like the bread, was going out of the window. Then, what can only be described as a remarkable sense of timing, and somehow managing to stare hard into us with his eyes half closed he explained,

"You could smell the shit on his breath as he died." John, for some reason only known to himself, was beginning to sound like Montgomery Cliff fantasising over his favourite steers, Indians, whiskey and broads. Slowly we turned back to face Campbell. Campbell however was clearly no longer able to face us. Like the girl next to me, he had suddenly taken an interest in the pot marked carpet. The jerks and fits were quite redundant and his left eye's opportunity to gleam was lost under a wedge of greasy brown hair. Any further explanation was not forthcoming. Instead he nervously offered,

"The other clients haven't been informed yet. We'll have a community meeting this afternoon. Perhaps you John, can lead that?"

"Sure," agreed cowboy John.

"One good thing that does come out of all this," continued Campbell, seemingly back in control, *"is that we're to get a new client this afternoon from Curney Ward. Perhaps you Olga, with one of the students, can keywork him. His name is Derek Clayton and he has a diagnosis of schizophrenia."*

"Surprise, surprise," interrupted Olga sarcastically. Campbell pretended not to hear her.

"Now students, what symptoms do you think we can expect to find in a person diagnosed with schizophrenia?"

"Same as what all the other bastards have," John giggled, shaking his head from side to side in merriment.

"I'm asking the students, not you John," the manager snapped and stole the briefest of glances across the room to the back of John's head. "Now what symptoms would you expect to find with the condition schizophrenia?" My mind had by now begun to wander. Poor Little Joe, what a nightmare life and now what a nightmare death. Little Joe had somehow survived Treblinka and all its horror. Cold, famine, mud, raw rotten potatoes, pulled gold filling, gas and death. He had seen his family systematically wiped out. Somehow and no-one exactly knows because little Joe went mute, he passed through the chaos of post war Europe and ended up in England, where the authorities in all their wisdom treated his trauma by placing him in an asylum. Little Joe progressed then from one institution to another and little Joe as the doctors and nurses knowledgeably informed us became hopelessly institutionalised. The only time you heard little Joe say anything was when he was restrained for his weekly suppositories. Forced to lie face down on his bed he would swear,

"Nazi bastards, fucking Nazi bastards," as the capsules were inserted into his KY'ed anus. The nurse in charge of the operation would reassure that it was for his own good and in turn we would reassure little Joe. Little Joe though never looked reassured. Quite rightly as it turned out. He would just look us in the eyes and hiss,

"Nazi bastards, Nazi fucking bastards." Treblinka - Causton, Causton - Treblinka. It was probably all the same too little Joe. As I sat there pretending to listen, pretending to be interested but submerged in my own thought, I remembered how it had actually been little Joe who had enlightened me. It had happened one morning about a month before his death and I had been delegated, as students are delegated, to take little Joe to Hyde Park for a picnic as part of his therapy. As we strolled through the park Joe scrunched up and lost in his heavy great coat, hands in pocket and focussing directly on the path we were following, I compensated for his conversation by rambling on about everything and nothing. I was feeling decidedly pleased with myself at giving Joe such a good time when it occurred to me in one brief unremarkable moment that it wasn't Little Joe that needed me but quite the reverse. I needed Little Joe. For it was in this split second of time that I first understood the primary objective of the *relationship between a therapist and their client. It is not to address the needs of the patient as all good therapists would have you believe, but is in fact to focus on the subconscious and conscious needs of the therapist. This is achieved through a mercenary manipulation of the patient's problem in order to reach the therapist's own desired goals. By doing so the therapist, hiding behind a patronising cloak of condescending jargon and an even sturdier wall of care and concern, takes on all these psychological qualities that combine to produce human satisfaction; power, fulfilment, experiment and growth. It is secondary and probably pure accident if the client has any success. So Joe, when I greeted you in the morning with the obligatory,*

"How are you today?" I wish you had said,

"Well, not bad for a man who's had no home, no money, watched their mother raped, their father and brother shot, their sister gassed and then pumped full of tranquillisers for the next 40 years for no apparently good reason." No doubt some fool would have said, "You seem to be a little upset."

At the boating lake we stopped to eat our packed lunch which had been provided by the hospital. Inside the white bags along with the standard Spam sandwiches, individually wrapped sultana cake and apple was inexplicably a violently red plastic knife, fork and spoon wrapped in a white paper napkin. Across the napkin was inscribed in bold blue letters 'We're sorry you are ill.' I looked at Joe clutching his cutlery and staring blankly at the serviette. Behind him a group of lads were rocking a rowing boat whilst an attendant from the shore was shouting to them to stop. In the foreground the cutlery was expressing its sorrow that Joe and I were ill and immediately I felt a wave of repulsion at not being able to share that sorrow. The boat behind capsized.

"Perhaps you can arrange that after the handover" Campbell was staring at me. I didn't know what he wanted but I nodded my agreement. He smiled, thanked me and then in one swift movement removed himself from his throne and cantered out the room.

"What is the treatment for acute impactation?" The petuli girl next to me shouted out after him but Campbell quite wisely was gone. One by one the others followed. John turned in the doorway.

"We'll do it at 3, ok?"

"Ok," I replied.

"Ok," he echoed and strutted off unshaven, smoking and sweating beer towards the nurses' station. I was alone in the room with Olga. She was still preoccupied with events outside as opposed to events within. Slowly I left my chair and walked over to where she was, aware of the commotion coming from the garden and looked out knowing what to expect. The men from the ward beneath half dressed and with their faces cut from a daily ritual of systematic shaving were fiercely fighting over the bread as if their lives depended on it. In the corner of the garden a nurse sat under a large oak tree reading his newspaper comfortably oblivious of what was happening around him. Olga was targeting patients as a child will pursue a bird that they consider has not had their fair share.

"I'm not sure you should be doing that," I said, looking at the chaotic scene below.

"Why not?" she turned to look at me. "I'm meeting their needs, I'm feeding them." her smile was attractive, warm and caring. "Here," she continued "why don't you help me," and forced the remains of the loaf into my hand. I briefly examined what was left before tossing it casually out of the open window.

X

Seb gets it wrong

"You're not Catherine Kenton are you?" I plucked up the courage to ask her "and you didn't work at Causton Hospital 10 years ago." The vinegary red wine was taking its toll.

"Well, in answer to your first question, I am not Catherine Kenton, I'm Catherine Dawson and secondly, I've never heard of Causton Hospital let alone worked there." She smiled at me.

"Oh" I said rather foolishly, and thought of the Saki short story.

"Who is Catherine Kenton anyway?"

"Oh nobody really. Just somebody I use to be acquainted with."

"I see."

The conversation changed direction to multi-cultural schools and sexism within the church, topics that both Liz and Catherine were hesitant to talk about. As at breakfast there was suddenly a large thump on the table; the Bishop had risen.

"Tomorrow is the Via Dolorosa, the Way of Sorrow," he announced gravely, "the route Jesus took from the Antonine fort to his death on Calvary. Now having talked to Rachel it will be hell all of us trying to get up together so what we'll do is split into six groups, each led by one of the priests on pilgrimage. So that's myself, Peter, Liz, Catherine, Judith and Terry." He had missed out dad, but dad didn't seem bothered. I leant over to him.

"It sounds like a Japanese endurance test," he smiled and responded

"Something like that Seb, something like that."

CHAPTER 5
Tuesday (The Old Walled City of Jerusalem)

I

The Scorpion V's The Bee

At about 10am we found ourselves weaving through a small souq outside the Damascus gate having walked from the Knights Templar down the Solomon Road. The market traders attempted to blind us with their bargains but we were under strict instruction not to be sidetracked.

"We are on a very tight schedule," Rachel had warned us earlier at reception again dressed all in black; urban gorilla, I thought. The sun was already shining high in the sky when we entered through the gate but was immediately blocked out by the imposing wall and the narrow streets inside the Old City. I thought as I walked along about the disembowelment of Judas Iscariot and having read the report of his demise in the Acts of Apostles the previous night felt that his suicide couldn't have possibly occurred at Gethsemane but somewhere else. I was also feeling disappointed, not even a whiff of psychosis.

The Old City was thick with the smell of stale kebab - the morning after the night before and the sound of the Minarets calling the faithful to prayer added to a sense of alienation and a time gone by. We walked, almost in single file, along King Solomon Road, passing the Austrian Arab Community Clinic before turning left and entering the Convent of the Sisters of Zion and finding ourselves in a long thin room with a terrace of fine oak stalls that we were requested by one of the sisters to sit in.

"Ok, here we are in the Sisters of Zion Convent and through there," said Rachel quietly and pointing to a doorway to our right, "will take us down to the Antonine Fort where Jesus was clothed in purple and a crown of thorns put on his head. So this means to he has been taken from Caiaphas's house marked by the spot of the church Peter in Gallicantu, he has been condemned by his own people, and handed over by Pilate to the Roman soldiers for crucifixion. There are 14 Stations of the Cross each depicting something that happened as he struggled along the Via Dolorosa to Calvary. Remember Calvary at that time was outside the City Wall and only probably came within the city when Suleyman the Magnificent rebuilt the walls in the 15th century – probably," she repeated herself. "Ok, let's move on." Slowly we left the stalls and followed a steep stone stairway down into the Antonine fort. The light was again poor but it was easy to make out the magnificent flagstones and the impressive whitewashed arches that hung flabbily from the low curved ceilings. Progress through however was slow as a group ahead of us who we had earlier replaced in the stalls decided to stop and pray every few feet, and the narrowness of the environment did not allow us to pass.

"Bloody typical," said Robin to me quietly. The Bishop's request had clearly after a nights sleep been forgotten. "Bloody, bloody typical. This shouldn't bloody well be allowed." The veins on the side of his neck were standing out the schedule was under threat. After what seemed an eternity, we inched through into an anti-chamber and gathered around our guide.

"This is where prisoners were kept before being marched off to Calvary. Here would be played the Game of the Kings and a crown of thorns put on the condemned heads. This didn't just happen to Jesus, the Game of the Kings, it happened to many if not all who were going to be executed. I didn't know what the rules of the game were only that the condemned always lost. Now, look at the floor." As one we looked at the flagstones.

"Rachel has us well trained," I whispered to Sally who I found myself next to. She didn't reply, either to involved in the flagstones or not bothering with such a stupid remark.

"See over there," Rachel was pointing again, "that is a scorpion carved into the floor, the symbol of the 10th legion. I didn't know if it was the legionnaires of this legion that escorted Jesus, maybe, maybe not, but the life at this time for a legionnaire, if not at war, was so boring. There was really little to do. That's probably why they played the Game of Kings. Now look above the Scorpion. That is a bee. The reason for the bee is probably from the Greek, Buzilaus, which is Greek for King. So you know even though we don't know the rules of the game maybe there is some kind of battle between the bee and the scorpion – the condemned v the legion – and of course the scorpion has the biggest sting. Over to you Bishop."

"We're going to start at Station three where your group leader will say an appropriate reading from the bible. Before we go through to the anti chamber that leads us to the Via Dolorosa – The Way of Sorrow –

I wish to quote from the bible what has passed for the first two stations.

"*Then they led Jesus from Caiaphas to the Praetorium.*
Pilate took Jesus and scourged him.
Then he handed him over to them to be crucified
And the soldiers led him away, into the hall called the Praetorium, and clothed him with purple and plaited a crown of thorns and put it on his head.
And Pilate said to the crowd "Behold the man."
Let us pray ....Our father........"

I was still looking at the floor, at the bee and the scorpion and tried to conjure up 'the Game' but couldn't. To each side of the etched figures were engraved in similar fashion the Star of David and I couldn't think of any significance. *Thought block.*

"The power and the glory. Forever and Ever. Amen."

II

On the Via Dolorosa with Peter

The group started to shuffle through into a light anti chamber and one by one, in groups of five or six, every three minutes descended through the large wooden doors onto the hidden street outside, until only our group, headed by Peter, (what an appropriate name I thought) was left in the anti chamber. He seemed nervous, as did the others.

"I think what we would do," he began in his Welsh accent, "is that we should all do a reading, take it in turns like, at each station, until we get there. Here, I've done some copies. Here Helen." He turned to his wife, a plump fresh faced woman who had been comforted by the Bishop at the Church of Peter in Gallicantu the previous day. "Pass them round. Now were going to go in a minute. So it's going to be busy. Stick close together. Don't lose me. But first let's sing," and in the next second Peter had burst into song.

"*Guide me O though Great Redeemer,*" quickly Helen joined in.

"*Lead me through this barren land,*" and all of a sudden I found myself singing as loud as I could.

"*I am weak but though art mighty,*" and probably, like Peter, I was transported to the rugby changing rooms of my youth where prior to taking the pitch I would implore for one last time and the 15 of us would scream as we ran on the spot,

"1, 2, 3, 4, 5," before charging out into what was usually a pre-destined lost cause – a bit like the fate of the bee.

"Bread of Heaven
Bread of Heaven
Feed me till I want no more,
Feed me till I want no more."

"Right follow me," yelled Peter and with a lot of huffing and puffing and with tears rolling down Helen's cheeks, we poured out of the Antonine fort, out of the Game, into sunshine, now directly overhead…….and a completely empty street. Peter came to a quick stop, and in true keystone cop fashion we all bundled into him and then looked around, left and right, into the emptiness and wondered which way to go.

"Look," said Helen after a couple of seconds, "right down there Peter. Isn't that the group ahead of us?"

"It could be, let's take a closer look," and we marched off. It didn't take us long to realise it wasn't however.

"Well it must be the other way."

"What are you looking for," a voice behind us suddenly said. We all turned around and faced a happy looking hawker with his basket of goods.

"We're looking for the 3rd station of the Via Dolorosa," Peter informed him authoritatively.

"Is that your wife?" said the man still smiling

"Why, yes it is," replied Peter, becoming slight agitated.

"Do you think she would like one of these?" he asked and pulled from the depths of his basket a small wooden camel.

"I don't know, I'll ask her." He turned to Helen. "Would you care for a small wooden camel, Helen?" briefly she considered the offer.

"Yes, why not, a small wooden camel," Helen answered. I watched on thinking *surreal*.

"How much?" asked Peter

"Oh 3 shekels or 2 for five."

"No, I think one will be enough," and rummaging around in his pocket, produced the correct money. The two men made their transaction.

"Really is a most beautiful camel," Peter confirmed dumbly.

"Yes it is," answered the trader, "and yes the third station of the Via Dolorosa, it's down there at the corner. You were going the wrong way." We all laughed and enjoyed the moment.

III

Sun flowers

After a little more confusion we found the third station, a depiction of Christ falling under the cross above the entrance to a Polish Chapel.

"*Jesus falls under the cross the first time,*" shouted Peter. "*He who would console me and give me back my life is far from me*", right onto the fourth." The next station was not much further on. However the narrow street was significantly busier with there being groups of logoed pilgrims now all over the place.

"Right Sebastian, you read the fourth now."

"Sorry," I said.

"Remember, we're taking it in turns."

"Oh yeah, yeah sure," and I fumbled in my pocket for the piece of paper that Helen had recently distributed back at the Antonine fort.

"*Jesus meets his mother,*" I said awkwardly, "*all you who pass, look and see: is any sorrow like the sorrow that afflicts me?*"

"Thanks Sebastian," Peter acknowledged. "Tradition says that our lady stood by the roadside in order to see her son. Here, in this little Armenian Chapel her grief and her sadness are remembered. Now a quick reading."

A group of Americans in white tee shirts and yellow sun hats went past us and turned the corner as Peter read. The reading wasn't so quick because about two minutes later a group of Japanese pilgrims, also in yellow sun hats and white tee shirts, went past us around the corner. I saw in the group the two Japanese women I had sat with briefly in the Church of the All Nations the previous day.

"Ok, let's press on." Peter had finally finished and led us around the corner towards the fifth station on a road that was considerably narrower. Instantly we registered pandemonium. The road was blocked with confused Americans and Japanese in yellow sun hats and white tee shirts. There was a lot of shouting including from the guides who appeared to be arguing about who should go first.

"Blimey," said Peter. "Wasn't expecting this. Now what to do?" He paused. "Right we'll do 5 and 6 together. Single file let's squeeze past on the far wall." Squeezing past wasn't so easy. The amount of bodies made it near impossible and progress was slow as the shopkeepers tried to entice us into their shops which on occasion we did due to a basic process of physics that doesn't let one form of matter pass through another. We literally popped into them. And then, just as we were about to emerge, a Japanese/American compromise was met and we were swept up the narrow street on a tide of yellow sun hats. At the sixth station they stopped again.

"Come on, come on!" Peter shouted, to his straggling team. "We'll do it all at the seventh," and through the mass we charged and finally broke through safely out of the melee. "Ok, the seventh is at the top of this street. In a chapel. Sanctuary, sanctuary!" He smiled at us and we all smiled back.

We carried on up the narrow street at a reasonable pace not wishing to be swept up by the tide of yellow sun hats a second time. I was beginning to relax when suddenly I felt a thump in the back of my head. Instinctively I stood to one side and turned. A man with eyes fixed, chanting and surrounded by a group of women charged past me. The man was carrying a large wooden cross, the top of which had knocked me on the back of my head.

"Man with cross coming up behind you oblivious," I shouted rather foolishly ahead of me. Our group turned, pressed themselves against the wall and the man with the cross with his entourage passed safely by. I walked up to Helen.

"This following in the footsteps of Christ is a pretty risky business."

"Not half," she answered somewhat breathless, "but apparently it was like this you know. It was a holiday, shopkeepers would be selling their goods and the sight of men with crosses was not uncommon. They wouldn't have been bothered."

"Who wouldn't have been bothered?"

"Why, the shop keepers, silly!"

"No I suppose they wouldn't have."

Shortly afterwards we arrived at the seventh station within a Franciscan Church and plonked ourselves down in one of the ornate pews.

"We've got a bit of catching up to do. I'm just wary of time so I'll take us through it. Station 5 Simon the Cyrenian is forced to carry the cross," he boomed. " *'They enlisted a passer by, Simon of Cyrene, father of Alexander and Rufus, who was coming in from the country, to carry his cross.'* Station 6, about half way up the last road, Veronica wipes the sweat from Jesus' face. *'May the Lord's face shine upon you,'* and here station 7, Jesus falls for the second time *'With their affliction, he was afflicted. In his love and his pity he redeemed them'."* Peter looked at his small congregation and sensed their disappointment. "See that column over there, that's exactly where he fell just as he was leaving the city. Remember Rachel said about the walls moving and Calvary being out of the city wall in those times. Apparently his death notice was posted here. Hence the Christian name for this site – Judgement Gate." He patted his bible and again I was reminded of my strange dream on the Piccadilly line.

There was a commotion behind us.

"Oh God," said Peter as we turned around. It was the sun hats. "Quick, let's go," and instantly we were on our feet as the newly formed international alliance swarmed over the pews. It took a couple of minutes to battle through the tide though once emerged it didn't take long to reach the eighth station. *"Jesus consoles the women of Jerusalem,"* said Peter, and then with an after thought said "Sorry Helen, you should be reading this." Helen looked at him with love and said,

"Jesus consoles the women of Jerusalem. *'Daughters of Jerusalem weep not over me. Weep rather over yourselves and your children. For if green wood is treated thus, how will the dry wood be treated'."* She looked at him with love. "Ok, on we go". By the time we reached the ninth station at the site of a Roman column we had caught up with the group ahead that included Rachel, the Bishop, his wife and dad. Peter made a decision to join up with them and so it was the Bishop who rasped, "Jesus falls for the third time. *'I have come to do your will, O God.'* Now look over there. You can see the roof of the Holy Sepulchre Basilica, a reminder that Jesus collapsed within the sight of the place of his crucifixion. The last five stations are all in the Basilica and hopefully the forward groups will be waiting outside for us, so let's move on and meet them." I strolled behind with dad.

"How did you find it?" he enquired

"Dangerous," I answered. "Bit intense really."

"Crucifixion, terrible thing. Terrible way to die," he changed the subject. "Apart from the agony of being nailed to wood, the weight of the position you were in would eventually break your back or neck, pull your arms and legs out of their sockets and make breathing near impossible. The worst thing of all though was the time people could take to die, days sometimes, dehydrating as bits of you simply break up. If the soldiers felt compassion they would break your legs and arms to speed up the process. Remember Kirk Douglas and Tony Curtis in Spartacus, the best of friends trying to kill each other by the sword so their mate wouldn't be crucified. Crucifixion, terrible thing, terrible way to die."

IV
Golgotha

By this time we had reached the Courtyard of the Holy Sepulchre Church. The earlier groups, true to the Bishops words, were waiting for us unprotected from the very warm midday sun and we merged together around the Bishop, his wife and our guide.

"As I said to my group," the Bishop began, "the remaining stations are inside the Basilica. The first four are all on the hill of Calvary, close together, and marked by four glorious altars. The fifth is the site of the tomb beneath. After Rachel gives us a bit of history we'll go inside and see the site of Christ's crucifixion, burial and resurrection. Rachel."

"Ok, thanks Bishop. This then is the centre of Christian Worship. The church you see was built during the crusades, though there were plenty of other religious buildings there before this including a temple to Aphrodite. The church, like the Nativity Church, is managed by a number of Christian denomination, actually six in total, Catholics, Greek Orthodox, Armenians, Ethiopian and Copts."

"That's only five, Rachel," somebody in the throng shouted out.

"Is it, let me see," and she started counting on her fingers. "Catholics, Copts, Greek Orthodox, Armenians, Ethiopians, so it is only five. Ah yes, I know, Syrians. I forgot the Syrians," she smiled as the sun lit up her face and for the first time it struck me that Rachel, decked out in black, was also an extremely beautiful woman. "Now where was I, oh yes, well all these denominations manage here and yes you guessed it, they don't really get on. Occasionally they gang up on each other. For instance at the beginning of the last century after a fire the Ethiopians were expelled because it was thought that one of their monks caused it when he was, how shall I put it, enjoyed a bit too much of the sacramental wine." A light tittering omitted from the group. "So, anyway each denomination has control of the church at certain times of the day. It works," she shrugged unconvincingly. "It will be too busy for us to tour all together inside so I'll say a bit about the interior here. Inside is the Stone of Anointing where Jesus was removed from the cross though the Catholics say it is the spot that was anointed before burial. Then to the left is the Stone of the Three Women where the Armenians believe Jesus' mother Mary, her sister and Mary Magdalene stood by the cross. To the right of the Stone of Anointing there is a staircase. Make your way up there and assemble with the Bishop to finish the remaining Stations of the Cross. This is Calvary or as we say in Hebrew, Golgotha meaning the place of the skull. You may kiss the rock if you wish then come back down the stairs and go to the left of the Stone of Anointment. You will see 18 columns supporting a dome above the ground. Below this is the Holy Sepulchre, the tomb of Christ. You may queue to go in. Ok let's go."

The group ambled forward encouraged by the shade that loomed ahead.

"I want you to take a photo of me kissing the rock," I heard a voice in front of me say. I recognised it to be Deirdre's, a woman who had been at my breakfast table earlier that morning, who talked shrilly throughout and I concluded by the time I had finished my scrambled egg was opinionated, usually wrong and a bit stupid.

"Martin, did you hear me," she repeated as we entered the church, passed the Stone of Anointing and headed up the stairs to Golgotha (a word that had struck me as very pleasant). "I want you to take a picture of me kissing the rock."

"I heard you, Deirdre. Don't worry, I'll get the picture." The atmosphere as we assembled at the top of the stairs was, for some reason, like the souq we had walked through in front of the Damascus Gate, though nobody was trying to sell us anything except of course religion. Maybe I thought to myself, maybe it is all the lamps everywhere, dangling throughout the church but more in abundance over the significantly holy sites.

"Jesus is stripped of the garments." The Bishop was off and pointing to an altar, " *"from the sole of the foot to the head are bruises and sores and bleeding wounds".* " There was a pause: "Jesus is nailed to the cross." He moved his still pointing finger a few degrees, *"they have pierced my hands and my feet. They have numbered all my bones,"* he came to the place of the skull (Golgotha) where Christ was crucified, "and they put a sign on the cross that said *Jesus of Nazareth, King of the Jews* and shouted". Again the Bishop moved his pointing finger. "Jesus dies on the cross. Jesus cried '*Eli, Eli, lama sabachotoni?*' that is '*My God, My God, why hast thou forsaken me?*' Once more, uttering a loud cry, Jesus gave up his spirit". Immediately a wail went up from the group, not a long wail, but a collective from the faithful that rose into the gloomy basilica and vanished. I looked at the pilgrims. Some had their heads bowed some, men and women, were crying. Dad was looking into space. Then there was a rasping which grew and grew from the Bishop until it had developed into the hack of a person who can no longer breathe properly. His wife supported him as a charged coughing fit, like the wail, came and went. Composing himself he pointed over the balcony to the Stone of the Anointing and said calmly,

"Jesus is taken down from the cross," and then pointed to the Sepulchre itself saying, "Jesus is laid in the tomb." At this point the pilgrims began to sing, holding hands. I left them and walked over to the edge of the balcony. The sun hats had arrived en mass and from up above they had the look of faceless sunflowers floating through the air like magnificent pollen. I turned round and saw the pilgrims joining the queue to kiss the rock. At the front, at the rock, there was a lot of pushing and crying as impatiently the Zenith of meaning was reached by those imploring salvation. The sun hats were joining the queue by now, the impact of which was that the queue was disappearing and other rogue queues were forming resulting in a scrum at the point where Christ was crucified. In the centre of the scrum was Deirdre, knelt down with her extended lips placed on the rock and her eyes to the side looking for Martin. Another pair of lips joined her on the rock. She lifted her head.

"Martin," she shouted.

"It's ok." I heard a gruff voice from somewhere to my left. "Just kiss it." I took out my camera as Deirdre returned her lips to the rock and took a picture of the scrum ahead of me with Deirdre as the hooker.

V
Seb talks to Roma and Fred

Twenty minutes later I found myself sitting in the sunshine of the courtyard outside. I had decided not to go into the Sepulchre, itself, and had opted for a small Coptic Chapel at the rear of it, which no doubt the Copts thought of as the last resting place and which no-one else seemed interested in. The wooden chapel, probably 2 metres square, was occupied by the obligatory lanterns and a Coptic monk clad in a thick brown habit covering his entire body including his head. I sat opposite him and nodded. He didn't nod back but I could see his eyes scrutinising me. He seemed like a character out of Disney. So there I sat with him quietly. It was a relief, an oasis from the chaos and intensity of the outside and a brief chance to recharge. Ten minutes or so later believing for no real reason that I may be outstaying my welcome, I left the Copt to his thoughts, took a David Hockney style photo of an impressive mural depicting the crucifixion and subsequent entombment, and then went out into the courtyard.

Around the perimeter of the courtyard were large stone benches. I found an empty one in the sun and looked at the view around me. Leaning against the wall of the Basilica were a dozen or so crosses of different sizes and I wondered whether the one that stuck me half way up the Via Dolorosa was amongst their numbers.

"Do you mind if we join you." I looked up and saw an elderly woman who I recognised to be from our party and her husband.

"Yes, please do, please do." I answered pointing to the empty part of the bench next to me. "I'm Sebastian, it's nice to meet you."

"I'm Roma," she acknowledged me sitting down, "and this is Fred. Oh it's great to have a seat. It isn't half getting hot and all this charging around."

"Yeah, its pretty tough going," and we recounted our earlier experiences along the Way of Sorrow before turning to more mundane things at home.

"The traffic in our village is getting worse and worse," Roma complained. "I've been trying to get a bypass built for the last 30 years, but no, nobody listens. So these darn articulated lorries charging through at God knows what speed. A child was killed in '91 but still nobody listened." 30 years trying to get a bypass built. I wondered why they didn't move but then why should they have to. Keith walked by helped by his mum and dad and through the direct impact of the sunlight on his sunglasses I could make out the whiteness of his blind eyes. And then Jan emerged. Her hair was wet.

"Jan," I said dumbly, "your hair's wet!"

"I know," she said, "I just washed it."

"You just washed it!" I couldn't hide the amazement in my voice.

"Yes, I found a tap at the back of the Basilica and I had a sachet of shampoo in my bag so I thought why not?"

"Why not indeed," I answered aware of Roma's quiet tutting in my left ear and contemplated if any other pilgrim in history had ever been taken by the urge to wash their hair at the site of Christ's crucifixion and resurrection and concluded that, in a strange way, I may have witnessed history. At this point there was a sound of commotion on the alley that led to the courtyard and a cat hurtled past us, its tail splayed and into the gloom of the Basilica.

"Have you noticed that every time we visit a site we always see a cat, though never more than one?"

"Can't say I've noticed that, son," piped up Fred.

"No, nor can I," said Roma, "but I'll look out for it from now on." Jan lay down on the bench next to us, her hair laid out behind her to dry. However she was only just settled when Rachel cried,

"Ok everybody, come together, come together," and obediently we gathered around.

"Damn," Jan whispered to me. "It's going to go frizzy. It always does if I don't dry it in a certain way."

"What did you say?"

"My hair, it's going to go frizzy."

"You should have bought your hair dryer with you," I joked and thought of my lovely wife and the amount of times I had dragged her hairdryer round foreign shores in my back pack both of us knowing full well that we would have the wrong fitting plug.

"Ok," Rachel began, "It's time for, wait for it, wait for it, lunch."

"Hooray," the group cheered as one. It had been a long morning and we followed her away from the Sepulchre Basilica to a street café at the junction of David Street and the Souq, ordering Shavara kebabs and ice cold water.

VII
Profile

Across the square was a small shop selling newspapers and before I sat down to my kebab I nipped across and bought the latest edition of Jerusalem Today and returned to my table. There was nothing in the headlines about the Caring Christians, but then further inside I stumbled on an article:

Profile: 'Mastermind: Joshua Fisher III.'

It read;

'Jerusalem has been a natural target for cultish activity for centuries and really that is understandable. They come and they go but generally they never stay around that long. So what is all the fuss about the Caring Christians and in particular their leader, Joshua Fisher III. Surely, now they have come, like the others, they will eventually disappear and be replaced. Well maybe not this time, because it seems that Fisher is intent, as one of the two end times prophets mentioned in Revelation Eleven, to create havoc at the end of the Millennium including inciting a bloodbath in significant Holy Places to provoke, it would seem, the Second Coming of Christ.

Fisher was born on January 3 1950 and raised in a small farming community in Tanningtown, near Philadelphia. Apparently he excelled at school where it was reported he had 'a gift of persuasion'. His family did not attend church but he converted to Christianity after listening to a number of leading theologians including Bill Bright and Billy Graham. Fisher claims to have no formal theological training, in order to learn solely from God.

Fisher started the Caring Christians in the Philadelphia area in the early 1980s to combat the New Age Movement and the Anti-Christian bias he considered to be in the media. Early issues of their newsletter 'Report from the Caring Christians' touched on such topics as feminist spiritually, New Age trends in the Christian Church, and alternative medicine. Fisher also lectured frequently in Philadelphia Churches about the New Age Movement.

Fisher's deviation from Orthodox Christian doctrine and practice allegedly began in the middle of the 1980s. Former member of the cult, Sam Johnson recalls that Fisher claimed to regularly speak with God in the morning. Jake Sharkey, also an ex-member recalls Fisher rationalising that 'his previous service to the Lord entitled him to freely solicit from his followers' and remembers a phone call in 1996 when Fisher started talking in triplicate, saying 'I'm speaking in the voice of God'. 'If he had done that before', Sharkey said, 'I'd have told him he was nuts."

The first clear sign that Fisher was becoming separationist in his theology came in the 1988/89 issue of 'Report from Caring Christians', in which Fisher voiced that patriotism constitutes apostasy, or religious defection and attacked numerous established Christian organisations including the Roman Catholic Church. He wrote,

'God views their pledges of allegiance to America as spiritual adultery. Instead of restoring America, the Christian right is helping to build Babylon'. Other articles that year included 'Whore America: Love of the Harlot Church' and 'Fighting Doctrines: Sons of Light vs. the Sons of Darkness." In the early 90s things went quiet but Fisher reappeared in 1996 when he began production on a radio programme called 'Our Foundation', from a radio network in Utah. The network however ceased airing the program in November of 1996 after Fisher sent a letter to radio stations on which his programme aired stating,

'For most of you, you have already become familiar with a significant part of the message that the Lord has given us to share: that American patriotism is not of God and that to truly serve God, one must come out of one's love for America. Now the Lord is requesting me to make one more request of others that is highly unpopular. You are to begin airing the programme for free on the air. Do not laugh, this is serious...we will not be sending you any more funds. It is time for you to serve the Lord with all your heart, soul and mind.'

Shortly afterwards having claimed that God had told him not to pay for any previous airings, Fisher declared himself bankrupt.

Records from the United States Bankruptcy Court, District of Pennsylvania, showed Joshua Fisher III to have assets at $142,628 and liabilities totalling $748,852. In addition to being indebted to radio stations on which 'Our Foundation' aired, Fisher also owed in excess of $100,000 to the Internal Revenue Services. Fisher reportedly demanded money from his followers. Refusal to pay would result in not only the families but also attendees of their bible study, going to hell. Much of the money he was given was apparently invested in Michael White Construction of Palm Springs.

It was also during this period that Fisher began to openly channel messages from God. He would preach about America being Satan and about the imminent apocalypse. It was now he proclaimed to be one of the two witnesses of Revelation Eleven, that he would be killed in Jerusalem in December 1999 but would be resurrected three days later. He also prophesised that the Apocalypse would begin after Philadelphia was destroyed by an earthquake in October 1998.

So what does the future hold for Fisher. Well, he may well die in December 1999 because that, it would seem, is what he wants. To the masses and to you Joshua I would quote Deuteronomy 18 that states 'A prophet who gives an erroneous prophecy is not to be feared.'

Next to the article was a picture of the man himself. He had black hair with a side parting, a large pair of glasses and a thick jet-black moustache. He was wearing a yellow open collared shirt. He reminded me of an ageing DJ.

"You're reading about Joshua Fisher III," a voice wheezed from behind me and I knew from the essence of cigar smoke that now engulfed me that it was the Bishop. I turned round.

"Yes, that's right." He had been looking over my shoulder. "I would say he has completely lost the plot, he's psychotic."

"Maybe," said the Bishop, "Maybe, but there again, maybe not," and he ambled off towards another bible. *Maybe not, that can't be right. A man who claims to be speaking God's direct words and thinks of America as a 'whore'.* The Bishop somehow registered my thoughts and turned back towards me.

"It may all be a sham. He might be making it up."

"Ok, we have to move on now. I hope you enjoyed your lunch," shouted Rachel, over the noise of the Souq. "The plan for the afternoon is that we'll go from here to the Wailing Wall. After that it is up to you. Those of you interested I will take to the Hurva Synagogue. Those of you not interested can have time to yourself, do what you wish. Unfortunately it is not possible at the moment to visit the Dome of the Rock or the Al-Aqsa Mosque. I'm not sure why, but that's Israel for you. Ok follow me." We followed Rachel into the busy Souq before bearing left along what was called the Street of the Chain. After a short period we turned right and into the Jewish quarter of the Old City. It, unlike all the buildings we had previously seen, had been redeveloped. There were modern tenements surrounded by communal areas of grass where ice cream vendors tried to seduce us with their numerous flavours and succeeded. Then under a bridge and in front of us, directly beneath, stood the Wailing Wall, the solitary remains of the second temple, where Christ, nearly two thousand years ago had preached.

"We have to go through a security check before we can go down to the Wall. Security is increasing in Jerusalem because of the significance of the year 2000." Rachel informed us of what to me was becoming strikingly obvious.

VII
The Wailing Wall

We joined the queue that snaked down the path to a small checkpoint, where young Israelis searched the bags of the pilgrims, constantly smiling and I was reminded of our smiling interviewer at Heathrow. Eventually our turn came and went uneventfully and we congregated in the large open area in front of the wall.

"This", began Rachel "is probably the most sensitive spot in the world. It is where Christianity, Islam and Judaism meet, the religions of millions upon millions of people. By the Jewish people it is considered to be the spot nearest to the holiest of holy. If you look you will see the Jewish people facing the wall. They are crying for the destruction of the temple, or as we say, they are lamenting and are praying for the rising of a third temple." A group of children walked by towards the Wall. They were being led by a man wearing civilian clothes and with a rifle slung across his shoulder. "If you wish to go up to the wall enter over there to the left if your men or right if you are a woman. The attendants will provide you with the proper head gear." I decided not to go directly to the Wall but stayed at the perimeter fence. The people at the Wall were truly lamenting some almost to the point of frenzy. The Bishop stood next to us and started reciting the Shema;

"Listen to Jehovah your God, Israel: Jehovah is one. Love Jehovah your God with all your heart, your soul and your might and take these words I am commanding you today to heart: Instil them in your children and talk about them when you are sitting at home and when you are walking down the street, when you go to bed and when you get up. Tie them as a sign on your arm and tie them around between your eyes: write them on the doorposts of your home and your gates."

Keith was being led up to the wall by his father. I could see them holding each other's hands, praying. Then Keith took a small piece or paper and pushed it into the crack of the wall.

"What's Keith doing?"

"He's putting his prayer into the wall," answered Rachel, stood the other side of me. "On this the holiest of holy site, the Jewish people put their prayers into the wall and wait for them to be answered. You can even send an e-mail. The people at the desk download them, print them off and put them into the wall for you. All very modern." There was something very odd about e-mailing prayers.

"How often do people come here to pray?"

"Depends," she replied. "The Ultra Orthodox, they may come up to 5 times a day to pray. Others maybe just once, like the women," she pointed to the right hand woman's section. "They'll do their work then come here to pray."

"How can they come 5 times a day?"

"What the Orthodox?"

"Yes, the Orthodox."

"They don't work?"

"They don't work. How do they survive?" I was beginning to feel very ignorant.

"They are supported by the state. They're job I suppose is to ensure religious enlightenment for Israel and its people through prayer and the study of the scriptures."

"What do you think about it?" She turned to me and shielded the sun from her eyes.

"Why, I don't think anything about it. What's the point." She smiled the smile of a person who has answered the same question a million times and before I could return it she had walked past me and started talking to the Bishop. I stood and watched the scenes in front of me: the lamenting, the wailing, the praying, the women walking backwards from the wall, the Orthodox, the non Orthodox, the children and the man, their leader, with a rifle slung over his shoulder. The Wall made up of its vast slabs of stone, oozed respect, tradition and the worst sorts of conflicts that people both willingly and unwillingly die for.

"I'm going back to the hotel. Could do with a bit of shuteye. Are you going on to the synagogue?" It was dad

"No, I don't think so, I'll come back with you, make sure you don't get lost. I'll just take a quick picture, you know, of them lamenting and all that."

"I wouldn't bother, it may cause offence."

"Why?"

"Because in their eyes you are making a graven image. They may not like that. Come on, let's go."

We left the scene behind us and headed up the path and passed the checkpoint. At the top, just before the Jewish Quarter, an Orthodox man was playing a small organ and out of it wailed a version of the Frank Sinatra song 'Strangers in the Night'. We walked back through the Jewish Quarter, resisted the temptation of the ice cream sellers and found ourselves back on the Souq. The narrow pathway was full of tourists being encouraged by traders to sample their goods, mainly clothes, leather, perfume, jewellery or other tacky souvenirs. At the junction of David Street we turned left and headed for the Tower of David situated at the Jaffa Gate and it was here, at this impressive citadel, that I noticed him.

VIII
Seb meets John

Stood at the entrance of the gate, with the beginnings of a beard beard and wrapped in a white robe that may have been a bedroom sheet was a man preaching.

"Let's go and have a listen to what he has to say. It may be fun."

"I don't know," answered dad uneasily. "Nobody else seems particularly bothered. I'll wait here, you go and listen," so up I went to him and listened. He looked at me briefly then took his bible and started reading in English.

"And there was given me a reed like unto a rod: and the angel stood, saying Rise and measure the temple of God, and the altar and them that worship therein.

But the court which is without the temple leave out, and measure it not; for it is given unto the Gentiles: and the Holy City shall they tread under foot forty and two months.

And I will give power unto my two witnesses, and they shall prophesy a thousand two hundred and three score days, clothed in saccloth."

I was stunned, amazed.

"What is this your reading," I stared at him. "What is it?" He didn't answer but carried on.

"These are the two olive trees, and the two candlesticks standing before the God of the earth.

And if any man would hurt them, fire proceedeth out of their mouth, and devoureth their enemies: and if any man will hurt them, he must in this manner be killed. These have power to shut heaven, that it rain not in the days of their prophecy: and have power over waters to him them to blood, and to smite the earth with all plagues, as often as they will.

And when they shall have finished their testimony, the beast that ascendeth out of the bottomless pit shall make war against them, and shall overcome them and kill them.

And their bodies shall lie in the street of the great city which spiritually is called Sodom & Egypt, where also our Lord was crucified."

I stood there mesmerised. He stopped reading, looked at me and said,

"We know it as Jerusalem."

"Sorry," I answered.

"Sodom. Sodom is Jerusalem."

"Oh, I see. What were you reading then?"

"I was reading, should you care to know, from the Book of Revelations."

"Revelations Eleven?" I asked.

"Yes, quite correct, Revelations Eleven."

"Why were you reading that?"

"It's what needed reading, don't you think."

"Yes, I suppose so. You're English aren't you?"

"Countries don't count," he answered. "I may seem English today but tomorrow I may be French or perhaps Mexican."

"Who are you? Who are you!" I gently probed.

"I am the Essene called John."

"John who?"

"I am the Essene called John," he repeated, this time quite assertively.

"John who?" He looked at me and considered his answer.

"I am John.....but some call me the Baptist," almost whispered staring straight at me. I gulped in air and lent my arm on the wall of David's Tower. I could hardly get the words out.

"John the Baptist?"

"Yes, that's right. The Essene, John the Baptist." I had to think quickly. "Who are you?" he went on. *Don't challenge, don't confront.*

"I'm Sebastian Carrington from London, Seb to my friends. I'm pleased to meet you, John," I said. "That's a lot of responsibility."

"Yes, it is a responsibility," he was calm. "I have a lot of work to do: Satan is all around and the people need saving before it is too late". Instinctively I took the copy of Jerusalem Today out of my blue bag and opened it at the profile of Joshua Fisher III.

"See this man, he proclaims to be one of the witnesses you just talked about, you know in Revelation 11." He took the paper and looked at the photograph of the cult leader.

"I know that man, Fisher," he hissed. " He is the Anti-Christ. Satan is all around."

"What do you mean he is the Anti-Christ?"

"The Caring Christians. They're a cult – the Caring Christian Cult. CCC, he's the leader."

"So what. That doesn't make him the Anti-Christ." After a few moments he handed back the paper and said,

"Have you got a pen and paper?" I fumbled around my bag wondering what was next and passed him the loose leaf pad and biro that dad had given me when we arrived. On it in large letters he wrote "Caring Christians Cult." He turned the page and wrote 'CCC' with the bottom of the C being exaggerated so what he actually wrote was 666.

"There," he said "the sign of the beast. Remember Satan is all around." I looked at the paper disbelievingly.

"What do you mean Satan is all around?"

"Exactly what I said. Satan is all around."

"Fisher is he here, in Jerusalem?"

"Yes, he is here in Jerusalem."

"How do you know?"

"I've seen him."

"When?" I asked. "Where?"

"A couple of days ago. I saw him on the Mount of Olives."

"Have you told anybody?"

"I tried to tell the police, but they think I'm mad. What would they know, anyway?" We stared at each other for a few seconds.

"I've got to go now. Goodbye John. Good luck." I turned and marched out of the Jaffa Gate and heard above the noise of the Jaffa Road,

"Save yourself sinner, save yourself Sebastian! Before it's too late, before you......" and then his voice vanished in the traffic.

I walked up the hill past the Bristol Garden in the direction of the New Gate.

"Sebastian, Sebastian wait for me. Wait!" I had completely forgotten about dad.

"Gosh dad, I forgot about you."

"What was that man saying to you? Who was he, Seb?" He asked breathlessly.

"He's John the Baptist."

"John the Baptist? What do you mean, John the Baptist. That's impossible."

"Yep, John the Baptist, at least he thinks he's John the Baptist."

"That's incredible."

"Not really, he's sick. He's suffering from Jerusalem Syndrome. He's psychotic."

"Is he dangerous?"

"No, he's not dangerous. Most people who are psychotic aren't dangerous. He's fine. Just mad." I took the profile of Joshua Fisher III out of my bag.

"Now he's dangerous," and pointed at the photograph of the man with large glasses, jet black moustache and the open collared yellow shirt, "very dangerous."

"Oh that cult thing we were talking about on the plane."

"John the Baptist says he's in Jerusalem. He says he saw him on the Mount of Olives."

"Oh ridiculous. He can't possibly have. What do you think?"

"I think he's probably telling the truth."

"Did he tell anybody, the police, the authorities?"

"He said that he tried to but, dad," and I stopped and turned to him, "sane people don't listen to the insane. Anyway, I doubt he did try and tell the police, they would have locked him up."

"Maybe he's on the run or something."

"On the run from what. Hardly, he's just declared war on Satan."

"Should we tell somebody?"

"No I don't think so. It's too complex. Imagine walking up to the authorities and saying a man who believes himself to be John the Baptist has seen the leader of a cult who believes himself to be one of the Witnesses of the Revelation on the Mount of Olives – it's too much, dad."

"Yes. I see your point, it's too much." We had reached the New Gate by now. I stopped at the shop and bought a couple of Maccabis and a tonic for dad's evening gin.

"Perhaps it's just as well we're leaving Jerusalem tomorrow," dad considered as we walked back to the Knights Templar.

"Perhaps," I replied "or perhaps not. It's just getting interesting."

IX
Return to Bethlehem

That evening we returned to Bethlehem to have supper with a group of Palestinian Christians. I hadn't been aware of such a group of people and when they arrived at the restaurant where a meza and red wine had been prepared they looked nervous and uncomfortable. One of the group, who looked like Bernard Cribbins, sat at our table and the conversation was dry. I sat drinking red wine with Sally who was sat next to me and her friend Sue, and by the time the Palestinian Christian leader stood up and made a powerful speech about working with others and the work of the group in Bethlehem I felt quite pissed. I recounted the earlier events to Sally and Sue who I could see did not know whether to believe me or not and I couldn't blame them. All of a sudden the room burst into a lively praising song, one of course that I didn't know and before I knew it a woman, a priest called Judith, on the table behind me grabbed my hand and had risen it into the air. The whole room, arms raised, was celebrating and, through the wine and the events of the day, I briefly felt their faith as if it was channelled through their arms as electricity is channelled through pylons.

Later back at the hotel, dad had gone to the bar to have a drink with Jan. I returned to our room drank both Maccabbis and phoned Laura. I told her about John.

"How much have you had to drink. Your sound sloshed?"

"I am sloshed," I answered "But it's true."

"I'm having the girls round on Thursday. Abby, Devina, Kate, Wands, Jane maybe a few others. An Ann Summers type thing."

"That's nice," I answered dumbly

"And you mum's coming on Friday for a couple of nights. She thinks I could do with the company".

Dad came into the room "Look I'm going now. I love you loads. I'll phone you tomorrow when I get to Tiberias. Ok."

"Ok. Love you to."

"We better get to bed," dad said after I had hung up. "We've got a really long day and we need to leave by six. Thank God that's Jerusalem over."

END OF PART 1

INTERLUDE

"You are going to be crucified for being a two faced shit. There is your cross. Just take it outside and the soldiers will help you on."

"Will you help me on?"

"Sure. Just lie on it and we'll nail you on. This may hurt a little."

"Now we'll raise you up. There we are."

"Sebastian, you shouldn't have thought of myself and my wife as Siamese twins."

"Bishop, I'm thirsty. I need a drink."

"You shouldn't have talked like that about your mother and me. You've had this coming to you for a while now."

"Dad, I can't breathe."

"I saw you looking at Rachel. You won't have her stuck up there, will you?"

"If you love me break my legs."

GALILEE

"Take the potion like they used to in Ancient Greece and step over quietly. Because we are not committing suicide – It's a revolutionary act."

Jim Jones, Guyana, 1978

CHAPTER 6
Wednesday (Masada - The Dead Sea - Qumran – Jericho - Tiberias)

I
Early Rise

"Christ, what's that?" I shouted. It was pitch black, I couldn't see anything, but a screeching that sounded like chalk being dragged down a blackboard was piercing the blackness. The lamp next to Dad's bed flicked on and the screeching stopped.

"My alarm clock, very effective," he said dozily. Clearly some of his night medication had not totally been through its life cycle.

"You use the bathroom first – we've to be out by six."

"What time is it now?"

"Five," he answered.

I sat up in bed and immediately became aware of feeling terrible. My tongue felt dry and swollen, my stomach was churning and my head throbbing. "Five O'clock," I said to myself. Dad had started snoring again.

I stumbled into the bathroom and looked in the mirror. The combination of red wine and Maccabi beer had made my eyes bloodshot. I turned on the shower and then knelt down in front of the toilet, put my head over it, stuck my fingers down my throat and vomited into the bowl. A mixture of fluid and phlegm slid down the sides and into the water. I then took two Neurofen and two paracetamol and swallowed them with a litre of bottled water before cleaning my teeth. I stood under the lukewarm stream of water of the shower for a couple of minutes, zombified. I could remember talking to Laura the previous night but what about exactly had gone – 'but I am sloshed' fleetingly came back and then I recalled my meeting John. Eventually I summoned the energy to wash my hair and body with a lemon soap bought from Sainsbury's and by the time I had cleaned myself up I felt the recovery process attempting to kick in. I dried myself and went back into the hotel bedroom. Dad hadn't moved. Having dressed I went over to him and shook him quite vigorously.

"Come on dad, we need to get sorted. We haven't packed." He tried to respond, but was finding it difficult. "Come on dad, go and get a shower. That will freshen you up." I encouraged him and this time he managed to throw both legs over the edge of the bed and push his bulk into the standing position before waddling into the bathroom eyes half closed. Hearing the shower go on I took out our two suitcases from the wardrobe and packed them up untidily. Dad re-emerged.

"Are you ok, dad?"

"Tired, but I'll be ok. Are you ok?"

"I had a weird dream. I dreamt I was crucified. Too much vino I expect."

"Probably. You haven't packed my clothes for today?"

"No, they're on the chair."

After breakfast of fresh fruit only we said our goodbyes to Mohammed the proprietor and his family and headed out into the cobbled streets of the Old City, which proved hazardous in the dim light of the new dawn.

"The weather's changed," dad said as we plodded through the New Gate.

"It's because the sun's not up. It just feels colder."

"No, its changed," he repeated.

II

The lowest point on earth

"Good morning to you all. How are you all this morning? Are you ok or too much wine last night?" Rachel laughed into the microphone. We had left the Old City behind us, driven past Bethany and taken the road towards Jericho. "It doesn't look so nice today, there's a lot of cloud. It will be colder perhaps but there again things change rapidly in Israel, so we will see. This is our plan then for today. First we will go to Masada, about 100kms from here and then to Ein Gedi, a spa resort where you can float on the Dead Sea, or have a mud treatment. We will lunch at Ein Gedi. After lunch we will head north to Galilee and en route will make stops at Qumran, where the Dead Sea Scrolls were discovered and at the ancient city of Jericho before we arrive in Tiberias tonight. So we have a long, but lets hope enjoyable day." Rachel sat down. Ahmet the driver put some music on. It was Palestinian music that to the lay ear sounded Greek and haunting, like the music they played on Katapagea. One night there myself and Laura had climbed high into the mountains above Lavidea to a small

Cycladic church and listened to the shrill of the baliki and accompanying voice of a male islander who sang of his love for the island. We drank Oozo bought from Evangalia's and talked of interbreeding on the island that produced huge abnormalities in some of the islanders. Those, for example, who could not move their heads and so their eyes were constantly fixed towards the heavens or others with feet that protruded at right angles to their ankles. Then Laura had performed fellatio on me and when I exploded in her mouth some minutes later, the dreamy effect of the oozo and music echoing around the mountainside, finding its way into the small cycladic church with its icons and incense, left me with a moment of unbearable pleasure. The next day, sober, we thought we should be repentant. Instead, lying on the beach, we took pleasure in our wickedness and we plotted to return to the scene. This time I would perform, if perform is the right word, cunnilingus on Laura with Laura sat on the small alter amongst the lanterns and icons, with perhaps a candle or two lit, whilst I knelt in front of her, licking her clitoris to the point of orgasm. It never went further than fantasy.

The coach was descending quite steeply through the sparseness of the Judean desert we were now in. Scattered here and there were large tents occupied by Bedouins and surrounded by their livestock, camels and usually a myriad of different coloured petrol cans.

"These tents you see," Rachel was back on the microphone, "this way of life is dying out. It will be gone soon, extinct. This is because of the changes in International Borders. In Israel and the Palestine territories it is better to live in a house than a tent these days. In the old days if you were wandering in the desert and you wanted a drink you could call at a tent. If you were given a full cup of water that meant you were not welcome but if they gave you just a sip of water that meant you were welcome and afterwards you would get a big mug of tea which would quench your thirst. Now, when we left Jerusalem we were 800 metres above sea level. You can see the hills of the Judean desert has vanished and that means we are on the valley floor of the Jordan. When we reach the Dead Sea we will be 400 metres below sea level – the lowest point on the earth." The coach came to a crossroads and turned right. "If we went straight on," Rachel went on, "and the borders were open then in an hour we would be in Amman, capital of Jordan. King Hussein built the road when Jordan occupied the West Bank of the river. Now straight in front of you is the northern shore of the Dead Sea. Currently the sea is evaporating because a dam was built south of the Sea of Galilee to irrigate the northern Israel territories. Remember I said 'water causes war'. Well Jordan has very little water, in fact almost no water. So we give them water. If the Israelis decided not to given them water then their existence and survival would be threatened. They would have to fight for it."

"How much do you think they give them?" I whispered to dad.

"Not a lot I should think. Just enough."

"Risky business."

"Risky indeed."

We travelled along the shores of the Dead Sea. Large date and banana palm plantations were flanked by mountains of different shades of red and then nothing until the next plantation. Occasionally we would pass a Dead Sea resort, which, in the sparse red landscapes looked like a natural oasis and fed by the wadis that dissected the almost lunar landscape.

"In a way the Dead Sea is all part of the Great Rift Valley from Syria to Uganda." Rachel was stood at the front of the coach. "Two massive plates exist, one north to south and one more east to west which push and pull at each other. That means we are now in an earthquake zone. The sea is called a sea because of the haze the atmosphere throws up. Even though the other side is only a few miles away it often can't be seen so it gives the impression of being a huge sea. It is called Dead because nothing can live in it. And here towards the southern edge of the sea is the biblical site of Sodom where Lot came to live with his wife."

"That's strange," I whispered again to dad. "John the Baptist told me Sodom was in Jerusalem."

"He's interpreting. Sodom according to the Bible was a wicked place – orgies, boozing, you know generally wicked. God's angels destroyed it in true fire and brimstone fashion but had told Lot to escape with his family and not turn back. His wife did and she turned into a pillar of salt. He's saying the wickedness of Sodom has been transferred to Jerusalem."

"I see, I see. That makes sense." Rachel was also recounting the demise of Sodom.

"When the angles arrived at Lot's house all the men besieged it and insisted that Lot bring out the strangers, *'that we may know them.'* This means that perhaps they want to have sexual intercourse with them and that is where the word sodomy comes from."

"Imagine wanting to have intercourse with an angel."

"They didn't know they were angels," snapped dad, "and another thing. Please stop referring to that man at the Jaffa Gate as John the Baptist – just call him John if you have to call him anything."

"Ok, dad," I answered, disappointed at my stupidity.

III
Herod

"That," Rachel announced and pointing over the shoulder of Ahmet, "is Masada," and in front of us appeared a huge red prehistoric monolith, plateaud on top which grew and grew and grew. Turning into the car park, which was unusually quiet, Rachel spoke again.

"When we get off the coach I will go and buy the tickets. You can have a look at the tourist shops. We will then go up on one of those yellow cable cars. If you look you can see they are building a new cable car system so that they can carry more people up, but it's not ready for us so we'll have to go on the old one." The coach came to a halt. I was relieved feeling quite queasy from the travel and the night before. Outside it was overcast and humid and having walked briefly around the expensive tourist shops we sat near the entrance of the cable car and waited for Rachel.

"Did you feel that?" dad said.

"Did I feel what?" I answered.

"I don't know, but I thought I felt a spot of rain."

"It doesn't rain here dad. It's one of the driest places on earth, if not the driest. Were a quarter of a mile beneath the Mediterranean. You're imagining it."

But then a drop of water landed on my forehead and from my eyes I could see it roll down the bridge of my nose until it dropped off the end and vanished into the desert. I looked up. It certainly was very grey. Then another drop, as I stared into the heavens, landed directly in my eye and made me wince.

"You're right. It is raining."

"Come round," Rachel had emerged from the ticket office. "Come round." We gathered round her. "I can't believe it," she said. "It hasn't rained here for 5 years and now look," and she stretched out her hands to catch one of the drops. "It won't last. Ok some history before we go up. Up on top are a number of buildings. The original fortress was built for Jonathon Maccabi but really what we will see was the work of Herod the Great. Now Herod, he wasn't 'Great' because he was loved by his people. Quite the reverse is true. He was loathed. 'The Great' refers to the magnificent buildings he built in Judea and Galilee and on Sunday at Caesarea we will see one of his great viaducts that brought water from the mountains to the coastal city. Herod lived from 74-4 BC becoming King of Judea in BC31 having found favour with the emperor Augustus. He was a treacherous man and ruled by the sword. Anybody he thought opposed him he had killed and this is important because as he got older he was less and less able to determine who was for or against him so he just killed. This is famously illustrated of course by the Slaughter of the Innocents in Bethlehem though of course Jesus, Mary and Joseph had found safety in Egypt. He also killed his wife, Marianne and his two sons by her. Whenever there was trouble in Judea or when he thought there may be trouble he would flea to Masada because obviously," she pointed up, "obviously it is very safe and nobody could get to him. He built, as you will see, his own little community up there, and thought about who was against him and plotted how to get rid of them. I suppose today you would say he was paranoid. When he died he ordered 70 Rabbis to be killed so the Jews had nothing to celebrate. Now here's the cable car. Let's go and I'll talk some more whilst we ascend."

I knew as we boarded the yellow cable car, that Herod was clearly a psychotic. A psychiatrist today would have little hesitation in diagnosing him as suffering from paranoid schizophrenia and I thought of the people who had died because of his illness, especially his two sons. The cable car lurched out of its station and we were climbing.

"This site," Rachel went on, "is the most visited archaeological site in Israel and that is primarily because of the famous siege that happened in 70AD. It came at the conclusion of the Roman-Jewish war. The Romans had regained control of Judea and this was the last outpost of Jewish resistance, a group of 1000 Zealots who were determined to scrap it out to the death. Now the story has become exaggerated over the years. It is commonly said that the siege was 3 years but it was more like 4 months. In the end the Zealots made a suicide pact to avoid being made slaves. The men killed their wives and children with swords. Then, the story goes, ten men were selected to kill the other men and then lots were drawn to determine who would complete the slaughter before falling on his own sword. The story says however that two women and five children who had hidden themselves in the massive water cisterns survived. To Israel the story of Masada is hugely important. On top you will see school children and army recruits being told the story of the bravery of Masada. The story always finishes 'Masada shall not fall again'."

At this point, half way up, there was a huge roar and the cable car shook quite violently. The pilgrims, including myself, looked around nervously.

"Don't worry. It is just the airforce. They practice around here." The first roar was followed by a second and we looked out of the window and saw three grey fighters in formation sweeping over Masada and onto the desert.

"Looks like a French Mirage to me," dad offered.

"No way, Derek," Robin challenged, "they're F.10s, no doubt about it." Who cares, is all I could think.

IV

The Golden Shot

At the top the rain had stopped. It was clearer to see how a severe path, the snake path, had been cut in the rock for those who wanted to climb up. It was steep and looked dangerous. We turned left and walked to the remains of the Northern Palace with its three terraces. The view beyond was sparse and huge. Below we could see the site of the Roman army camps etched out in the sandstone – huge barracks that surrounded the site completely. Rachel talked more of the history, and explained how people were able to survive on this desolate rock high up beneath the level of the sea.

" I think now you should walk around on your own. There are clear information signs at various points. We'll meet back at the top of the snake path in an hour, that's ten thirty." I walked back through the palace and came to a bathhouse.

"The principles are the same as the great bath houses of the Roman Empire." Rachel was saying to the Bishop." Beneath the bath," she carried on pointing at the large stone bath in the middle "would have been channels of water heated by a furnace. Water would evaporate but when it reached the ceiling it would condense and roll down the circular walls to........," I walked on past the bathhouse to a tower perhaps fifty meters to the south east. A group of pilgrims were already in there looking out at the impressive scene below including Keith and his parents. Pam, his mother was talking to Deirdre.

"....he plays bowls and is good at archery."

"I won a tournament last September." It was the first time I had heard him talk.

"How do you do it, archery, when you can't see? Isn't it dangerous?" Deirdre asked insensitively what I was also thinking.

"Well," Keith replied, "you listen to instructions from an aid, like distance, left a bit, right a bit, on target." It sounded like the Golden Shot.

Far beneath me I saw a bus move away and wind up the distant hillside. A boy was chasing it and after a hundred meters or so gave it up as missed. The bus carried on for another mile and then stopped. It then reversed back down the winding road and picked the boy up.

V

Seb and Sally catch up

I left the tower and saw the six priests on pilgrimage assembled by the remains of a Byzantine Church including dad. They were praying

"Did that really happen yesterday?" a voice behind me said. I turned and saw Sally.

"Sorry Sally what was that?"

"You know, the stuff you told me and Sue in Bethlehem last night about that man who thought he was John the Baptist and the leader of that cult."

"Yes, it did happen."

"What will happen to them?"

"I don't know really. The cult leader will probably be arrested if he's in Jerusalem, they've got pretty good intelligence. As for John the Baptist, well I expect he'll be deported eventually. Did I tell you he was English?"

"No, no you didn't."

"Yes, he had an English accent. It was very Home Counties."

We wandered around the perimeter fence.

"How the hell did the Romans manage to get up here?" I asked not really expecting Sally to know.

"They built a ramp and climbed up."

"A ramp. It would have been to steep surely."

"No, look out here," she pointed. "You can see how they did it. They probably started nearly a mile away and just built it up. The soldiers wouldn't have built just supervised. It was probably the prisoners from the Jewish war, so when the Zealots up here tried to stop the builders of the ramp from building it, they could have been killing fellow Jews, people who they had earlier fought alongside."

Maybe Rachel was wrong about the length of time that the siege lasted. The ramp looked like it would have taken an age to complete. We walked in silence around the perimeter, passed the Southern Bastion and other Byzantine remains until we were back at the Snake Path Gate. Most of the group had returned and Robin started counting heads.

"49. One missing. Anyone know whose missing?" It turned out to be Jan.

"Bloody typical," and then Robin put his hands around his mouth, filled his lungs with air and yelled as loud as he could, "JAN!" and scanned the scene in front of him. The astounded pilgrims scanned him. "JAN, WHERE THE BLOODY HELL ARE YOU?" Other groups of tourists, pilgrims, school children and soldiers looked around at us "JAN, WHERE THE......."

"Shut up, Robin!" Barbara interjected "Just shut up." She was bright red. From behind the remains of the Byzantine church where I had earlier seen the 6 priests praying Jan emerged and trotted up to the group.

"I am sorry," she said "I was lost in a world of my own. It really is amazing."

"Ok," said Rachel, "Back to the cable car. We need to get to Ein Gedi." We turned back to the snake path gate to the cable car.

"Damn cable car," I heard the Bishop say to his wife "Does nothing for my vertigo."

VI
Ein Gedi

We arrived at Ein Gedi, a health spa on the shores of the Dead Sea shortly after eleven O'clock. As we pulled into the resort, an unusual concoction of palm trees, grass and what looked like a huge Municipal English swimming pool circa 1970 set against the ferocious red background of the desert, Rachel explained the process of rejuvenation.

"There are four parts to the process. First have a hot mineral shower and then cover yourself in mud. The mud is full of minerals that will rejuvenate your skin. Let it dry. Then walk down to the seashore. It is quite a long way, remember it is evaporating, so if you like get the train," and she pointed to a train on wheels with a few little coaches that gave the impression that it should be driven by Noddy. "Then at the Dead Sea just have a good float and the mud will come away. If you've got scratches the sea might sting a bit because of all the salt and when you've had enough take a dip in one of the sulphur pools before rinsing in the large freshwater pool. This of course isn't compulsory," she laughed. "Listen be back here for one for lunch and then we'll go onto Qumran."

The pilgrims descended out of the coach

"Are you going, Seb?"

"No. Are you?"

"No I don't think so."

"I've done all this before and it doesn't do anything for me." In Turkey the previous year myself, Laura & Jack went to a place called Dalyan, hired a boat one day, which took us to various sulphur pools and mud baths. The smell was terrible, you had to breathe through your mouth but eventually the sulphur stuck to the back of your throat. Eventually it made us wretch. Jack and Laura liked the mud bath. I sat and watched them and I remembered Jack covered in baked mud like a swamp monster whilst I sat drinking Carlsberg on what was a very hot day. "I thought I might go and read my book for an hour or so, chill out."

"Fancy a coffee?"

"Ok, yes, why not."

We headed for the self-service restaurant that looked out over the sparse landscape towards the sea itself. It was empty apart from the bustle of young waiters and waitresses preparing themselves for the onslaught of seriously cleansed tourists. Dad came to a window seat where I was reading my book with a tray of coffee and some biscuits and poured each of us a cup.

"It's only half eleven. It feels like four or something," he said.

"It was the early start."

"Did you find your answer in The Acts of the Apostles?"

"What answer?"

"About Judas Iscariot."

"Yes I did, thanks."

"And what do you think?"

"I think he could not have hung himself from one of the old olive trees in Gethsemane. But of course we don't actually know if those trees were the witnesses to the betrayal. If they were you could definitely say that he did not hang himself at Gethsemane, not a big enough drop. If they weren't well who knows, maybe, maybe not, though I think whatever its highly likely that the act," I paused "the act of that Apostle did not happen there."

"I think you're probably right." He paused. "What are you reading?"

"It's a book called 'the last King of Scotland'." I showed him the cover.

"Why is there a picture of Idi Amin on the front?"

"Well according to Idi he was the last King of Scotland. As well as of course being a dictator he amongst other things also considered himself to be the conqueror of the British Empire and the ruler of all the fishes in the sea."

"Is it biographical?"

"It's a novel tracking Idi through the eyes of his doctor, who just happens to be Scottish."

"Sounds good."

"It is good, very good. Thinking about Idi and his power, and then Herod the Great, there are a lot of similarities, aren't there? You know getting rid of people, scale causing perception to go out the window."

"Was Amin mad?"

"Absolutely, big time and cruel with it, really cruel. Have you heard of the photographer Don McCullin?"

"Yes I have."

"Well he covered numerous war zones, Cyprus in the 70s, the six day war when the Israelis entered the Old City and Uganda. In Uganda he ended up in some prison, well a death camp. John Simpson was there also. They thought they were going to die and witnessed Idi's secret police taking his political enemies into a courtyard. They would lie them on the floor and then smash their brains out with these massive metal mallets, I suppose to save on bullets – you know mallets that you see at fair grounds to test your strength. Just smashed their brains out." There was a brief silence between us.

"It's difficult to grasp."

"It is difficult, but it's all down to security, isn't it. You know, back home, it's all safe. I mean life is perceived as hard, but it's not, not really. We don't experience the scale of trauma of other societies whether its famine, disease, poverty, I don't know political oppression."

I looked out of the window. One by one the pilgrims were emerging on the terrace outside in swimsuits, flip-flops and covered form head to foot in mud that made them hard to recognise. I recognised Deirdre by her horn-rimmed glasses and presumed the man holding her hand was Martin but couldn't be 100% sure. Even old Mrs Thornton, who was in her 90s and being accompanied by her 3 daughters all in their 60s, was being helped towards the Noddy train.

"That's the problem with faith," I went on still staring out the window and oblivious of who I was talking to. "How can I have faith when everything is laid on a plate for me? I know its corny, but think about Sodom and Lot and the wrath of God and Christ as you told me the other day, as the Great Redeemer, and the bridge between man and God. So why all the suffering still? Why all the killing? Why the Genocide? And why should I want to be part of a faith which is about individual salvation where the end goal is to get to heaven? That's selfish. I can still live my life properly can't I?"

The Noddy train was disappearing with the swamp people into the distance. Dad was quiet, sipping his coffee, and I realised the questions I had asked weren't directed at him or his faith that he shared with the people on the train but at myself. It struck me I had never spoken so passionately or openly to him in my life.

"I'm sorry dad. I get carried away. It's just that sometimes I think it is the *thought* of God that makes people feel safe in a pretty unsafe world." I paused. "No doubt on judgement day I'll be proved wrong and meet my maker at Sodom."

"Sometimes," he replied "you can over think. Sometimes its best just to carry on, you know let things happen."

"But that's denial"

"No, not necessarily. Now I'm going for a walk. Do you want to come?"

"I think I'll read a little bit more about Idi."

"I'll be back in a hour or so and we'll have some lunch."

"Ok dad, bye." I watched him leave the restaurant and felt an overwhelming affection and didn't know why. What did he mean, *not necessarily?* I looked around the now completely deserted restaurant and it struck me that it was only dad and myself who had not taken on the sulphur and mud ordeal.

VII

Jallopino Peppers and Carlsberg

True to his word dad returned an hour later. The Noddy train had also brought the pilgrims back with red arms and virgin white bodies; *what strange shapes*, I thought to myself, and soon the cleansed were decanting into the restaurant. Dad and I sat in relative silence as we ate salad with large jallapino peppers and shared a Carlsberg. The extent of Idi's atrocities had evaporated any remnants of my hangover and I needed a beer to be able to stomach them.

By 1pm Robin and Rachel were encouraging us to get back to the coach.

"We've still plenty to do, Qumran, Jericho. We need to get going," but the Bishop had only just returned from his mud and sulphur odyssey and it was nearer two before we headed north towards Qumran. "That's the power of the church for you," I joked to dad as we sat on the coach and he smiled.

VIII

The war of the Sons of Light against the Sons of Darkness

As we approached Qumran Rachel was again talking to us.

"Ok, we'll soon be at Qumran. It is at these historic caves that the Dead Sea Scrolls were found by the son of a local Bedouin shepherd in 1947 and they are thought to be the oldest Hebrew books in existence. They can mostly be seen in the magnificent Israel Museum in Jerusalem in what is called 'The Shrine of the Book'. The story goes that the boy was looking for a lost sheep. He came to the cave and threw a stone in and heard it strike pottery."

"That's amazing," I whispered to dad "Imagine if that stone had not hit the pot."

"So hearing it strike the pot, he climbed down into the cave and found 50 cylindrical jars containing all of these scrolls. We now know that the scrolls, which were written on animal hide, date from the first century BC. Unfortunately when found the scrolls were fragmented, torn. So clumsy," she reflected quickly as if no one else was around. "So here we are. First we will watch a brief film about the life of the people who wrote the scrolls, the Essenes, and then walk around the renovated site of where these men lived and finally we'll look into the cave itself."

"Who did she say wrote them?" I asked dad

"The Essenes," he answered as we left the coach.

"But dad, that's what the guy at the Jaffa Gate kept saying."

"I don't know what you mean."

We were walking up some stairs past a sign directing us to 'The Audio Visual Show.'

"John. I asked him who he was. He said, *"I am the Essene, John"*. I asked him again who he was and again he said, *"I am the Essene, John"*. So I asked him again and this time he said *"I am John...some call me the Baptist.'* I asked him three times who he was."

"That's because, Seb John the Baptist was an Essene, probably. Maybe Christ also."

We entered the small seatless cinema. It went dark and a picture flicked on the screen showing bearded men, wearing only one small white garment that covered their genitals and buttocks, writing, bathing and praying. The accompanying script was provided by a deep voiced American that reminded me of Boomer at the Church of the All Nations at Gethsemane.

"The Dead Sea Scrolls," the commentary began "were written by the Essenes. The Essenes were an ultra devout Jewish sect who left Jerusalem to live out this devotion in the harshness of the desert. They were disillusioned with the way others lived their lives, such as the Pharisees and Sadducees, and the wealth and corruption of the Temple of Jerusalem. They lived life in strict accordance with biblical law which included work, exercise, prayer, bathing. Spiritually, they believed in the imminent arrival of Christ. Qumran was destroyed by the Romans in 68AD during the Jewish Revolt." The text finished and for 5 minutes or so the film featured the Essenes at work to a background of haunting music. Suddenly the American voice filled the room again.

"You may now pass through to the exhibition. Thank you for visiting Qumran, original home of the Dead Sea Scrolls." The light flicked on and a door opened to the side of the screen. One by one we trooped through.

"What the hell is that supposed to mean, 'Original home of the Dead Sea Scrolls'?"

Dad ignored the question.

"Right," Rachel said, "have a walk round for twenty minutes or so and we'll have a look at the excavation and cave."

The exhibition featured Greco/Roman clay pots, how the Essenes made their ink, how the animal hides were treated and a history of the discovery. There were also impressive blown up illustrations of the scrolls with their magnificent penmanship. There were fragments from the Books of Leviticus and Esther, but the one that caught my eye was the Essene description of the final battle, the one that currently Joshua Fisher III was planning for the Mount of Olives which read:

"*The War of the Sons of Light against the Sons of Darkness.*"

IX

Dead Sea Scrolls

Outside we toured the excavation which included a kitchen, a lookout tower, storeroom, and an aqueduct that ran behind the pottery workshop to the Mikum or ritual bathhouse. We then walked to an observation point and looked out over a sheer valley at the cave where the original scrolls were found. Looking at the arid landscape I became aware of the thousands of caves that dissected the mountainside, and of past oppressions that made people hide in them.

"Well there it is, son." There was a voice behind me. I turned. It was Fred who I had spoken to with his wife Roma, in the courtyard at the Basilica of the Holy Sepulchre the previous day.

"What do you mean Fred?"

"Look at the entrance of the cave son," I turned back and looked at the opening some 50 metres away.

"What about it Fred?"

"What do you mean 'what about it?' Can't you bloody well see? There's your bloody cat for you." Quickly I dug into my blue Loving Dove Christian bag and produced my binoculars. Raising them to my eyes I focussed on the cave entrance and sure enough there was a large white cat sitting proudly erect and camouflaged by the mountainous background. It appeared to be staring at us, but when I felt its deep yellow eyes piercing the binoculars and burning into my own I realised I was wrong. The cat was staring at me.

X

Casino

On the coach I felt disturbed and would not allow myself the thought that I so much wanted. At the Church of the Nativity, Dominos Flevit, Peter in Gallicantu, The Basilica of the Holy Sepulchre and now here, Qumran. Always one, never more, just one.

"We are running late, very late and it's quite far to Tiberias," Rachel interrupted my thoughts, "so we won't be able to stop at Jericho. I will point a few things out and give a bit of history. We're about 40kms east from Jerusalem. This is the lowest town on earth and dates back to 9000 BC. Its success has been due to the springs that make the land fertile and you can see all the date palms around you that reflect this fertility. But sometimes in the past the springs dried up so they just moved the town to the next spring. Jesus would have stopped here on his journey from Galilee to Jerusalem. His usual route would have been Capernaum, where we'll visit on Saturday, Jericho, Bethany, and Jerusalem. Now the main site I wanted to visit was the Monastery of Temptation, but we haven't got time." Briefly I felt resentful of mud, sulphur and the Bishop. " You can see it to your left over there." I looked left across what had struck me as a very bland town, I never thought Jericho would be so bland, and high cut into the mountain cliff was the Monastery.

"It's like the one in Katapagea."

"There's a Monastery like that on Katapagea?" asked dad

"Yeah, cut high in the cliff overlooking the Aegean. The monks give you Turkish Delight and Rakki when you get there."

"What's Rakki?"

"It's a local spirit to which you add honey," and I remembered staggering up the mule track with Laura after a night of Rakki in the port.

"The Monastery of the temple is where Christ was tempted by the Devil," went on Rachel. The Bishop grabbed the microphone.

"*If though be the Son of God, command that these stones be made bread,*" and handed it back to her.

"Thank you, Bishop. Now if you look to your right, you will see Jericho's newest development." We turned and saw a huge casino. "Should we stop for some Black Jack, Bishop?" Rachel joked and then just as quickly as we were into Jericho we were through.

As we travelled towards Tiberias the scenery began to change. The starkness of the desert and its dried up wadis was gradually becoming greener and greener and the amount of arable land was increasing. There was also reminders of conflicts passed – the occasional stranded tank or bus. As night crept in the silhouette produced as we hurtled along the banks of the Jordan reminded me of the Isle of Skye, North of Portree to the Old Man of Stoor and onto the grave of Flora McDonald.

XI
Seb watches Breaking News

About 7 o'clock we reached the shores of the Sea of Galilee at Tiberias. Rachel advised us to be ready for supper at 8 o'clock. In the hotel room we sat, I with a Maccabbi, dad with his gin and watched CNN (Israel) in silence. Unlike the Knights Templar, there was a television in this hotel room. At eight, as instructed, we went to the restaurant where again we sat with the two female priests, Catherine and Liz. They were both pissed having drunk a bottle of Bombay Gin with the Bishop and his wife. Liz was very free speaking saying she had 3 children through IVF, that they were a pain and she would prefer to be a recluse in Scotland. After supper dad went for a drink with David Brown, the miserable man from the first evening's supper. I went back to the room and rang Laura. People were dropping out of her party planned for the next day. She sounded fed up. I turned CNN (Israel) back on. The reception was poor and I fiddled with the aerial to little avail and sat down with another Maccabbi to watch. The picture flicked and jumped. The ads were on, but then returned to the studio. At the bottom of the screen were two words in bold red. They said "Breaking News," and then it was over to the presenter.

"As we said before the break we are getting information through related to a body that has been found in Jerusalem, more precisely on the Mount of Olives. We know only the person to be male nothing else at the moment except the police have not ruled out violence."

I couldn't believe it. Where we were two days ago a body had been found. Somewhere between Pater Noster and Gethsemane where the Essene, John had spotted the Caring Christian, Joshua Fisher III somebody had died, and instinctively I feared the worse because I knew it had been violently.

CHAPTER 7
Thursday (Cana – Nazareth – Mount Tabor)

I
Water into Wine

For the second morning the shrill alarm of dad's clock penetrated the darkness ridiculously early. I was in bed, half asleep, when dad came back from the bar and didn't relate the breaking news of a body being found on the Mount of Olives. More alert this morning we washed and dressed quickly and went for breakfast.

"I was watching the news last night,"

"Anything of interest?"

"Yes, there was, they found the body of a man on The Mount of Olives."

He paused and asked,

"Who found the body?"

"I don't know, they didn't know anything else apart from that – maybe we'll find out today."

At around seven o'clock we were back on the coach and Robin was counting heads.

"50 – Ok Ahmet we can go," and the coach climbed out of the hotel forecourt, past the football stadium and out of the town. It was raining.

"Morning, morning," Rachel said.

"Morning," we wearily replied.

"No, that's no good. I said Good Morning," and she shouted it into the microphone

"Good Morning!" We shouted back.

"That's better. Ok let me outline the day. First we are going to Cana to the site of Christ's first miracle of turning water into wine and those of you who wish to can renew your marriage vows. Then on to Nazareth and the Church of the Annunciation. After Nazareth we will stop for lunch before going to Mount Tabor and the alleged site of the Transfiguration of Christ. I say alleged because, surprise surprise, there is some dispute. Then if there is time we will stop off at the River Jordan at the place that John the Baptist conducted his baptisms – so again a long but interesting day."

II
Judith asks for support

The countryside as we climbed had completely changed. It was a deep luscious green with clumps of pretty red poppies, dreamily looking down onto the Sea of Galilee.

"There was a bit of an argument in the bar last night," dad said to me discreetly.

"Oh yes, what about?"

"About the renewing of marriage vows. Deirdre wants to renew them but Martin doesn't want to."

"So what happened?"

"I don't think they're going to renew them."

"I suppose that's some sort of shame."

"Maybe," he answered.

"Ok, if you look behind you, you can see the Sea of Galilee clearly." Rachel was off again. "It is not really a sea but a fresh water lake. The Hebrew name for it is Lake Gennasaret." We looked back and agreed the view down to the lake was glorious. It seemed to be shimmering light even in the dullness of the day. "Those hills behind Galilee, these are the Golan Heights and just the other side is Syria. Where we are passing now is the ancient battlefield of the 'Horns of Hittin'. It is in fact an extinct volcano and is where Saladin defeated the Crusaders and brought Tiberias under Islamic control in 1187. Today Tiberias is a completely Jewish city. Now I think Judith wants to say something." Judith, the woman who had raised my arm in the air the evening we went to eat supper with the Palestinian Christians in Bethlehem walked up to the front of the coach and took the microphone.

"Before we arrive at Cana I just wanted to say that it is really important to support each other through the renewal of the marriage vows. It can be quite emotional and intense. I feel there has been a bit of tension around in the last day or so, so please support each other." She turned off the microphone and returned to her seat.

"What was that all about?"

"I'm not sure," dad answered.

III
Renewal

At the place in Cana where Jesus turned water into wine when the wedding had run dry there are two churches, one Roman Catholic and one Greek Orthodox, both of which claim to have the original jars in which the miracle was performed. When Rachel told us that I thought of my cousin who didn't know whether he lived the right side or the wrong side of the railway bridge. Who had the right jars and who had the wrong ones.

Close by is a Franciscan church which we planned to use for the renewal of vows but we were an hour late, and had to be sandwiched between two other groups of pilgrims which meant we had to stand in the drizzle in the courtyard waiting. Once in the church those who were renewing their vows stood at the front whilst those who were not stood around the flank. Judith conducted the service and beautiful it was too. She did it with meaning that made the couples dab their eyes with paper handkerchiefs. I noticed Deirdre and Martin on the front pew.

"Go and offer peace to those around you." Judith invited us after the renewal. I turned to dad and offered him peace.

"And peace with you also," he smiled. Barbara was the other side of me.

"Peace be with you, Barbara." She took my hand.

"Peace be with you." Next to Barbara was Keith, standing tall and erect with his white stick and sunglasses and who had won an archery competition last September. I walked around Barbara and took the hand that was not holding his stick. Then looking into the blackness of his sunglasses, I said,

"Peace be with you, Keith."

"Peace be with you too, Sebastian." I let go of his hand. How did he know it was me? I hadn't talked to him, or his parents or any of his family since I first spotted him looking out over Jerusalem. Barbara hadn't said my name. He continued to gaze straight ahead of him. Dad had now taken his hand,

"Peace be with you Keith."

"I'm not sure who you are. Is it Martin?"

"No, its Derek."

"Peace be with you too Derek."

I felt the need for some fresh air and went back out into the courtyard. We weren't due on the coach for ten minutes and I decided to go for a walk along the pedestrian only cobbles of Cana. I left the courtyard and turned right along a row of tourist shops selling primarily cheap wine when I heard a voice in the distance behind me.

"Sebastian, wait, Sebastian wait."

It was said with some urgency. Turning round I saw Sally running towards me. She was in floods of tears.

"Sally, what's the matter, what's the matter?" She caught up with me and struggling to catch her breath she blurted out,

"I've been married twenty seven years and he's not here to renew our vows. I really wanted him to be here. I tried to phone him last night and the night before but I couldn't get told of him." I put my arms round her.

"It's ok Sally, it's ok." She was sobbing into my coat. After a minute or so, with the shopkeepers and their wine looking on, she pulled herself away.

"I'm sorry, I'm sorry. It all got too much," she said as she dabbed her red eyes. Sally, unlike Jan, was trying to grow old gracefully and succeeding as there was a beauty about her that spoke of wisdom, experience and caring.

"Look I was going for a short walk before going back on the coach. Do you want to come?" and I put my arm out to her, through which she linked her own.

"It's a pretty intense place, isn't it?" I said as we strolled again past the shops.

"What here?" she answered.

"No the whole thing. All this conflict and religion, it warps your perception. Back inside Keith said "peace be with you, Sebastian", but I've never spoken to him so how did he know it was me?"

"I don't know."

"Twenty seven years, that's a long time." I changed the subject.

"I wish he was here," she went on. "You know, we've always done so much together. Brought the kids up, gone on holiday...." She was starting to get upset again, "and I couldn't get hold of him. I tried every half hour. He should have been home by nine. He was at the golf club AGM."

"Well it probably overran. Golf Club AGM's are very complex – they're more about power than anything else and well power can take a long time to sort out." This is sounding ridiculous I thought. I didn't have a clue what I was talking about.

"Yes, your right", she answered to my surprise, "he was up for vets captain." She changed the subject. "If your wife was here would you have renewed your vows?"

"I don't know. Probably not."

"Why not?" she seemed shocked.

"I've only been married seven years. It feels like were still at the beginning. I don't feel ready to renew them."

"I see," she said "that makes sense. Why did you come here with your dad?"

"I don't know, its complex. It's about a lot of things, our relationship, him asking me, my lack of assertiveness." It all sounded corny.

"Are you glad you came?"

"Yes, I am."

"Do you believe in all this?"

"In all of what?"

"In all of this, you know, do you believe in God." I was stunned by the question.

We stopped and I turned to her and heard myself feebly saying,

"I don't know."

At the moment of truth my agnosticism had held firm – *I have no firm belief about God.*

"When I was a kid I was an altar boy, whatever it's called at this church in Bath. I use to dread it because I always had difficulty fitting this bronze candlestick into its stand. Then one Sunday it just wouldn't go in so I offered up a little prayer, you know a bit of a divine intervention. But it didn't come. So I swore at it."

"What did you say?" she interrupted.

"I told it to get the fuck in." She smiled and I noticed that her eyes were still moist from when she had been crying. " But it didn't and everybody heard and my days as an altar boy were thankfully numbered. Anyway since then I have been suspicious of anything to divine, if you see what I mean."

119

"I do see what you mean and I can understand that," she responded. "It's all very far fetched. The thing for me is that it's a way of life, always has been. I never challenged it, just accepted it from when I was a kid. I don't feel I can challenge it now, I'm getting too old." I thought of the people refusing to go through the children's memorial at Yad Vashem, dad saying not to think too deeply at Ein Gedi and here at Cana, where Jesus turned water into wine, Sally was saying she was too old. Three forms of denial in the land where Jesus was denied three times by his closest disciple.

"You're not too old, Sally, far from it. You should just go with what you feel best with. Life's too complicated otherwise."

We turned around and walked past the church where twenty minutes before we had witnessed the renewal of vows and returned to the coach. Twenty or so minutes later we arrived at the town of Nazareth. Nazareth reminded me of Bethlehem. Busy, bustling and a mess as it prepared for the millennium celebrations in the town where Gabriel announced to Mary about her miraculous conception. Our first stop was at the Greek Orthodox St Gabriels, a church that marks the spot where that denomination believes the annunciation took place. By this time many of the pilgrims had needed to relieve themselves but couldn't because of the contamination with the toilets and so took comfort in drawing up small ladles of water from the deep blue spring within the church that marked this holiest of holy site. Rachel tried to reassure the group that the facilities at the Basilica of the Annunciation were considerably better and attempted to cheer the desperate pilgrims up with a tale of an inter-denominational punch up that took place one year when Easter and Passover fell in the same week.

IV

Jonathon Mautner

We left St Gabriels and entered the building site that was Nazareth towards the Annunciation Church. We followed a track of half- built pavements, wood and sand. I found myself walking with Emily, the wife of Robert who I had had breakfast with in Jerusalem a few days prior.

"You seem to make a lot of notes," she commented "have you been asked to write an article?"

"No. It's just, you know, you come on these things and then forget them. I just didn't want to forget."

"You could write a book about all this."

"I don't know, maybe."

We found ourselves next to a small supermarket.

"Emily, I'm just nipping in here. I want to get a paper, see what's going on." Inside I bought a bottle of water and a copy of Jerusalem Today. It was impossible to read walking along so I tucked it in my blue Loving Dove bag and chased after the others in the distance.

I eventually caught up with them in the courtyard of the Basilica of the Annunciation. Rachel was in full flow.

"This is the fifth church to stand on this site, this one being completed only 30 years ago. It is on two levels and you can look down into the grotto of the Annunciation when you are inside. The Roman Catholics perform many services here so try not to disturb them. When you walk round admire all the depictions of the annunciation sent from around the world. They constitute some brilliant art. Meet back here in an hour and we will go on to St Joseph's Church or as it is otherwise known the Church of the Carpenter's Shop." I retreated to one of the stone benches that surrounded the courtyard as the Bishop dispersed the pilgrims with,

"*The angel of God announces to Mary and the word was made flesh.*"

I was beginning to feel a bit oppressed by the churches, whatever the history, and took the paper out my bag and read the headline:

Body of Man Identified: Murder search commenced.

The article read:

The body of the man found on the Mount of Olives has been identified as Jonathon Mautner, 46 of Nedasseret Zion in Jerusalem. According to a police spokesman Mr Mautner's body was discovered in the garden of the Dominus Flevit Church. Mr Mautner had received multiple stab wounds to the body and he had been decapitated. Police also said that his head was facing the Old City with an ash tear painted beneath his left eye and the numbers 666 had been painted on his forehead.

"*The killing is of a huge concern to us,*" *reported Chief of Police for the Old City, Ben Regan.* "*It is extremely brutal, and very symbolic. Why anyone should want to kill this family man in this way is unclear. Currently our investigation is working with a number of other institutions including religious and psychiatric establishments to profile what we may have here."*

Mr Mautner, a restaurant owner with restaurants near the Tomb of the Prophets and the Old City would often walk between the two following a route that took him down Mount of Olives, past Dominus Flevit and Gethsemane, along the Ophel Road to the Dung Gate. He leaves behind his wife, JoKaty and 4 children.

At the bottom of the article was printed a rather unremarkable picture of Jonathon Mautner, clean-shaven and smiling outside one of his restaurants. I stared at the photograph for a few minutes and reread the article. *Wasn't Nedasseret Zion the suburb where the Caring Christians had been arrested shortly after our arrival in Israel?* I couldn't remember. And what about the head staring out over Jerusalem on the site where Jesus had done the same thing nearly two thousand years ago and wept for the incompetence of man. Except this wasn't Jesus but somebody presumably, with his three 6's, to be perceived as the Anti-Christ. *Satan himself.* Ash, Roman Catholics mark themselves with ash on Good Friday, or do they?

"Aren't you going to look round?" It was Rachel.

"Yes, I was just about too. Look at this." I handed her the paper and she read the article.

"Things like this happen here from time to time. It all becomes too much, the religion and the intensity. I can remember a few years back a number of women being killed all around the Old City. The killer broke their necks, stripped them and painted their bodies with snakes before tying them up to trees. When they caught the killer he said he was the father of Adam and protecting him from the sins of Eve. The reason he killed more than once was that he perceived Adam to mean man and Eve to mean women. He was protecting man from the sin of woman. It was all very suppressed, sexually suppressed I mean. Obvious really, but it baffled them at the time for a few days."

"Who was he?"

"He was a Roman Catholic Priest working at the Basilica of the Holy Sepulchre. The Roman Catholic community, as well as being ashamed, were amazed. He was truly respected in their community and other communities. You could say he took Genesis a little too seriously. Look, do you want me to show you around?" I wasn't expecting the offer but immediately answered yes.

"Not often we get a father and son combination, without their wives," she commented as we passed through the two massive wooden doors that marked the entrances of the church into which were carved significant events in the life of Jesus from his birth to his death at Calvary.

"How do you know I'm married?"

"I just expect you to be. Well are you?"

"Yes, I am," I answered as I stopped to look at the carvings not wanting to get bogged down in another father son bonding conversation.

"There's a picture in the National Gallery in London called 'the Betrothal of the Arnolfini'," I said to her. "Do you know it?"

"No."

"It's like this door in a way."

"How can a door be a like a picture?"

"The picture shows a couple getting married. The Arnolfini were merchants from Italy who came to the low land. In the fifteenth century Jan Van Eyk painted their picture of betrothal in a bedroom. She is wearing green and seems to have a lot of layers on, which gives the impression that she is pregnant. There's lots of symbolism about fertility and health. Behind the couple on the far wall is a wooden mirror. The mirror itself is circular but has an ornate carved wooden surround. What is incredible about the mirror is two things. Firstly you see the reflection of the backs of the Arnolfini. Beyond that you see Jan Van Eyk himself painting the two of them. The second thing is on the wooden surround the life events of Christ are depicted, just like this door, carrying the cross, the annunciation, the nativity except of course it is a hundredth of the size of these depictions here."

"Is it a beautiful painting?"

"Yes, it is. A wonderful painting. Oil on canvas, 1434. Above the mirror Van Eyk has written 'Johannes de eyck fuit hic' which means "Jan Van Eyk was here," or something like that. Art scholars interpret this as Van Eyk witnessing the wedding but sometimes I wonder if he is referring to the unborn child – was it his, if of course it was there at all. You should see it."

"Maybe, if I come to England. Your dad has invited me over to stay with him and your mother."

"Are you going to take the offer up?"

"I don't know. I may. It depends on my daughter."

By now we were walking in the church itself. It was large and surrounded on all sides by impressive mosaics from the countries of the world with their impressions of the annunciation.

"Do you know a lot about art?" Rachel asked.

"No, not really, I wish I knew more. Funny though I do know a little about Renaissance art. The annunciation was always symbolised with while flowers, the white to depict the virginity."

"Or perhaps the colour of sperm. You can't conceive without sperm." I was shocked.

"No," I spluttered "No, I don't think so." There was a brief, awkward silence. Latin echoed from a priest carrying out his duties around the basilica.

"No, perhaps not," she also was embarrassed, "I know very little about art."

We stood in silence looking into the grotto of the annunciation where a service was taking place. White flowers surrounded the grotto, an ejaculation of irises and daffodils. I couldn't shake out of my mind what Rachel had said.

"Right," she said, "I better go and round them up. I'll see you in the courtyard."

V

The Carpenter's shop

The Church of St Joseph's was a short and uneventful walk from the Basilica of the Annunciation. It was built on the site of Joseph's Carpenters shop but wasn't particularly impressive. I found myself sat outside again trying desperately to ignore Rachel's sexual interpretation of Renaissance art with a cat perched across the pathway staring at me. Deirdre and Martin came and sat next to me and we started talking. They were supporters of the football team Manchester United who had beaten Forest 8-1 a couple of weekends ago.

"Oh, it was so funny," ranted Deirdre. "It was a shame because we could only get tickets in the Forest end and in the end a Forest fan threw a cup of tea over my son."

"How old is he?" I asked.

"Twenty five. It's probably because we couldn't stop laughing."

"Probably," said Martin wearily. *Stupid cow* I thought, and remembered nearly ten years ago to the day, standing on the Kop at Hillsborough, drunk and watching 100 people having their lives crushed out of them. I got up and walked away.

VI

Joshua and Jonathon

We stopped for lunch at a large self-service cafeteria where the Horns of Hittin was re-enacted around the salad bar. Myself and dad sat on our own, and though briefly disturbed by Fred who informed me of every cat spot he had made in the previous 24 hours, enjoyed relative quiet. After lunch I took out my copy of Jerusalem Today and showed him the article of the murder on the Mount of Olives. He was at a loss for words and so re-read the article and looked at the photograph.

"Have you got a pen. Can I borrow it?" he eventually said.

"Yes, of course, what are you doing?" but he didn't answer, he was deep in concentration. From my upside down angle I could see him start scribbling on the photograph. First of all he drew an open collar onto the tee shirt of the victim, then a moustache onto his round face and finally a large pair of glasses onto which he shaded a tint. He looked at the picture and nodded his head. Then he slowly turned it towards me. Before it had travelled through $180°$, I could see the resemblance. I felt sweat in the palm of my hands and my legs go weak. I could hear the thump of my heart in my brain as all of a sudden I found myself staring into the face of Joshua Fisher III. I took a swig of Carlsberg.

"I don't believe it. I don't believe it," I repeated, "it's him. I didn't see it, I didn't see it."

"But you don't see things," Dad answered slowly. "You didn't see the crosses in the cistern at Peter in Gallicantu, just as you didn't see the face of Joshua Fisher III in the face of Jonathon Mautner." There was silence between the two of us. "I thought you said he wasn't dangerous."

"What do you mean?"

"The man at the Jaffa Gate. Didn't he say to you he had seen Fisher on the Mount of Olives?"

"What are you suggesting, dad. This isn't Fisher, it's somebody else."

"No it's not Fisher is it, but it's somebody who looks like Fisher who just happens to have been decapitated on the Mount of Olives."

"This is ridiculous. What are you saying, that John the Baptist from the Jaffa Gate marched up the Mount of Olives and chopped a mans head off who happened to own a couple of restaurants, who just happens to have a slim look of Joshua Fisher III."

"Is it that slim?" I looked back at the paper. If I hadn't been so amazed I was having the conversation I was having I would have laughed at it. Dad was silent, also looking down at the paper. Mautner did look like Fisher, *very like him.* Eventually he said,

"Look, he walks between his restaurants. The same route, the same time. This killing its not instinctive, somebody just decapitates somebody else for the fun of it. This is planned and with motive – the death of the Anti-Christ who is left to weep out over Jerusalem. John would have thought Fisher would have disguised himself. He wouldn't have expected Fisher to look how he does in the papers. You wouldn't, would you?"

"No, I suppose not."

"You suppose not! Come on, Seb. You *know* full well that Fisher, if he came into the country would change his appearance. He wouldn't stand a chance otherwise. And John knew that as well, except he's gone and got it horribly wrong."

"Ok, dad, ok. So what do we do? Go up to the nearest policeman and say we think John the Baptist chopped of Satan's head on the Mount of Olives?" He tapped his fingers on his lips.

"No, I don't think we should do that."

"Well what should we do?"

"Nothing."

"Nothing," I answered.

"We don't want to get caught up in anything over here. It's only a hunch anyway. We just carry on. We'll be home in a couple of days. I thought you said John wasn't dangerous," he repeated.

"Well maybe I was wrong. I underestimated it all, you know 'the war of the Sons of Light against the Sons of Darkness'. Perhaps they're both dangerous."

VII
Seb falls asleep

The coach stopped halfway up Mount Tabor.

"Ok," Rachel said "the road becomes very steep so we have to go up in taxis the rest of the way". The taxis held 7 comfortably and we started the steep ascent to the summit. I was obviously deep in thought about the revelation of lunchtime. I was thinking about the Roman Catholic Priest who broke women's necks, painted them with snakes and tied them up to trees and the additional symbolism of Adam as man and Eve as woman. I knew whoever killed and beheaded Jonathon Mautner on the Mount of Olives and signed him off with the sign of the Beast and the weeping of an ash ear, would most likely repeat the act. The act of a psychotic Apostle.

"He must have been pretty fit," Barbara said, squashed next to me.

"Who must have been petty fit?"

"Why, Jesus of course. He wouldn't have got a taxi. He would have walked up."

"I guess he must have been fit." A cow suddenly ran out in front of the taxi causing the driver to break viciously.

"Ah ha" continued Barbara, "it truly is the land of milk and honey." At the top of Mount Tabor the group gathered outside the Franciscan Basilica.

The Bishop began. "This is where Jesus came with Peter, James and John and '*was transfigured before them: and the face did shine as the sun, and his raiment was white as the light. And, beyond there appeared unto them Moses and Elijah talking with him*". Thank you Rachel."

"Ok thanks, Bishop. There is like most of the sites in the Holy Land dispute about whether this it he exact site of the transfiguration. It may have been on Mount Hermon in Caesarea Philippi or on the Mount of Olives itself, though this site was dedicated by Pope John

Paul II just a few weeks ago, so if he says it happened here, it must have." The group laughed.

I left them and went to sit under a tree. The weather had improved and it was a reasonably warm afternoon. A sign in front of me said 'Keep Mount Tabor tidy' and, as I watched the pilgrims enter the Basilica, I was aware of the rubbish that littered the site. I lay down and, caught in a hypnotic breeze that dissected the afternoon, fell asleep and dreamt of John. He was preaching at the Jaffa Gate, reciting Revelation eleven, except it seemed to be in slow motion.

"And I will give power into my two witnesses. These are the two olive trees, and the two candlesticks standing before the God of the Earth. And if any man would hurt them, he proceedeth out of their mouth and devoureth their enemies: and if any man will hurt them, he must in this manner be killed."

John stopped reading yourself." At this point a man with a crown of thorns and a cross on his back struggled and looked at me. *"Sinner,"* he said silently *"Sinner, save between the two of us, fell, picked himself up. Slowly he turned his head towards me. An ash tear was painted beneath one of his eyes that pointed to the man's straggling beard. "Save yourself, sinner,"* Jonathon Mautner told me, *"tell Joanne I love her. Tell the children that I love them."* Then he walked on with his cross and out of my vision.

"Seb, Seb, wake up, wake up," my eyes shot open. "Are you ok?" Dad's face was peering into mine.

"Yes, I'm fine. At least I think I'm fine. I fell asleep. I was dreaming."

"Come on we're going, get in the taxi."

On the coach Rachel informed us there was enough time to stop briefly at the River Jordan, "at a location South of Galilee where John the Baptist worked," as she put it. I was tired emotionally and physically and wanted to get back to Tiberias, but half an hour later we pulled into yet another car park packed with tourist coaches.

VIII

Seb meets an old friend

Once again we descended out of the coach and walked through a complex of restaurants and shops until we arrived by the riverbank itself. Into the bank of the river was built a number of wooden terraces on to which groups of pilgrims stood, praying, singing and weeping. People dressed in white robes descended the terraces to be met by their pilgrimage leaders and were thrust into the water in the name of "Father, Son & Holy Ghost." In the distance I saw Boomer of the Agony, booming baptism into his flock.

"Actually John the Baptist didn't do any baptising here," Rachel whispered to me as I watched our Pilgrims assemble on a terrace. "He did it all in the Judean Desert, but don't tell the others."

"Is that right," I enjoyed her honesty. "So what's this site?"

"This is straight Israel exploitation, big time," she answered stretching her arms in front of her.

"What about the rest that you've said over the last week, is that Israel exploitation, big time?"

"No, not really, some is, some isn't. But the point is people don't know what is the truth and what isn't. You tell people what they want to hear and you tell people what they need to hear."

"I know you do. Look Rachel I've had enough for the day. I'm going back to the coach. I'll ask Ahmet to put some more of that music on."

"Before you go, before you go." She looked at me and asked the question, "Are you an atheist?"

"No," I answered.

"Well, are you Christian?"

"No," I answered again.

"Then what are you?"

"I don't know," and with that I turned around and walked off back to the car park.

The car park, full of coaches but empty of people, was hidden from the main highway by a thicket of trees some 10 metres wide. I approached our coach and from the bottom of the stairs asked Ahmet if he could put some music on when from the thicket I suddenly heard or thought that I heard,

"Sinner, are you saved?" I turned towards the thicket but saw nothing.

"Did you here that Ahmet?"

"What?"

"I thought I heard something from the thicket." I was really unsure whether I had heard anything or not. "I'm going to take a look." I walked over cautiously.

"Hello sinner, hello again," a voice came from within the thicket.

"Who is it? Who's there?"

"Just a little closer and all will be revealed."

I walked into the thicket a little further, glanced over my shoulders at the coach and remembered the woman at Heathrow who asked if I was ever going to leave the group.

"Here I am sinner. Here I am."

I peered through the gloom of the early evening and saw, covered in a white robe similar to those used for baptising at this, the epicentre of Israeli exploitation, the Essene who called himself John.

"John, is that you?" is all I could find to say. He walked forward. "What are you doing here?"

"I've come to baptise. Baptise sinners like you." He looked different. The holes in his eyes shone of the blackness and chaos of a live psychosis. He was unkempt and it didn't look like he had slept for days – *sleep depravation*.

"How did you get here?"

"That doesn't matter, does it?"

"No, I suppose not. I just thought you were working in Jerusalem."

"My work there has stopped for the time being. I've been watching you. "

"Your work, but I thought you baptised in Jerusalem?"

"I baptise here, sinner." I stared at him, into the void of his eyes.

"What is your work in Jerusalem, John?" *Be careful now, be careful.*

"Saving sinners, through the destruction of darkness."

"Through the destruction of darkness?" I repeated after him.

"That's right, sinner, through the destruction of darkness." Briefly we were quiet starring at each other.

"How do you destroy darkness, John?"

"You destroy Darkness, sinner, by killing the Anti-Christ. By defeating Satan."

"And have you defeated Satan, John?"

"Partly, sinner, partly."

Again there was a silence between us for a few seconds.

"A man died on the Mount of Olives last night."

"A man didn't die," he answered.

"Yes he did. Do you know about it John?"

"I know about the death of Satan."

"The picture I showed you at the Jaffa Gate, the one of Fisher, the man who died looked like Fisher".

"What do you mean looked like Fisher?" his voice was raised and his face twitched. "What do you mean looked liked Fisher," he hissed. "It was fucking Fisher. Fisher the Anti-Christ! Satan!"

Please legs work, turn around get on the coach but my legs wouldn't move. They to were tree trunks in the thicket.

"How do you know it was, Fisher?" I asked, and very slowly he replied,

"Because when I sliced his head off his body the Lord said to me *'I no longer weep, the Anti-Christ now weeps. Fisher weeps'.*" I paused for breath.

"What now?" I whispered

"Oh sinner, Satan is still strong, there is another who pretends to be a witness," and I remembered the symbol of Eve as woman and Adam as man. He was going to kill again. I leant onto a tree and said as calmly as I possibly could.

"You killed the wrong man," and, at that point, that moment on the banks of the unimpressive Jordan, my whole world went topsy turvy – what did I mean, *you killed the wrong man*? "The man who died on the Mount of Olives wasn't Fisher. He was a Jewish family man with children. He owned two restaurants, one in the Old City and one near the Tomb of the Prophets. He was called Mautner, Jonathon Mautner. He had a wife, Joanne and four children. Jonathon Mautner, Joanne Mautner and their children. They were a happy family, John." John's expression didn't alter. He starred with his psychotic black eyes. I could see saliva around his mouth and on his beard.

"Are you doubting the Word of the Lord, Sinner," he retorted aggressively and I knew his psychosis was too deep to be confronted by the concepts of reality. "Are you doubting the word of the Lord, Sinner," he walked towards me.

"No, John. I'm not doubting it."

"Do you doubt my word?" He was very close. I could see his madness and smell his breath and on his neck I could see a tattoo that said 'England'. And then, from within his robe, he produced a photo, and thrust it towards my eyes and I was staring at the severed head of Jonathon Mautner with his ash tear and 666 emblazoned like a tattoo on his forehead.

"Christ," my legs began to collapse. "No John, I didn't doubt you!"

"SINNER!" he screamed through his scrunched up face and the back of his hand flew across my face, knocking me to the floor where, head down, I waited for the knife to be stuck into the back of my neck, and briefly wondered in which direction he would point my decapitated head. "You are a sinner, are you not? I saw you talking to that woman, that pretty little tour guide. You want to fuck her, don't you? You want her pussy!" The knife didn't come. Instead, lifting my head, I saw Ahmet in the thicket who struck out at the Essene John. He too fell to the ground and Ahmet shouted something at him in Arabic. John the Baptist got up, pointed at me and screamed,

"Sinner, you're fucking dead. Do you hear me, dead. You're dead, Carrington!" before running out of the thicket in the direction of what I thought to be Jerusalem.

Ahmet helped me up. He gave me a handkerchief as there was blood coming out of my nose.

"Look Ahmet, nobody needs to know about this."

"Don't worry. Everything's ok."

On the coach I cleaned myself up. *I'm losing it. I'm losing it.* Ahmet put the music on and the rest of the pilgrims appeared into view, baptised.

IX

On the same spot

Back at the hotel I felt myself settling, though I was frightened. I decided not to tell dad about the incident – I was nearly killed possibly as a false Witness of the Revelation, by a psychotic John the Baptist was again too much. We talked briefly of the day and then turned to the article in that day's edition of *Jerusalem Today*. I recounted to him the Roman Catholic Priest and his lethal interpretation of the tale of Adam and Eve. The effect of a couple of Maccabis was having the desired effect when slowly, very slowly it struck me.

"Oh no, oh no," is all I could hear myself say.

"What's the matter?" dad asked.

"The person who killed Jonathon Mautner, he'll kill again or try to."

"Yes, I should think so."

"But not only will he kill again, he'll kill again at the same spot."

"What makes you say that?"

"Because it is that person's belief that this is the final battle. Sons of Light v Sons of Darkness and the battle is taking place on the Mount of Olives." Dad paused for a moment.

"Do you think they know?"

"Who, the authorities?"

"Yes, yes, they will know." I was agitated.

"What do you think will happen?"

"Well," I answered turning to him, "I suppose they'll kill him."

X
Laura goes to Camden

Laura phoned me.

"I cancelled my do. Well I haven't. It's just nobody would come. They all dropped out."

"Slow down," I said "Slow down!"

"I'm at Mark and Jane's. Jane and me are going out in Camden. Mark's going to babysit Jack and Madeline. I need to get out. I really miss you." At that point I was desperate to be home "I miss you too. I'll be home in a couple of days". I skipped supper to watch CNN and to watch for any breaking news. By 11.30 none had broken so when dad returned from the bar we both retired to bed and waited for Friday to arrive.

CHAPTER 8
Friday (Mount of Beatitudes, Tagbha)

I

Jonathon Mautner's head

I was awoken by tapping on the window. It was light, no early start today. Getting up I walked over to the window and drew the curtain. Sparrows were the cause of the tapping and to my surprise they didn't fly off in fright but rather carried on with their business, whatever that was. The day was dreary and I looked out over the hills that were the Golan Height and then back to the hotel's swimming pool which was empty of water and uncared for. Briefly I remembered the journalists in the Killing Fields sat around their hotel pool and waiting for the arrival of the Khmer Rouge in Phnom Penn. I walked over to dad's bed and picked up his clock. Eight thirty.

"Dad," I shook him, "It's eight thirty. We've got to be on the coach by nine." Slowly he came to life.

"What time did you say it was?"

"Eight thirty."

"My, that's good."

"We obviously needed to catch up a little. I'll go and use the bathroom while you wake up."

Though I had slept for nine hours or so, my sleep had been restless. The image of Mautner's severed, photographed head, with his tear of ash and the sign of the beast kept intruding in and out at will. The head was smiling, perched on a bench where its body should have been. The eyes were stuck looking down, the opposite to the interbreeds on Katapagea, and they were quite lifeless. When dad was in the bathroom I fought with myself to put CNN on. I was desperate to know if anything else had happened but allowed that fabulously ambivalent trait of denial to kick in. *Just settle down, take it easy, it's over* and then I rationalised that my denial, in this, the land of denial, was about my fear of what had happened and what may happen in the future. I was scared.

II
Christian alliance

We ate a rushed breakfast with Robert and Emily. Robert reminded me of the rugby international to be played the following day and we agreed to walk into Tiberias as according to the itinerary Saturday afternoon was our own though, hardly surprising, I wasn't that interested.

"You know I think its great what you're doing," he suddenly piped up sipping his coffee.

"What's great?" dad asked

"What you two are doing. I'd love to do this with my boy, but no, not a chance I shouldn't think."

"How old is he?" I asked

"Twenty two."

"I don't think I would have done this at twenty two. Things change don't they – experience, maturity". I was sounding a bit silly.

At nine we left and took a route north along the western shore of the Sea of Galilee. It had started to rain and the atmosphere of the day seemed matched by the quietness on the coach – I sensed the pilgrims were ready for the pilgrimage to head home.

"How's Idi?" dad enquired.

"Killing a lot of people," I answered. "It's a funny book because you start thinking your in a biography, then a travel guide of Uganda and then you realise you are actually in a terrible tragedy. It's really horrific."

"Good morning ladies and gentlemen."

"Good morning," the pilgrims answered Rachel's greeting.

"That's good you sound brighter today. Listen, I'm going to read you an article from today's local Jewish paper that's printed in Tiberias. It relates to our trip to Nazareth. Remember I told you all that the Christian Denominations they don't get on, you know, Catholics, Greek Orthodox, Syrian, Copts and the others well just listen to this. The headline says;

'*After 2000 years the Christian churches in the Holy Land go on Strike,*'

Ok and the article reads;

'*Christian Pilgrims to Israel later in the year will find they cannot enter many of the churches that are sited at the scene of Jesus' miracles. This includes the Basilica of the Annunciation, the Church in Nazareth allegedly marking the spot where the Archangel Gabriel first told Mary she was with child and the Basilica of the Holy Sepulchre in Jerusalem where Christ was crucified.*

Christian leaders in the Holy Land issued an announcement yesterday that all their famous holy sites and sanctuaries will be closed for a two-day period sometime in November. The shutdown of the sites when Israel is expected to be swarming with Christian tourists is protest against a decision by the Israeli government to allow a mosque to be built near the Basilica of the Annunciation in Nazareth. Such is the threat that the local authorities are increasingly concerned about the likelihood of civil unrest. The Pope has cancelled his visit to Nazareth in the spring of 2000. The statement, signed by the patriarchs of the Greek, Roman Catholic and Armenian churches as well as the Franciscan 'Custos of the Holy Land' reads as follows,

'Ever since the period of Ottoman rule some 500 years ago, this city has also lived in an atmosphere of peaceful co-existence between Christians and Muslims. This arrangement in Nazareth – now an Arab city, where the Muslim population outnumbers the Christians has left the city shaken by a series of sad events which has unfortunately raised the level of intolerance and tension.' The Mosque's cornerstone is due to be laid at the beginning of November.'

So here you have it, simple really. As one rift decreased another increased. The rift between Christians heals so the one between Christian and Muslim widens. That's Israel for you," she paused, "Powder keg," and into the microphone she mimicked the sound of a bomb going off. She was deadly serious. "Anyway let's talk about today, not yesterday. If you look over to your left," she pointed to a village in the distance, "that is Majdal or Migdal. In the New Testament it is called Magdala and is the birthplace of Mary Magadalene. It is also widely believed that the robes worn by Jesus after his crucifixion were made here. The village in antiquity relied on its weaving. There's not much about the place today. So today we will go to the Mount of Beatitudes. Then we will walk in Jesus' footsteps from Beatitudes to the village of Tabgha and visit The Church of the Primacy of St Peter. Then, I'm not sure, it depends on the weather but we will visit the Church of the Multiplication of the Loaves and Fishes. We have a service booked there for four but the forecast is heavy rain so we may have to return to the hotel after lunch for an hour or so." She switched off the microphone and sat down.

"Interesting what she said. One rift decreases allows another to increase. I like that," mulled dad.

III
No Guns

Shortly afterwards the coach pulled into a lane that wound up to the Mount of Beatitudes. We left the coach behind us, passed a sign that said "No Guns" and entered the garden of the Beatitudes with the Octagonal Chapel away to our right along with a magnificent view of the lake. We gathered around Rachel.

"Remember I said that for me the children's memorial at Yad Vashem was the most moving and powerful place I have been on earth. Well I think this is the most spiritual and beautiful. If I were Christian this place would be the place I most wanted to visit. Not the riot on the Via Dolorosa or Bethlehem or Nazareth. Here, on the Mount of Beatitudes, with the greenness of the hills and the lake with its little fishing boats on it, and no buildings. It would have been very, very like this 2000 years ago. We're now going to walk down the steps to the Church and the Bishop will speak to you." The pilgrims started down the wide stone step that dissected the garden. I took out my camera from my blue bag and took a picture of the pilgrims descending with the small church and Galilee as a backcloth and knew that the picture would not do any justice to the beauty sprawled in front of me.

IV
The Second Coming

We gathered around the Bishop who coughed into his hand before saying in his deep English rasp,

"The Beatitudes are the blessings said by Jesus in the Sermon on the Mount which took place here. The word Beatitudes comes from the Latin 'beati sunt' which means 'blessed one'." I noted that all the clergy, Peter, Liz, Catherine, Judith, Terry and dad, were stood behind him. The Bishop with his disciples I thought. As one they spoke:

"Blessed are the poor in spirit, for theirs is the kingdom of heaven,
Blessed are those who mourn, for they shall be comforted,
Blessed are the meek, for they shall inherit the earth,
Blessed are those who hunger and thirst for righteousness, for they shall be satisfied,
Blessed are the merciful, for they shall obtain mercy,
Blessed are the pure in heart, for they shall see God,
Blessed are those who are persecuted for righteousness sake, for theirs is the kingdom of heaven,
Blessed are you when men revile you and persecute you and utter all kinds of evil against you falsely on my account. Rejoice and be glad, for you rewards is great in heaven, for as men persecuted the prophets who were before you."

They stopped together in unison. I noticed Helen and the Bishop's wife crying. The other pilgrims had their heads bowed. A few moments later the Bishop rasped quietly, "Here on Beatitudes we also listen to the other fundamental teachings of Jesus," then dad said,

"Think not that I came to destroy the law or the prophets: I am not come to destroy but to FULFIL." He was stunning, I was stunned. This was followed by Liz and Catherine,

"Judge not that ye be not judged." Then Peter and Terry,

"Whosoever shall smite thee on they right cheek turn to him the other also," and then Judith.

"Love thine enemies, bless them that curse you and do good in them that hate you," and then all of them,

"Our father who are in heaven
Hallowed be thy name…"

I looked out over the hills and lake and felt a peace that was so oppressive that I couldn't understand it. "Don't think too deeply," said dad at Ein Gedi. "Don't think too deeply."

"The Power and the Glory, Forever and ever. Amen."

There was silence for at least 30 seconds which was eventually broken up by our guide.

"Ok we're going into the chapel next. It was designed by the Italian architect Anton Barluzzi. Apparently Mussolini ordered it, but I don't know. Quick question group, which other churches have we seen designed by Barluzzi?"

"Dominus Flevit," Roma shouted out

"That's right. One more though." Nobody knew. "Maybe I didn't tell you." I thought of Boomer.

"The Church of All Nations at Gethsemane," I said.

"That's right. The Church of the Agony. Ok, on this church the eight sides represent the first eight beatitudes of Matthew that we have just heard. Inside you will see a pavement that runs around the altar, it represents the seven virtues." We went into the light chapel. It was busy with all 50 of us crammed in so I sat at the back and waited for it to empty. Then I walked up to the pavement Rachel had referred to and started around it. Occasionally I would come to one of the virtues painted in gold leaf onto it:

Justice....Charity.....Prudence.....Faith.....Fortitude.....Hope.....Temperance and then I was back at Justice. I looked out into the garden. I could see Sally smelling roses, and the Bishop further on smoking a café crème and choking.

"An oasis of peace," a voice said over my shoulder. It was David Brown, the man we had supper with on the first night.

"Yes it is," I answered.

"It's not always like this. Sometimes the wind funnels down from the hills and the Golan Heights and whips up the lake into a tempest. It can be very sudden."

I left him looking out the window and briefly felt for this sad old man and his father, a soldier, killed in action. I walked around the tranquillity of the garden, its roses and beautiful grapefruit trees and sat on a reclusive bench that looked towards the chapel built by Barluzzi. A group of Americans were close by and suddenly the peace was fractured by a loud voice, the group's preacher,

"We find Beatitudes in Matthew, Luke and John," he boomed and yes, it was Boomer from the Agony. At this point I jumped as a cat, a tabby cat as if from nowhere, leapt into my lap and looked directly into my eyes. "We're going to consider the Beatitude of Luke 6:20-23," I heard Boomer continue.

"My God," I whispered to myself. "Another cat."

"*Blessed are the poor, for yours is the kingdom of God.*" The cat's piercing yellow eyes continued to stare at me. It started to purr.

"*Blessed are you that hunger now, for you shall be satisfied.*" The cat stretched its paws, flexing and retracting its claws in the joy of the moment.

"*Blessed are you that weep now, for you shall laugh.*" The cat continued staring and then rubbed its head onto my breathless chest.

"*Blessed are you when men hate you, and when they exclude you and revile you and cast out your name as evil, on account of the Son of Man!*" Boomer was shouting, "*Rejoice in that day, and leap for joy, for behold, your reward is great in heaven,*" and I allowed myself the thought that Christ was here, sitting on my knee. *Where is dad. I want a picture, a picture of Christ sitting on my knee? It's not everyday this happens. One to show off. Where is he, where is he?* The cat stared at me then leapt onto my shoulder and over the back of the bench. I turned quickly, but never saw it again. I scanned and scanned the garden but to no avail.

"Are you All right, Seb? You look like you've seen a ghost?" It was dad, stood in front of me.

"Where have you been?" I snapped aggressively back. He was taken aback.

"I've been in the garden enjoying the peace."

"I needed you!"

"What for?"

"I needed you to take a picture."

"Well I'm here now. I'll take it now."

"No, you can't. It's too late."

"Too late? What do you mean it's too late?"

"I needed you to take a picture of me with Christ on my lap but now he's run off."

"Sorry," he gasped. "What did you say?" He looked amazed. I caught my breath.

"I wanted you take a picture of me with a cat on my lap but now he's run off." I said. There was a silence between us.

"I though you said something else," he said eventually.

"What did you think I said?"

"Oh it doesn't matter, its too far fetched."

V
Seb considers his sanity

Ten minutes later we were walking single file down the mount towards Tabgha. I was at the back as usual, and reeling from the experience was unable to focus on the beauty of the deep red poppies and golden daises that dominated the countryside or a nest of caterpillars that intrigued the rest of the party. *I'm going insane* I thought to myself with what level of diminishing insight I had. *I came to look for madness but madness found me first.* The Caring Christians, John the Baptist, the fiasco on the Via Dolorosa, Jan washing her hair, the head of Jonathon Mautner weeping over Jerusalem, and of course, Fisher. Where was Fisher? I hadn't given him any thought for a while. The newspaper report had said he was in London. John had said he was in Jerusalem, but of course John's Fisher turned out to be the luckless Mautner. We arrived in Tabgha and proceeded into the Gardens of the Church of the Primacy of St Peter.

"This," Rachel began, "was built by the Franciscans in 1933 on the site of a 4th century church. Over there," she pointed to a large flat rock, "that is known as the Mensa Christi, the table of Christ on which Jesus, when he was resurrected, cooked I suppose his disciples a meal." The Bishop interjected, he too pointing, this time towards the lake

"*As soon then as they were come to land, they saw a fire of coals there and fish land thereon and bread*"

"This then is also where Jesus three times offered the primacy to Peter," went on Rachel and again the Bishop cut in.

" '*Feed my sheep,*' Jesus said to Peter '*Feed my sheep,*' he repeated and then '*Feed my sheep*' again and he accepted."

"Over there, those rocks are called the thrones of the Apostles……." I decided I had had enough and left the group back to the coach which Ahmet had driven from the Beatitudes to Tabgha. As I approached I could hear the pilgrims singing 'Kum bi ya.' The rain that had stopped on Beatitudes started to come back gradually.

VI
Mrs Thornton's cats and dogs

On the coach I spoke to Ahmet.

"Thanks for yesterday. I should have thanked you earlier. That was a strange affair."

"It's ok. How would you say it in your country? Nutters," he tapped his head with his finger and laughed. I laughed with him. "This place is full of nutters," he carried on laughing and it struck me I was probably one of them.

I looked down at the chair behind Ahmet where Rachel sat. The paper she had quoted from earlier in the day about the closure of Holy Sites was on it. I picked it up.

"Ahmet, are you able to read this?"

"Yes I can read that."

"Is there anything about Jonathan Mautner the man killed on the Mount of Olives a couple of nights ago?"

"Let me have a look." Almost immediately he said, "Yes, it's here on the front page."

"What does it say?" He scanned the article

"Not much really. They are looking for a man as opposed to a woman. That he is very dangerous. He is probably very sick. They quote a psychiatrist who says it is likely the man suffers from an illness called 'Jerusalem Syndrome' and here, here is a picture of the family."

"Let me have a look." He passed me the paper. It was a family shot of the Mautners in their Saturday best, mum flanked by her two daughters sitting in the front row, and Mautner standing behind her, his arms resting on her shoulders, with their two teenage boys, one on each side of him. All of them wore large smiles. They were it would seem a very happy family. Not any more. Mautner had no head, she had no husband and they had no father. Repulsion swept over me. Suddenly the heavens exploded and the rain fell with an intensity that lashed against the windows of the coach. I could see the pilgrims charging back from the Primacy church. I started off back to my seat.

"Are you interested in the Mount of Olives?" Ahmet shouted after me against the sound of the deluge.

"Yes I am."

"There's something else here."

I stopped in my tracks and turned slowly and walked back.
"What?" I asked
"It's nothing much. There at the bottom of the page."
"What does it say?"
"It says newsflash, ah, it's a newsflash. They were probably too late to print"
"Ahmet, what does it say?"
"It says: *'Israeli intelligence marksmen late last night shot a man dead at Gethsemane on the Mount of Olives: more to follow'*."

I sat in my chair and stared vacantly at the one in front of me. The pilgrims piled on to the coach, they were soaking and their dripping made the gangway slippery. Dad sat down next to me. Water trickled down his face. He took out his handkerchief and wiped it.

"Ahmet translated some of Rachel's newspaper to me."
"Oh yes," he said.
"They shot a man on the Mount of Olives last night." He paused.
"Who shot a man on the Mount of Olives?"
"Israeli intelligence. It's only in a newsflash. It must have just become available for the late edition."

Neither of us knew what to say

"Look, why don't you forget about this," dad broke the silence. He sounded annoyed. "Forget about the news, CNN, papers – just stick to the coach and the hotel. We're going home in two days. You'll be back with Laura and Jack." He was clearly concerned for me and I felt touched.

"Well its raining cats and dogs as you English would say." Rachel was on the microphone. "Why do you say that, cats and dogs?" Nobody answered and then a tired old voice piped up,

"I know why." It was Mrs Thornton who I had last been aware of being escorted covered in mud by her three daughters to the Noddy train at Ein Gedi.

"Why don't you tell us, Mrs Thornton?" Rachel asked. She turned to one of her daughters and said something inaudible.

"Rachel, she thinks she needs the microphone." One of the daughters shouted.

"Ok, bring her up, bring her up," and old Mrs Thornton was escorted up the slippery gangway to the front.

143

"It's a long time since I've done any public speaking," she joked grasping the microphone and the pilgrims smiled. "The reason we say it's raining cats and dogs is this. It's nothing to do with cyclones or tornadoes lifting them off the ground, nothing quite so grand I'm afraid. When I lived in the subcontinent more years than I care to remember ago there was a very long dry season then a short, sharper monsoon – a bit like this." The pilgrims laughed as she gestured to the streams of water that meandered down the windows of the coach. "In the dry season the cats and dogs when they had had enough would go and find somewhere remote to die, some nook or cranny in the countryside. Anyway when the monsoons came because the drainage was so poor the place would flood horrendously and the dead cats and dogs would be dislodged from their resting places and be flushed out of their holes. When the floods receded there would be corpses of cats and dogs everywhere. That is why we say raining cats and dogs." The coach burst into spontaneous applause and Mrs Thornton was helped back to her chair.

"Ok we'll go for lunch and then back to the hotel for a couple of hours before going back to our service at the Church of the Multiplication of the Loaves and Fishes."

VII

Seb goes for a drink

Back at the hotel after the usual scrummage at a self-service cafeteria between Tabgha and Tiberias for lunch most of the pilgrims rested in the large lounge next to the reception waiting for the rain to stop. I borrowed an umbrella from reception and decided to go for a walk in the town, to pick up some beer as much as anything else. Tiberias was a bland town though quite busy and I strolled past the main bus station into the centre avoiding the large pools of water that were seeking Mrs Thornton's cats and dogs. There I found a shop and brought 4 Orangebooms, which I hadn't had since my college days, some tonic and some peanuts. Walking back the rain had eased off. I passed an alley from where I heard music. 'A bar,' I thought to myself, 'a bar'. I went to investigate and there at the end of the alley was indeed a bar called rather unimaginatively, 'Sports Bar'. I went in. It was empty and I didn't recognise the music. A television was on high up in the corner and to my surprise it was on an English speaking channel. I went up to the bar and ordered a Becks and then sat myself down. The TV was showing highlights of a football match, Haifa Macabi against Tel Aviv. I turned to the barman.

"Are you going to have the rugby on?" I asked. He shrugged his shoulders and I remembered Rachel saying Tiberias was a completely Jewish town and so I considered it was likely he didn't speak English. Then the music went off and the voice of the barman said,

"Sorry, I couldn't hear you. The noise of the music was too loud."

"I said are you going to have the rugby on tomorrow. England V's Scotland," and I was overwhelmed by that dreadfully shamming British arrogance that perceives the world as British.

"What's rugby?" he answered.

"It's a game. England are playing Scotland tomorrow. I thought you might have had it on."

"No, sorry."

I turned back to the TV.

"I'll turn it off. It's only the news coming on." The barman pointed the remote control towards the television.

"No, hold on. Can I watch the news? You're not exactly busy."

"Ok, if that's what you want."

VIII

John Gutheridge

The shooting on the Mount of Olives was the third headline behind Kosovo, and a proposed peace summit prior to the next Israeli election. By the time the shooting story came I had drunk my Becks and ordered another.

"And now," the female broadcaster began, "we turn to last nights late night shooting on the Mount of Olives where it has become clear that the Israeli Secret Service shot dead a man whilst, it would seem, he was assaulting a women. This is turning into a remarkable story and its over to Aiyesha Lavit at the Mount of Olives for full details." I could hardly breathe. Aiyesha came into view with the Dome of the Rock behind her and I recognised the spot as where we had stood at Dominus Flevit and remembered Christ crying for the incompetence of man and where dad had taught me about Christ, the Great Redeemer.

"The man shot," she began, "has earlier today been named as John Gutheridge. Gutheridge, 39, was here on holiday from his home in Hemel Hempstead in England. Apparently he came with a group in an organised pilgrimage from churches in the area of Hemel Hempstead, but dropped out two weeks into the pilgrimage. The leaders of the pilgrimage reported him missing 10 days ago and said they were concerned for his well being. Apparently he had been behaving strangely for a while in Israel. It was also reported that Gutheridge suffered from manic depression, an illness that can bring massive mood swings and very grandiose behaviour." Then up on the screen flicked the face of Gutheridge. It looked like it had been taken from his passport. I looked at it, normal eyes, not psychotic, trimmed beard, the picture of a well man. But without doubt it was the Essene called John, and I remembered him at the Jaffa Gate, "I am the Essene John…..some call me the Baptist,". I started to cry.

"Are you ok?" the barman enquired surprised.

"No, not really. Let me just watch the end of this and I'll go."

"Don't worry about that that there is no one around. Are you sure you are ok?" The shot had moved back to the Mount of Olives.

"Now with me," Aiyesha recommenced, "is Chief of Police for the Old City, Ben Zelkine. Ben can you tell our viewers exactly what happened here."

"Well, Aiyesha at exactly 2.30am today, Israeli intelligence shot John Gutheridge killing him instantly."

"How many shots were fired?"

"Just one. It entered through his cranium and also exited. As I said he was killed instantly."

"And why was he shot?"

"At the time Mr Gutheridge was assaulting a woman. He was trying to, it was our opinion, to kill her. He was armed with a knife and a machete. We briefly tried to negotiate but he would only say, "This is God's work." For the safety of the woman a very difficult decision had to be made."

"Who was the woman?"

"I am not able to disclose that at the moment."

"And did the incident happen here?"

"No, it happened at Gethsemane. This area we are standing at the moment is a police only area and is where Jonathon Mautner was murdered two nights ago here in the gardens of Dominus Flevit".

"Are you saying the two cases are related?"

"Yes I am. We found what we would call a trophy of Jonathon Mautner's murder on the clothing of John Gutheridge."

"And what was that trophy?"

"A picture of Mr Mautner's head." He spared the graphics of the picture I had seen in the thicket the previous day.

"Ok, thanks Ben. Back to the studio."

"I have in the studio with me today," the news presenter continued, "Dr Sam Ronnell, a psychiatrist from the Kfer Shaul Mental Health Centre here in Jerusalem. Welcome Dr Ronnell."

"Thank you," answered the psychiatrist surprisingly relaxed in an open collar shirt.

"What's happened here, Dr Ronnell? What has happened to John Gutheridge?"

"Well actually its quite straight forward," he beamed into the camera. "This is a man with a known psychiatric condition, in this instance manic depressive psychosis. The condition is stabilised through what we call mood stabilising medication such as Lithium. Now depending on the degree of illness other medications may be added such as an anti-depressant. What seems to have happened to Mr Gutheridge is that at some point he has decided to stop his medication. Looking at the details this was probably just before he came on pilgrimage. He probably was a devout man, possibly a *very* devout man,' and he emphasised the very, 'and he was probably confident his faith would protect him particularly in this, the centre of the Holy World. His devoutness probably stemmed from earlier conflict and turmoil in his life.

Whenever I interview people with psychosis who have killed I ask two fundamental questions. The first is simply 'didn't you go to far?' This gives me an idea of the depth of psychosis I may be dealing with. More importantly it helps to measure the degree of remorse that someone feels towards their victim and this helps make a prognosis about how likely it is, given a certain set of circumstances, that the person is likely to re-offend. The second area I look at is unnatural marks on the body such as scars usually caused by violence to others, accidents or of course attempts to kill themselves. Another example is tattoos. I ask them to interpret these marks, be it a scar or tattoo. It tells me a lot about the person. I am never ceased to be amazed by those who kill who paint their body with their undying love for their mother or father, though seldom both.

Gutheridge we know had tattoos including one on his neck that said 'England' and others that depicted violence and were overtly racist. He also sported the obligatory 'mum' tattoo. We also are aware from our sources in the UK that he was involved in racist agitation in the 70s and 80s. He was an active member of the skinhead movement in the United Kingdom. But his faith hasn't been enough. It hasn't given him the protective layer that he needed. As his mood has swung he has become confused by the intensity and conflicts of Jerusalem and eventually religion and psychosis has overtaken him and he can no longer tell if he is right or wrong. His perception has gone. It has left him if you like. When he killed Jonathon Mautner his psychosis probably mistook him for somebody else. Last night he said he was doing 'God's work', so maybe, on the Mount of Olives he was probably fighting out Good v Evil, or the Sons of Light v the Sons of Darkness. He obviously saw himself as a son of Light and Jonathon as a son of Dark. Perhaps the woman last night was in his view a daughter of Darkness."

"Is there a name for this?" the newsreader enquired.

"Well I talked about manic depression but this is something a little bit more. It is called Jerusalem Syndrome. It's more common than we think but most people aren't lethal with it."

"How would you know who is lethal and who is not?"

"Well I would reiterate most people who get the syndrome as with any mental health condition are not dangerous to the public. However in Gutheridge's case we have a number of factors that may have caused him to kill and it is this, the combination of factors that is likely to determine how dangerous the person is. In this instance the first factor is that he suffered with a pre-existing condition, manic-depressive psychosis. Secondly we have learnt he was part of a violent organisation, a bit like Burgess' Clockwork Orange where alcohol and drugs would have been an important part of that culture. He would have witnessed and been part of violence against others at this time. He was also probably the victim of violence periodically. Now what we could also say very broadly is what sort of person would join a group like this. Research shows personalities that are generally disordered, anti-social and share a common theme of failing to recognise boundaries. That begs the question why are some people like this? Well there may be a number of reasons. Partly perhaps because of the way they were brought up. A child's house is its society and if boundaries are lacking there then it will have difficulty in maturing when laws are enforced beyond parental care. Maybe the child has been abused psychologically, physically or even sexually. Or maybe the child has had an accident that has caused some cerebral damage and led to a deterioration in the way that the child behaves.

Gutheridge, while we don't know precisely about his childhood, was a member of a group with a disproportionate amount of people with what is described as a personality disorder. He had a severe psychiatric condition and probably used excessive alcohol and drugs in the past. He then at some point in his life tried to change and this was through his new found faith. This is an enormous transformation, a transformation of extremes if you like resulting in an explosion of faith. The result of this was that Gutheridge stopped medicating himself, he dismantled that protective shield that had been built to protect him against what can only be described as a terrible psychosis. So as the shield wore down and his perception left him it may be that he was unable to reconcile the idealistic subconscious image of Jerusalem as a holy place with the war torn city it is in reality. These two concepts, holiness and war, in Gutheridge's mind, merged. He was literally fighting a holy war."

"It all sounds very complex."

"People are complex."

"Moving on, the millennium must be an important date?"

"Well its well documented the increase in the amount of cases of Jerusalem Syndrome correlating with the increase in tourism to celebrate the anniversary of Christ's birth. What we must be aware of is sufferers with a mission, like John Gutheridge."

"Finally, Dr Ronnel, if the police had not intervened in such a dramatic way, would in your opinion John Gutheridge have killed that woman at Gethsemane?"

Dr Ronnel looked directly into the camera and answered, "Yes, without doubt."

IX
Christ's Agony

When I arrived back at the hotel the pilgrims were boarding the coach for the 4.30 service at the Church of the Multiplication of the Loaves and Fishes. After the news report the barman put the music back on and I drank a couple more Becks. I toyed with the idea of retreating to my bedroom with the Orangeboom but decided to go. Dad was already on board.

"Are you ok?"

"I'm ok. I went for a drink. I found a bar."

"Any good?"

"Yeah, I suppose so. I saw the news."

"I thought you might try and avoid that."

"Well I didn't," I snapped. There was a silence between us. Then he asked,

"Ok, tell me what happened."

"The man shot dead last night was a bloke from Hemel Hempstead called John Gutheridge. He was the same man I talked to at the Jaffa Gate, the man who said he saw Fisher on the Mount of Olives. The news story is saying that Gutheridge killed Jonathon Mautner. When they shot him yesterday he was trying to kill a woman at Gethsemane," and slowly I added, "the place of Christ's Agony".

Again he was silent, and then he put his hand on mine and said softly,

"Seb, it's over now. It's over. Like I said we've got just two more nights. It's over." and he turned and looked out the window.

X

Seb takes communion

Fifteen minutes later we arrived at the church. As I got off the coach I asked Rachel if I could keep the paper she had read to us from earlier that day as a souvenir. It was huge inside the church, its size exaggerated by the fact that it was empty of pews and we formulated a crescent around the far side of the altar, said to be the rock where Jesus fed five thousand with a couple of loaves and a few fish. Apart from us the church was empty. Then, through a side door, came the Bishop. He looked, even in the turmoil of my mind, magnificent like a medieval Cardinal, Medici style, or even the Pope himself. He briefly mentioned how the site of Tabgha was famous for its miracles. 'The calling of the First Apostle, the Healing of a Leper, the Miracle of Multiplication, the Sermon on the Mount, Walking on Water,' he rasped and then said, "let us pray." We buried our heads to pray and he began the intercession. Half way through he said,

"And now we remember those we have left at home," and out of the blueness of the flicking sinister light he said, "Jack and Laura of Winsmoor Hill." I wanted to cry again and fought back the tears as he listed the other relatives left at home. I saw Sally across the crescent from me. She was crying; crying for her lost husband. When I looked up I noticed the church was now full of pilgrims. They had just arrived hundreds of them, maybe thousands, and they flashed their cameras at us as we stood behind the alter where Christ performed a miracle. The Bishop said,

"We will now sing Psalm 23, The Lord is my Shepherd," and he immediately burst into the first line. His voice echoed around the Church and was joined by the beautiful soprano of Catherine and Liz bouncing above my head. Then the other pilgrims, the hoards who seemed to come from nowhere, also started joining in, so by the last verse the church was roaring, "Goodness and mercy shall follow me all the days of my life."

We stood for the communion. The Bishop distributing the thin wafers, Liz and Catherine assisting with the wine. I felt really dry after the Becks and unstable on my feet. Eventually he reached me, took a wafer and put it in my open mouth.

"The Body of Christ," he rasped café crème at me and then, for the first time in my life, the Celebrant of Communion smiled a great big grin.

"Amen," I whispered as he moved on to his wife stood next to me crying. Before I had swallowed the bread, Liz had arrived with the goblet of wine and stood in front of me waiting for me to swallow. It felt like an age and then instead of me sipping from the goblet as I was use to she handed it me. I was shaking – *Oh Christ. I'm going to drop it*. I looked into the now packed church. Flashes were going off. Everything seemed to be spinning. Liz smiled at me.

"The Blood of Christ, Sebastian," she almost sang. I put the goblet to my mouth and took a swig of vinegary red wine and handed it back to her. She wiped where I had drunk from with a cloth. I stared at her before responding, "Amen".

The communion finished with the Bishop saying,

"Peace be with you."

"And also with you," the church responded and I remembered being a server in a church in Bath some twenty years before. We arrived back at the hotel at about seven.

"I'm going to skip supper. I'm exhausted."

"All right Seb, you do that."

"Have you got any sleeping tablets."

"What for?"

"So I can sleep, dad. I'm feeling a little perplexed. I need a good nights sleep."

"In my wash bag there's some Temazepam. Just take one."

"Ok," I answered. I went upstairs and phoned Laura.

"How did you get on with Jane last night?" I asked her

"I went mad when I went to Jane's. I lost it. Your mum's here. She's just coming down the stairs."

"What do you mean, you went mad?"

"I'll tell you when you get home."

"What about Jack?"

"He's great. He sends his love."

"Oh yeah." I swigged on an Orangeboom

"How are you?" she asked

"Looking forward to getting home," I answered.

"What's it like?"

"What, over here? Complex, really complex."

"I wonder what happened to that guy you told me about when you were pissed."

"John the Baptist?"

"Yeah, John the Baptist."

"I don't know," and I wondered what the English news was reporting. "Look. I'll speak to you tomorrow. I'm really shattered."

I hung up and went into the bathroom, I found dad's Temazepam and took two washed down with the Orangeboom. I got into bed and waited for sleep to take me to a dream world of headless people, crosses and Mrs Thornton's dying cats and dogs.

CHAPTER 9
Saturday (Capernaum – Sea of Galilee)

I
Change of Plan

I awoke to dad shaking me.

"Seb, Seb are you All right?" It took a while for me to come to my senses. In fact I had forgotten where I was such was the depth of my disturbed sleep.

"Dad," I said dozily. "How are you? What time is it?"

"Nine, you've slept for twelve hours. We're due off in thirty minutes."

"I'll go and have a shower, I'll be ready."

"How many Temazepam did you take?"

"One," I lied.

In the bathroom I felt a bit shaky. Lack of supper and too much Temazepam and Orangeboom had left me feeling weak. I packed my Loving Dove bag grabbed a huge bowl of fresh grapefruit in the restaurant and was on the coach within 10 minutes of dressing.

"There's a slight change in plan. We were going to Capernaum first then on to Ein Gev for lunch and sail back across the Sea of Galilee, but were going to do it the other way round, well almost. We'll sail from Tiberias to Capernaum, tour the site of Jesus' & Peter's home and then Ahmet will have brought the coach round and drive us along the eastern shore of the lake to Ein Gev for lunch." As we travelled through Tiberias to the harbour it was completely empty.

"Where is everyone?" I asked dad

"It's the Sabbath," he paused and added, "No work and no play on this their holy day." *Very poetical*. At the harbour we embarked onto a fishing boat staffed by two men. As we pulled out of dock one of the men put a record on an old wooden gramophone which suddenly burst into the English National Anthem, whilst the second man raised the Union Flag. Peter, the Welsh priest who had led me up the Via Dolorosa, attempted to sing the Welsh anthem, 'Land of My Fathers' over the top of the scratching and screeching of the record, but failed dismally.

II
Sailing the Sea

The day was clear and blue and ahead of us we could see clearly, as we chugged north, the Octagonal Church of the Beatitudes, Tabgha and to its right Capernaum.

"So much," said the Bishop, "in such a little space." Twenty minutes into the journey the wind changed direction and it swept down on to the lake from the Golan Heights, and I remembered David Brown's warning on the Beatitudes the previous day. The lake became distinctly choppy to the point that the waves crashed onto the boat and soaked the pilgrims in the process. Some were looking decidedly worried as they reached into their Loving Dove bags for their anoraks and struggled to stand up to put them on. When I fly in turbulence I look at the stewardesses for signs in their face that they may be worried knowing that their training doesn't allow for this. I decided to seek reassurance in the faces of the two sailors. They looked unperturbed. Emily, sat opposite me, was ghostly white and she sunk her head into Robert's chest and held on to his thick blue crew neck jumper. Barbara, next to me, held the hood of her anorak over her head in defiance of the wind.

"Didn't expect such a realistic re-enactment!" She was referring to Jesus calming the lake and saving the disciples. "But we'll be ok with the Bishop. He's God's representative!" and she laughed. The Bishop was the other side of me and attempted to light up a café crème until the top of a wave crashed over the side into him soaking the cigar. He threw it at the floor and with water dripping off the end of his nose he turned and said,

"There'll be no cleavage shown today."

I looked around the boat. The pilgrims were wet and cold. Some of them had chattering teeth. Emily vomited over Robert's thick blue crew neck jumper and then as quickly as the squall occurred, the wind direction changed again and the lake in seconds was as flat as a pancake; complete calm. The pilgrims looked dazed, and gradually one by one stood up and peered over the edge of the boat into the calm almost disbelieving.

"Lord be praised! Thought we were going to meet our maker en masse," laughed the Bishop and lit up a café crème. His flock tried to laugh with him

III
Seb talks to Derek, Jan and Rachel

Twenty minutes later we docked near the ancient city of Capernaum. At the end of the small wooden jetty was a café and the pilgrims sat four to a table drying out in the warmth of the sun and drinking coffee. I found myself sitting with dad, Rachel and Jan

"Do you ever go back to France, Rachel?" dad asked the guide.

"No I haven't been back for a long time. I may go back sometime. I usually go to Uganda to visit friends when I travel."

"I'm reading a book on Uganda about the time of Idi Amin."

"I didn't go there then," Rachel laughed and continued "Have you ever been to Switzerland, Derek?"

"We had a family holiday once there – a place called Grindelwald."

"I know Grindelwald – up the railway line form Interlaken."

"Yes that's right Rachel. Last year I met an old colleague of mine. He said that they had been to Grindelwald. I asked him whether he enjoyed it, "No" he said, "My son was killed, fell of a rock"."

"Oh dear, that's terrible."

"Yes, it was terrible, didn't know what to say."

"So what did you say?" I asked

"I don't know, I can't remember." I turned to Rachel

"I once hitch-hiked through Switzerland."

"Did you." She said unimpressed

"Yes. 1991 I think. We, that's me and my wife, Laura, though she wasn't my wife then. We had been visiting her aunt on an Island called Katapagea, in the Greek Cyclades. When we eventually arrived back in Athens we had very little money. There was a bus back to London in five days. I think we had enough for the fare but if we used the money then we couldn't survive until the bus went, so we decided to hitch."

"What happened?" Jan asked.

"Well we headed north towards Macedonia and Yugoslavia but the war started, so the borders were closing and trying to hitch through a war zone didn't seem very sensible. So we used some of the money to catch a bus back to Athens and then another bus to Patras. At Patras we bought two deck tickets to Anconna. The journey to Italy took two days. In Anconna I bought a map and it struck me that Euro route 14 could take us all the way to Calais.

At first things were really frustrating. Short little lifts, hops of little more than 20 miles or so, though we did eventually get a fairly decent lift to Piacenza from a couple of soldiers where we stayed overnight. The next day we were arrested for hitching on the motorway near Monza. It was really hot and they wanted a spot fine and of course we didn't have the money," the three of them appeared interested, "so they asked us to send it to them when we got back to England, though of course we never did. We eventually got a lift into the outskirts of Milan where we took the metro to the central station. We were both tired and fed up. At the central station was a train going to Calais and we thought about jumping it but we didn't. Instead we bought two tickets to Como, the border with Switzerland, where the lake is. We thought just to be in another country would raise our spirits.

When we reached Como we walked for a couple of miles back to the motorway. On the way I can remember stopping a woman and saying 'What country are we in?" and she answered 'Switzerland' and we were really relieved. Then we were lucky and this guy picked us up in his BMW and it seemed like we flew through the Alps. He didn't speak any English but stopped in the evening and bought us a meal. He dropped us at a service station, as he was off to Lucerne and we were headed for the French border at Basle. Though it was dark we decided to carry on and a bunch of hippies picked us up and took us across the border into France.

We slept by the roadside that night and were woken by what seemed at the time a pack of dogs. By mid morning we had reached Strasbourg, but after waiting 5 hours for a lift we decided to give up and we went to the police. They said we would have to go to the Consulate in Paris so we may as well just carry on. We made a big sign that said 'Metz, Reims, Calais, Great Britain'. I would say to Laura, 'we have to wait for THE LIFT. We haven't had it yet but it will be THE LIFT that gets us home.' Eventually we got a lift with a drunk Frenchman who told us jokes in French and laughed to himself. Whilst we were travelling along we went past a van with English plates. In the front of the windscreen of the van was a sign that said 'The Royal Mail.' I waved to the man driving and pointed to a bandana I was wearing in the red, green and yellow of the Rasta movement. He waved but I could tell he thought I had probably smoked too much of what my bandKaty implied." Jan laughed.

"Anyway at the next toll some ten minutes on we jumped out of the car and waited for the lorry. When it arrived we dodged the cars to the booth it went to. The driver wound down his window and recognised my bandKaty. We told him that we were desperate and that we needed to get back to the UK. Could he give us a lift?

"Well I'm not supposed to" he answered me "Against regulations."

"Please," cried Laura. "We were attacked by dogs."

He pondered and said to he would wait in a lay by he knew two hundred metres on. We thought he was saying that as an excuse, but fair play by the time we had huffed and puffed up there, he was waiting. This was THE LIFT. We crossed firstly west and then north thought the battlefields of Northern France, I suppose dad", I looked at him, "near to the memorial of The Lost and arrived in Calais that night. In Calais he made me his assistant so I didn't have to pay to cross the channel and Laura we smuggled through in the sleeping compartment in the cabin."

"How many lifts did it take?" Rachel asked.

"I don't know, 20 or 21 I suppose. When we got married Laura's dad opened his speech by saying "Last year Laura hitchhiked from Italy to London without spending a penny." Dad and Jan smiled. Rachel didn't.

IV

A lot of responsibility

Rejuvenated the group left the café and walked east along the shore towards Capernaum. I still hadn't fully absorbed the events of the previous 72 hours, though when I did think about it, it was the ethics that worried me most. Should I tell anyone, the authorities? Dad clearly felt we should just get home. Had we reported John Gutheridge when we first met at the Jaffa Gate where he read Revelations Eleven to me, then perhaps the Mautner children would still have a father; or perhaps not. However hard I tried to rationalise what had happened at the end of the process there was only one outcome – a dreadful and desperate feeling of guilt. Somehow, in some way, I had played a part in the death of Mautner. When Gutheridge said he was John the

Baptist I had tried to address the feeling of the delusion – *that's a lot of responsibility* – not confront it. But perhaps the perception in psychosis is one of collusion, not one of feeling. If that is the case did that line, 'that's a lot of responsibility' give permission to Gutheridge to decapitate Mautner or for John the Baptist to decapitate the Anti-Christ represented by Joshua Fisher III and believed by the Essene John to be a false Witness of the Revelation.

"That's a lot of responsibility."

The contrast between these exposed raw feelings and the gentle undulating scenery we walked through, where Jesus walked, was just too vast to be translated into any sort of sense.

"This then is Capernaum, the town where Jesus lived. This became the centre of his Galilean ministry. We are standing in the 4th century synagogue which is built over the one that Jesus would have preached from. It is from here that he would have started his journeys and returned to places like Phonetia, Caesarea Philippi, across the lake to the Gentiles, and of course most famously Jerusalem. Now what is also important is that Capernaum is on the trade route. We are at the point where 3 continents meet – Europe, Africa and Asia and people who had listened to Jesus would take his teachings along the routes. Nazareth wasn't on a major route, so you know, in terms of spreading the message this was a pretty good place to be. Now Bishop you've arranged a few readings….."

I decided to go for a walk and left the remains of the synagogue to explore the rest of the excavation. As I left I could hear David Brown's voice say,

"And they went into Capernaum and straight away on the Sabbath day he entered into the synagogue and taught…." And then it vanished in the wind which again had changed direction.

V

Fred performs a miracle

As I walked past the excavation of the homes of fishermen from 2000 years ago I heard a voice behind me,

"Hold on, there, Hold on!"

I turned and saw Fred who had pointed out the cat at the entrance to the cave at Qumran. He had a limp and walked awkwardly towards me.

"Hello, Fred."

"Hello," he replied, "aren't you staying for the readings?"

"No, I don't think so. I was going for a walk."

"Oh, can I come with you?"

"Please do, Fred, Please do."

In silence we walked towards the excavation of Peter's house over which was built a modern designed Roman Catholic Church. It was on large concrete buttresses.

"What does that look like to you, Fred?"

"It looks like a space ship," he stared at it.

"Or a crab maybe," I added. "It's terrible isn't it?"

"Yes," he agreed. "Awful." He tutted.

We walked on a little further and then he said,

"There's your cat for you," and pointed to a black cat sitting on the wall of one of the excavated Capernaum houses and again I began to feel overawed by the sense of it staring at me. After a moment Fred said,

"It's not like the one you saw yesterday."

"I don't know what you mean, Fred."

"Of course you do, son. The cat that sat on your lap at the Beatitudes." Then he turned and staring through his large framed glasses slowly said,

"The cat you thought was Christ." I blinked at him and didn't know what to say.

"How do you know?"

"I saw you."

"Saw me what?"

"I saw you staring at this cat. You were shaking and then started looking round as if you were looking for something or maybe somebody. So I walked round the back of the bench you were sat on and stood behind one of the grapefruit trees and heard your conversation with your dad."

"What about it Fred?" I asked seriously.

"You said to your father that "I needed you to take a photo of me with Christ on my lap, but now he's run off". You're dad heard that as well because he asked you to repeat it and you said "I needed you to take a photo of me with the cat on my lap, but now he's run off"." He was still staring at me. After a few moments he went on.

"Son, I'm not your father, so I can hear things without letting my emotions interfere, and the reason I know you said 'Christ on my lap' it that you said 'but now he's run off' on both occasions. How did you know the cat was a he. Why not a she – she's run off or an it – it's run off? But you were definite it was a he and to you that cat at that point in time was Christ."

He turned away and leant his arms over the wall of the excavation.

"So what about that cat over there?"

"What about it?"

"Is that Christ?" he asked

"I don't know," I answered staring at it. There was a silence between us.

"Or is it," he began slowly, "that one over there," and he pointed back towards Peter's home where another cat, this time white, sat washing itself. "Or maybe that one over there," and he pointed in the direction of the synagogue where we could see the Bishop reading from the Bible.

"Which one's Christ – I mean they can't all be, and they're certainly not father, son or Holy Ghost – became look there's another one."

"I don't know," I repeated.

"Well let me tell you which one, shall I?"

I was silent.

"I'm going to tell you anyway," He paused. "None of them are, son. They're just cats, like all the cats we've seen. They're just cats, son". He patted me on the back and added, "It takes more than a feline to be Christ. It's just coincidence. Come on now let's get back to the group," and we walked, him with his limp and his arm on my shoulder, and as we walked I felt a relief gradually take control, and with that sense of control I began to feel better.

VI
Seb eats lunch with the Bishop

We drove down the Eastern Shore of the Sea of Galilee, along the fringe of the Golan Heights, to a Kibbutz called Ein Gev for lunch. The rolling hills of the Golan Heights for some reason reminded me of Arthur's Seat, the extinct volcano that dominates the Edinburgh skyline, and I could picture armies swarming across them as they came in search of water because as we had learnt, water causes war. I remembered the man with the ginger beard on the train to Heathrow, the man who had worked on a Kibbutz called Ein Gev and had waited each day for the Arabs to come from over the Golan Heights to reclaim what they thought was rightfully theirs. He also had told me to keep my wits about me and I didn't know what he had meant. I did now.

At Ein Gev I sat with the Bishop and his wife for lunch.

"Fancy wine, Sebastian?"

"Yes, why not?" I answered and he ordered a bottle of red.

"Remarkable thing happened last night," he carried on, as we ate carrot and tomatoes in pitta bread and beautifully fresh Peter Fish that were conveniently farmed at Ein Gev.

"A woman came to the hotel," he went on. "She came to visit Fred."

"Why?" I asked, interested.

"Well let me tell you. After the war Fred was based in the navy at Trieste. The state of Israel wasn't founded but about to so it must have been '46 or '47. The British policy was to intern the traumatised Jewish population in refugee camps. Most of the Jewish population wanted to head to Israel. Apparently Fred just took his boat to Israel, full of traumatised Jews and dropped them off, and not to the camp in Northern Cyprus he was ordered to take them too. He could have been court martialled. It was extremely brave. The woman who came to the hotel was a child on that boat," the Bishop rasped. "She came to thank him." I thought of the day I sat in the courtyard of the Basilica of the Holy Sepulchre with Roma and Fred, where I had wondered briefly why they hadn't moved because of the traffic that made Roma campaign for a ring road for most of her life and learnt a lesson in humility.

That evening there was a group party. Earlier Robert and myself had wondered into Tiberias but couldn't find the rugby. I had brought some more Orangeboom and returned to the hotel where, whilst dad napped I read about the journeys of Jesus from a couple of books dad had bought at the Church of the Multiplication of the Loaves and Fishes. The party was hardly a swinging affair, only Sally, who looked the worst for ware for drink, but was particularly happy. She had managed to contact her lost husband. The other pilgrims sat and sipped their drinks in the knowledge that the next day they would be going home and back to their lives in England.

I was just about to go to bed when Rachel came up to me, smiling.

"So you must be an agnostic."

"What do you mean?" I asked her.

"Well if you're not a Christian and not an atheist either, then that makes you an agnostic, doesn't it?" I was reminded of our conversation at the baptism site.

"Bravo! But not to loud, it might cause some upset, " I answered. She sat down next to me and I turned towards her. "Rachel," I went on, "I have no firm belief about God."

"Is that what it means, agnosticism, having no firm belief about God?" I was aware of Barbara sat the other side of me listening in.

"Not necessarily, that's just my interpretation, nice and simple."

"Well what else does it mean?" More of the pilgrims were taking an interest.

"How do you fancy a walk?" She looked surprised.

"Ok," she agreed. I drank the dregs of my beer and we left the party.

VII

Seb and Rachel go for a walk

The evening was warm and Tiberias was still deserted. We headed towards the town centre. The moon, not quite full, shone brightly in the deep darkness and we could see it shimmering on the Sea of Galilee in the distance.

"Right, now we're away from prying ears let me tell you a bit about agnosticism. Well allegedly it was first used by Thomas Huxley, the 19th century biologist."

"I know who Thomas Huxley was," Rachel interrupted.

"Sorry, Rachel. Well Huxley, who was a big fan of Darwin, his belief was that nobody ought to have a positive belief for or against a divine existence. Once in debate at Oxford with Bishop Samuel Wilberforce, do you know about Wilberforce?" I asked conscious of my earlier comment.

"No," she replied.

"Well Wilberforce was a creditable theologian of his time and went to the university at Oxford to debate all these huge things with Huxley. During the debate Huxley stated that he would rather be descended from an ape than a Bishop."

"I wonder what our Bishop would say to that?" Rachel laughed.

"He would probably spark up a cigar and think about it. Anyway, I can't really get to grips with Huxley, so I just settle for the no firm belief bit." We walked on in silence for a couple of minutes and arrived at the shore of the Sea where the light of the moon continued to flicker on its surface and with the Golan Heights innocently silhouetted in the background. Rachel turned to me.

"Remember the other day in Jerusalem, at the Wailing Wall you asked me what I think about it. I answered nothing, what's the point."

"Yes, I remember," I answered.

"Well that wasn't quite true."

"What do you mean?" I looked into her eyes and fought the urge and feeling of wanting to kiss her – *Renaissance sperm* - and remembered my selfish and excluding love for Laura.

"I do think about these things."

"So what do you think." There was a brief silence.

"I think the Christian religion is wrong."

"Wrong, what do you mean wrong?"

"The writings, in the New Testament, they are wrong. Matthew, Mark, Luke, John, the Acts of the Apostles, they are all quite wrong. Good story, but wrong."

"Well what's wrong about it?" She sighed.

"Where do I start. Let me see. Well the Gospels were written after the Jewish revolt, which of course the Romans crushed, remember the mass suicide on Masada."

"Yes, I remember."

"Well Christ was crucified some thirty years earlier. After the crucifixion his followers split into two groups. The first was his family and friends, his disciples if you like led by his brother, James. They followed the law strictly as laid out in the Torah. The other faction was the one led by Paul who received his vision of Christ on the road to Damascus, though Paul never met Jesus in the flesh. Paul's belief was that this vision was more significant than Jesus' activity on the earth. Are you with me?"

"Yes, I'm with you."

"Ok. James' faction were based in Jerusalem whilst Paul's ministry was scattered across the Roman Empire. Paul however did not follow certain fundamental principals like circumcision or kosher preparation and eventually he was summoned to Jerusalem to I guess some sort of summit. There, James told Paul to pray at the Temple to show his devotion. But Paul was recognised by other zealots who literally attacked him as a heretic. To save himself Paul called out to nearby legionaries that he was a Roman and they did save him. So you see Paul was a Roman."

"No, I don't see. So what if Paul was a Roman."

"Well, don't you see. What would have happened if James and the Disciples had written the story of Christ, not Paul?"

"I don't know. I don't know what you mean, Rachel."

"Think about it. The Gospels hardly mention the Roman occupation. Pontius Pilate is seen as a nice guy who does everything to keep Jesus off the cross, for goodness sake he even offered Barabbas as a swap. But no those nasty Jewish priests want him dead no mistake. Now what we know is that the Roman Occupation was brutal and the people were oppressed. The situation was political. When Jesus asked Peter who he thought he was," she looked around her, "not far from here, perhaps at Capernaum, he answered the Messiah. But we know that Messiah had no divine meaning then, it simply meant King. And Christ is Greek for Messiah. All the divinity associated with the words Christ and Messiah it all came later. When he entered the Temple and attacked the traders he did so because the Romans controlled it not the corrupt priests – they were merely puppets. And of course Jesus was executed for blasphemy and if it was the priests had found him guilty then under Jewish law he would have been stoned. Under Roman law he would have been crucified and left to rot as a symbol of the power of the Empire."

"So are you saying that Jesus was a politician?"

"Not quite, but that politics and religion were hard to distinguish just like now. What Paul wrote or instructed was propaganda and anti Semitic with it. There was no Judas. That was the name of the state. Judas was Judea!"

"What did you say?"

"Judas, Judas Iscariot. He represented the state and people of Judea."

"But in the Acts of the Apostles it says that after the betrayal he hung himself so violently that his bowels fell out."

"Haven't you listened. The Acts of the Apostles is Paul's influence written after the Jewish Revolt. The bowels of a corrupt Judea fell out. It's symbolism. It makes a good story. You mix a little bit of truth with non-truth and in the end nobody knows what is the truth and what isn't. It's like the myth of Jesus being born to a virgin in Bethlehem. He was born in Nazareth, one of a number of children with James the eldest. So you see its all wrong, but it's better than anything James and his bunch came up with, not that I suppose they were trying to come up with anything anyway." For the third time I was reminded of the dream, *the vision,* I had on the Piccadilly line and in the silence of the warm Tiberias evening I glimpsed Mary Magdalene, whose village we passed the previous day on the way to Beatitudes and the Christ cat, and saw her ready to receive Jesus.

"What happened to James?"

"I don't know exactly what happened to James, I can't remember, but the faction lived on for a couple of hundred of years or so until Paul's writings were truly entrenched. Then they were outlawed as heretics."

"That's amazing, Rachel. I had no idea." She turned back towards the water's edge and then lifted her head towards mine.

"Well I suppose that's what makes you such a good agnostic." Briefly we laughed. "Anyway it's not worth getting up tight about, what's the point?"

"None, I suppose. No point whatsoever," I answered. Then I put my arm through hers and we walked back to the hotel in silence where the party had ended.

CHAPTER 10
Sunday (Tiberias – Mount Carmel – Caesarea – Tel Aviv – Winsmoor Hill)

I
Robin's successful itinerary

We arrived at Ben Gurion airport at 4pm precisely, exactly when Robin's itinerary said we would arrive. To that point it had been a strange day. Leaving the hotel we celebrated communion on the shores of the Sea of Galilee and in the clarity of the morning could see the Beatitudes, The Church of St Peter the Primacy and in the distance snow capped Mount Hermon, a contender for the location of the Transfiguration of Christ. Then we left Tiberias behind us and drove to the beautiful Mount Carmel where the prophet Elijah had gathered the people of Israel and demonstrated the supremacy of the true God over other false Gods.

"The reason he had to do this," explained Rachel, "was because there had been a drought for 3 years so there was famine and death. After he had convinced the people he killed the prophets of the other Gods and the rains came. I like coming here on the last day. All three religions honour this site; Judaism, Christianity and Muslim; it's a reminder that it all stemmed out of Abraham." We sat in the olive groves and enjoyed the shade. The weather had changed to how it was when we first arrived.

II
The four horsemen of the Apocalypse

We left Carmel and drove through the plain of Esdruelon.

"If you look to that wooded area," Rachel said, "behind the wooded area is Megidda. The other name for Megidda is Armageddon. We haven't time to stop, I'm sure you don't want to miss your flight, but again in the book of Revelation in your bible this is the supposed scene of the final battle between good and evil."

"I thought it was the Mount of Olives, dad. At least John thought it was the Mount of Olives."

"I don't suppose it matters really, here, the Mount of Olives, somewhere else."

"However it is likely," Rachel went on," that the author of Revelation chose this site because traditionally it had been the site of many battles and conflicts, for example where Deborah sang of her victory over the Canaanites and incredibly a battle between British and Turkish forces in the Great War. The British General responsible for victory was General Allenby, and as a result he was given a peerage and became Viscount Allenby of Megiddo."

"Viscount Allenby of Armageddon," I whispered "What a great title."

"Because of these conflicts the name Armageddon has now been applied to any huge slaughter or period of mass destruction. Has anybody got any questions?"

"I would like to know who wrote Revelations?" somebody from the back of the coach asked.

"Well it is thought to be John the Evangelist. He was one of Jesus' disciples and witnessed the Agony at Gethsemane and the Transfiguration of Christ on Tabor, remember, where Jesus shone and appeared in vision with Moses and Elijah. It was thought that John the Evangelist was exiled to one of the islands in what is now the Greek Dodecanese where he wrote it. And this would make sense because Revelation is an example of apocalyptic writing in the bible, and apocalyptic writing occurred when there was persecution happening, which John's exile suggests. The themes of apocalyptic writing are often similar – the evil age is soon to be ended, destroyed by God. The subsequent age, the Kingdom of God, will be ruled by God, and only those who were oppressed will be able to enjoy it. Have you any other examples Bishop?" she asked. The Bishop took the microphone stood up from his front row throne and rasped.

"In Daniel there is a message of impending defeat for the oppressors of the Kingdom of God. These detailed prophecies are supposed to date from 600BC but were actually written as a response to the persecutors of the Seleucid king, Anticohas IV in the 2nd century BC."

He sat down breathless.

"Thanks Bishop. And of course in Revelation John describes four horses all of a different colour. A red horse signifies war, a white one refers to civil strife, a black horse hunger and a pale horse, death. With their riders they make up the four horseman of the Apocalypse. Charming Bunch," she smiled.

I looked around me and thought that this unremarkable plain didn't look capable of hosting such a remarkable event.

III

Seb and Derek chat on the beach

By lunchtime we had arrived at the ruins of Caesarea on the Mediterranean coast. Standing on the beach, beneath Herod the Great's magnificent aqueduct, Liz was tempted, stripped into her swim gear and splashed around in the waves, whilst for the last time Rachel gave us the history.

"Ok back to the coach, well drive through the excavation of Caesarea on to a nearby restaurant for lunch." The pilgrims took off back to the coach. Dad and myself looked out over the sea

"Well that's it," I said.

"Yep," he replied "that's it."

"No more head counts for Robin." Dad smiled

"Where the bloody hell's Jan," he mimicked and we laughed. We turned, put our arms round each other and walked back up the beach to the coach.

IV

Airport

The departure terminal at Tel Aviv was heaving. El Al hadn't called our flight yet and we sat resting with the hoards of tourists returning to their homes throughout the world. I sat with dad chatting.

"There seems to be some significance about the number 3."

"What do you mean?" he said.

"Well three religions, three continents, three people crucified at Golgotha, three times the cock crowed and the primacy was offered to Peter three times, Christ was 33 when he was crucified….I even asked the Essene John his name 3 times." I could tell he wasn't listening. "Dad are you listening?" he didn't answer. He was staring over my shoulder, his eyes fixed and his mouth twitching.

"Are you all right? Do you want me to get you anything?" He again didn't answer. He just stared and I thought he was having some sort of seizure.

"Dad? What is it? You're worrying me. Do you need some tablets, some medicine?"

"No," he answered and continued to look over my shoulder. I turned my head and then literally in an instant saw him. Across the isle reading a book was Jonathon Mautner.

"Christ. It's Mautner," I gasped. "It's Mautner."

"It isn't Mautner," said dad slowly. "John the Baptist chopped Mautner's head off on the Mount of Olives. He's made a mistake."

"Who's made a mistake?"

"He has," and he continued to stare at the face of Jonathon Mautner.

"What do you mean he's made a mistake?"

"Have you got that old Jerusalem Today, the one you bought in Nazareth?"

"I think so, hold on," and I rummaged in my bag and produced the paper. On the front page was the picture of Jonathon Mautner which dad had sketched on as we ate our lunch *en route* to Mount Tabor. He examined it and then said quietly again,

"He's made a mistake. He's had a shave and put contact lenses in."

I looked at the paper and back at the man,

"Fisher'" I hissed, "It's Fisher."

Suddenly Fisher looked up catching our eye and instinctively we turned our heads.

"Don't look at him anymore, dad," and I could see out of the corner of my eye Fisher looking towards us again. "Just talk to me normally and tell me what's happening." Fisher started reading his book again.

"We should tell someone," he said "we should tell someone!"

"Dad, we can't. Let's go home, then we'll tell someone. We'll go to the embassy"

"Do you know what he's wearing – a beige hat, a white shirt, red trousers and black shoes."

"What," I whispered "Are you sure? It may be just a coincidence."

"Maybe, maybe not. We need to tell someone." We looked at each other.

"Dad, listen to why we can't do that. There are two reasons, dad. First we'll not get on our flight and if we don't we'll be part of an investigation into a group of people who are planing to kill." I thought of Laura's Uncle Jimmy and of how her family believed he was a spy and couldn't leave the country.

"The second dad is your right, you're absolutely right. He's made a mistake and doesn't realise it. Maybe he's just arrived because he looks the spitting image of Mautner and Mautner's face is all over the papers. Somebody else will see that and he'll be stopped."

"How can you be sure of that? The murder has been and gone. It isn't front page anymore, its old news. Anyway isn't that the wrong attitude," he stared at me and slowly said, "that's the attitude that lets genocide happen."

"Dad I need to get back." I was beginning to plead. "I need to see my family." He looked at me and then smiled.

"Of course you do," and patted my hand "and I don't know what your mother would say." We sat for a couple of minutes of silence and then dad patted my hand again.

"There's a man joined him. He's young looking and blow me.....Christ....he's wearing beige, red, black and white.....what are they like? Fisher's stood up, they're shaking hands. He's given him something."

"Who's giving who something?"

"Fisher to the other one. They're shaking hands again. Fisher's sitting down. The other guys coming this way. He's going to walk past us."

The man walked by. If ever there was a person who looked *normal*, then this was him. Average height and weight, dark hair, glasses and sporting the colours of the apocalypse. In a way he looked too normal, *ultra normal*. I watched him. He was moving quickly, heading towards the check in desks.

"Dad, wait here, I'm going to see where he is going. Don't do anything. Ok dad, don't do anything."

"I won't, don't worry." He picked up Thursday's paper and started to flick through it. Slowly I ambled towards the check in desks.

"Stretching your legs, Sebastian."

"That's right Bishop, stretching my legs."

The man was at the check-in desk for Air Olympus the national carrier for Greece. *Hadn't I read about the Caring Christians wanting to be sent to Greece.* I went over to the departure board and scanned it from the top: Istanbul, Cairo, Tokyo, London Gatwick, New York,

Athens: Flight AO 133 Athens departure time 19.00 hours from gate 15. Quickly I turned around from the board to see the man disappear into the security check to have his bags searched before getting clearance to go on to the departure lounge.

I went back to Dad, and sat down. Fisher was still occupying his seat, reading.

"He's going to Athens. Remember the morning we had breakfast with Robert and Emily, you know you joined me late, it said in the paper that the deported Caring Christians wanted to go to Greece."

"Ok everybody, get your bags, were going through customs as a group." It was Rachel, here to the bitter end. "Let's go." The pilgrims, started picking up their bags and followed Rachel to the El Al security and check-in.

"I'll catch you up, dad I've something to do."

"What are you doing? Don't be stupid." he snapped.

"Don't worry. I'll see you at the check-in desk."

Bending over I took the copy of the local Tiberias paper from my blue bag, the one where Ahmet had shown me the picture of Mautner with his family. There were a number of security guards in the terminal and I approached one who would have a clear view of Fisher. He was young and clean-shaven.

"Hi," I said approaching him. "Do you speak English?"

"Can I help you?" he replied seriously but smiling.

"I don't know."

"Is there anything wrong?"

"They're may be." He felt for his machine gun and was no longer smiling

"Where are you going?"

"London. I've been on a pilgrimage."

"So what do you want?"

"I want to show you a photograph," and I held up the paper.

"See this man," I continued pointing to the face of Jonathon Mautner, "he had his head chopped off on the Mount of Olives by someone who suffered with the psychiatric disorder Jerusalem Syndrome a couple of days ago."

"I know the story."

"Well," I said and I turned my body to face Fisher's and, taking a gulp of air, said,

"But isn't that Jonathon Mautner," and pointed at Fisher in his chair.

Fisher looked up from his book and saw me pointing. My arm was shaking. Fisher this time didn't look back at his book. Briefly, very briefly, a look of surprise covered his face. The soldier stared at Fisher and then at Mautner and then at Fisher again.

Fisher rose up from his seat and as normally as he could, *ultra normally*, he closed his book and headed for the exit. The likeness of the two, man and picture, registered on the soldier, and whistling to a colleague he trotted towards the exit. I walked briskly back to my bag and case and chased after the pilgrims, who were queuing up to enter the security gate. As I reached them the queue began to move and once in the door closed behind us. I couldn't stop shaking.

Once again we went through the rigorous ritual of questioning and bag search, this time for once by a young woman who had no eye contact and did not smile. Our bags were checked in and we headed for the second security check at the entrance to the departure lounge. Rachel stood here and kissed people on the cheek before shaking their hand goodbye. I wondered what she was thinking. When I came to her, having composed myself, we kissed each other on each of our cheeks and she put a polished brown stone into my hand with a Peter fish painted onto it. I fumbled in my bag,

"Here take this Rachel. It's a damn good read," and I gave her 'The Last King of Scotland'.

"You must send me a picture of that painting you talked about in Nazareth. You know 'The Betrothal of Arnolfini'." I was impressed that she remembered.

"That's right," I smiled, "'The Betrothal of the Arnolfini', I will send you a copy." I paused. "Goodbye, Rachel."

"Goodbye, Seb." she answered, smiling. I turned away and entered the departure lounge. It was the only time she called me by my name since the day we arrived. I never saw her again.

V
Seb shops for presents

"Have you got any money, I need to get Jack and Laura something. I'll square up when we get home." I had earlier explained to dad what had happened, how I had shown the picture of Mautner to the guard and how he had followed Fisher out of the building. He looked at his wallet and handed over a wad of shekels. I went into one of the tourist shops and bought Jack a red tee shirt, with a happy face painted on it as if by a child and 'Israel' written underneath. For Laura I bought some decorative candles in the shape of eggs and one particularly large candle depicting the Old City of Jerusalem. The Dome of the Rock was even impressive on a candle, though I thought she might think that these gifts were like my coffee – lousy.

And then I went to gate 15 where the passengers for OA 133 to Athens were congregated, waiting for their call. He, like Fisher, was sat reading a book. There was an empty seat next to him.

"Do you mind if I sit here," I asked.

"No, please, be my guest." He was American and he carried on reading.

"Been on holiday," I said to him smiling.

"No, not really," he smiled back, the sort of smile that suggests please I don't want to talk to you. "Business really," he added.

"I've been on a pilgrimage."

"Oh," he answered, "Did you enjoy it?"

"Yes I did. I don't think I believe, but it's a pretty incredible place."

"You don't think you believe." He looked at me more interested and I knew instantly he had taken the bait. He put down his book. "Well, maybe I can help."

"Help me with what?"

"Believe," he answered.

"Having spent 10 days with 50 Christians including a Bishop you may find that quite hard," I responded. "What business were you on?"

"Oh, that's not important"

"And where are you going, Greece?"

"Why, yes."

"Did you see the news story, about Jonathon Mautner." I changed the conversation

"I'm not sure."

"The one where a psychotic chopped off a man's head and faced it towards the Old City with an ash tear rolling down his cheek."

"Yes I did hear something about that. What's this all about?"

"Well I just saw Mautner at the front of the airport."

"You what, look I really think…."

"And you shook his hand. But it couldn't have been Mautner could it, because, like I said he had his head chopped off by John the fucking Baptist." I was becoming aroused.

"Look if you don't go away I'm going to call security."

"Good, that's what I want you to do. They'll just think I'm a religious nut and have me first in the queue on the plane back to England. You on the other hand, dressed in your colours of the apocalypse – you see I am a nut – they'll wonder why I'm hassling you." Sweat was appearing on his top lip.

"So if it wasn't Mautner. Who was it?"

I took out the *Jerusalem Today* bought in Nazareth the previous Thursday from my blue bag with the sketch of Fisher on top of Mautner. "Well it could have been this man, the man who John the Baptist mistook Mautner for. But who is he? Perhaps you could tell me?"

"You're crackers," he hissed.

"No, *I am not*. I am not and you know it. Well if you're not going to answer me," and I dug back into my bag and took out the profile I had read over a kebab minutes after Jan had washed her hair at the scene of Christ's crucifixion and put it on his lap, so that the spectacled man with jet black moustache and open collar yellow shirt stared up at him. He said nothing.

"What I'm wondering as well, is that why didn't he leave after he met you. I guess he must have been waiting for somebody else."

"Ok, ok that's enough." There was silence.

"I've got a deal for you, which you accept or I'll blow this fucking open now. I swear it." He stared at me and said,

"What is it?"

"Before I came through security I went up to a guard with a picture of Mautner with his family and I pointed out your man Fisher and suggested that Fisher must be Mautner even though of course Jonathon hasn't got a head any more."

174

"You did what?"

"You heard me. Now that seemed to freak Fisher out because...."

"Andrew, Andrew," a voice shouted in our direction "I couldn't...." a woman was fast approaching the man who the woman had called Andrew. Briefly he shook his head, the woman stopped looked at us and turned and walked away.

"..because, Andrew, it is Andrew isn't it?" I carried on, "the guard went after him and after that I don't know because like you I have a plane to catch"

The intercom came on

"OA133 to Athens boarding Gate 15".

"Now listen to me Andrew, are you listening?"

"Yes"

"Fisher's finished, gone. Forgot about him. Get your people to forget about him. You're not going to see him again. There isn't going to be no fucking resurrection in December, no apocalypse, Armageddon what ever you fucking well want to call it. So just go away and don't come back because my feeling is that it's you and yours that killed Jonathon Mautner. It's you, Andrew, it's you who slaughtered the innocent Jonathon Mautner."

He picked up his bag and took a stride towards Gate 15. He then turned to me and smiled,

"The Lord will save you sinner," and then added, "Fisher was just a piece of shit anyway. I'm coming back and there is sweet fuck all you can do about it. See you, sinner," and then he turned back towards the gate. The woman joined him. He said something to her and I could see her gasp and put her hand to her mouth and then they vanished through Gate 15.

VI

Seb says farewells

I stopped for a beer, settled myself and then joined dad and the rest of the pilgrims at Gate 22. Dad was reading a copy of the *Financial Times*. Eventually the flight was called and we took courtesy buses to the El Al flight waiting on the tarmac. I never told him about Andrew.

The flight back to London was uneventful and we arrived back at Heathrow at 11pm. Waiting at the luggage carousel the Bishop came up to me.

"Well, Sebastian, its been great having you along. Hope you enjoyed it."

"It was great – you were a great leader."

"See you at the Minster," he winked and went to collect his baggage. I thought briefly of Thomas Huxley and decided I would rather be descended from a Bishop than an ape. At the baggage reclaim I then found Fred.

"Thanks, Fred," I said to him.

"Thanks for what, son?"

"You know, yesterday."

"Don't be so daft, son." He held out his hand. "Take care, Sebastian."

Laura was waiting at the terminal. "I managed to get Uncle Jack to babysit," she said and we hugged each other strongly. I turned to the rest of the pilgrims who were coming through.

"I'll just go and say my goodbyes, darling."

"Ok," I walked up to dad. "Bye dad. I'll get the photos done and we'll come up next weekend."

"Bye, Seb," and we hugged. I saw him walk over to Laura and they kissed each other on the cheek. I turned to Sally.

"Bye Sally, I'm glad you got hold of your husband."

"Bye Seb, come and visit when you're up." I came to Jan.

"See you soon, Jan," and kissed her on the cheek. Finally I came to the blind man, Keith.

"Goodbye Keith. Good luck."

"Goodbye, Seb. Good luck to you to."

Then I turned round, took Laura's hand and headed for the car park.

Laura had brought me a couple of cans of 1664 which I swigged as we headed around the M25.

"What was it like then?"

"Oh I don't know. Amazing, dangerous. I'm glad to be home."

"Well that's not exactly giving anything away."

"I'm really tired, I'll tell you it all tomorrow. Can I put some music on?"

"Ok."

So I put the radio on. It was tuned into Capital Gold. The programme was featuring the band 'The Clash' and a song called 'Safe European Home' was blasting out. I began to relax and rested my hand on Laura's thigh

"How's Jack?"

"He's great, Seb" she answered, "I've got some news for you."

"What is it, love?"

"We're going to have another."

"Another what?"

"Another baby, stupid!"

I raised my arm from her thigh to her stomach.

"That's great, that's great," I repeated and we started talking excitedly about our new life with Jack and a baby

VII

Midnight News

"Hold on, darling, hold on I need to hear this." It was the midnight news on Capital. The first item was about the genocide in Kosova and the ongoing struggle in the Balkans and this was followed by other news of decreasing importance. My heart began to sink when in the predictably unpredictable fashion that epitomised the last 10 days the newsreader said,

"And we're just getting news that the leader of a Christian cult, the Caring Christians has been arrested at Tel Aviv airport. Apparently Joshua Fisher III, believing himself to be a Witness of the Revelation, planned to die in Jerusalem in December and then be resurrected 3 days later and incite the final battle between good and evil. Heavy stuff, Joshua! You should lighten up a little bit. Take a chill pill or something!" I smiled.

"That's a coincidence," Laura said "You flew from Tel Aviv didn't you," and so I changed my mind and told her the story about the Essene John, a Christian Cult out of control, a cat called Christ, Renaissance sperm and a man who lost his head and wept a tear of ash. By the time I finished I knew she believed me because it was just too fantastic to make up.

VIII
Laura and Jack

When we arrived at Winsmoor Hill she turned off the engine outside the 'cottage' style home, leant over and gave me a deep kiss. We went inside.

"I want to see Jack, I can't wait until tomorrow."

"Go and see him then."

"Are you sure? I don't want to disturb him. I don't want to wake him."

"No, go and see him," Laura insisted.

I climbed up the narrow stairs to his room, dimly lit in red to keep away the demons of the night. He was fast asleep.

"Hello Jack, I'm back," I whispered.

Immediately he sat up.

"Daddy, daddy." He was still asleep.

"Lie down, my darling, stay asleep." He lay down and pulled his quilt over him. He was beautiful and his beauty took me back to the Mount where Jesus wept for the incompetence of man and then to the lush pink heather of Exmoor where all that was needed was a lump of wind.

End of Part 2

LONDON

"Welcome this pain, for some day it will be useful to you."
Publius Ovidius Naso

Chapter 11
December 28th 1999

"Thank God that's over," sighed Sebastian Carrington to his wife, Laura as they pulled up outside their home in Winsmoor Hill. "Right you see the kids in and put the kettle on and I'll unpack the car."

"Do it quietly, Martha's asleep. Come on, Jack, let's go." Seb watched his family leave the car and go into the small terraced house. He then went around to the back of the car and started unpacking the boot of its Christmas contents.

"I can't believe how much stuff we've got," he moaned to himself as he attempted to disentangle a number of bags from a travel cot that Martha detested. Having succeeded he took the cot inside. As usual the television was on. Sebastian stored the cot in the backroom and went back to the car and started to unpack the rest of the luggage onto the pavement.

"Are you Sebastian, Sebastian Carrington?" a woman's voice said behind him. Seb turned to face a tall, elegant woman wrapped in thick clothing to protect her from the chill of winter. He guessed she was in her late thirties.

"I'm sorry, I don't think I know you."

"No, you don't know me. I've been waiting for you."

"Waiting for me. I'm sorry I don't understand. What do you want?"

"Sebastian," she said slowly, "did you know a man called John Gutheridge?"

"What?"

"A man called Gutheridge, Did you know him?" she repeated. Seb was silent. "I don't know why I'm asking you this because we both know the answer."

"He's dead."

"I know he's dead, Seb. Can I call you Seb?"

"Who are you? What do you want?"

"One thing at a time, Seb, one thing at a time."

"Who are you?" Seb repeated.

"My name's Alice. Alice Hunt. I wanted to talk to you, you know about John."

"Are you his sister?"

"No, I'm not his sister, I'm...."

"Seb, Seb come here quick. It's on the news! Come quickly, quickly!" Laura's voice was raised with excitement and immediately he dropped the case he was holding and ran inside.

"What is it?"

"Who is that woman?"

"I don't know, something to do with Gutheridge. Now what is it?"

"Gutheridge, what do you mean Gutheridge?"

"Gutheridge, John Gutheridge, the man who killed Mautner."

"I know who you mean. What does she want?"

"I don't know, Laura, I really don't know. Now what is it!" Laura turned towards the television.

"Look," she pointed, "somebody's been shot in Jerusalem."

"What?",

"He was shot on Temple Mount," she replied, "look." Sebastian turned to the television and saw a camera shot of Temple Mount. The newsreader was having a telephone report from his colleague in Jerusalem.

"So, Bob, what's happened?"

"Well the facts aren't 100% clear at the moment. But it would seem a man armed with a fully loaded machine gun managed to get onto Temple Mount and when he refused to hand over the gun and then made gestures indicating that he was about to start some sort of carnage, then Israeli troops shot him."

"How did the man manage to get onto the mount?"

"Well, Neil that is a complete mystery. Temple Mount is of course of extreme importance to two major religions, Judaism and Islam. I can't underestimate the religious significance and the authorities of course are very aware of this. Hence security is tight, very tight particularly for the Christian New Year celebrations just around the corner. How this man managed to break the cordon is just not known."

"And do we know anything about the man shot dead?"

"Not much concrete at the moment. His name was Andrew Mortimer, an American from Philadelphia and apparently he arrived in Israel from Greece a week ago or so. That's about it though there is some speculation linking him to a fanatical doomsday cult called the Caring Christians. The leader of the cult, Joshua Fisher III was arrested at Tel Aviv airport last February and is still in custody in

Israel. Fisher had planned to spark off the end of the world this December by inciting bloodshed at Holy sites in Jerusalem. But as I said it's all speculation."

"Ok, Bob, we'll come back to you at the end of the programme. Now for today's other news." Sebastian continued to stare at the television and then turned to his wife,

"I don't believe it, Laura. I just don't believe it. That was the man at the airport. He was called Andrew. He called Fisher a piece of shit. Fisher was going to die and be resurrected three days later to fight the final battle. Mortimer's replaced him. He said he was coming back. Now he's dead. He tried to get the Jews and Muslims fighting each other and no doubt he expects to be back in three days time." There was a brief silence between the two.

"New Year's Eve," whispered Laura.

"Yes, New Year's Eve."

"These things don't go away do they, Seb. They simply follow you around." Sebastian turned around. Alice had come into the house. He stared at her.

"Who are you, Alice? What do you want?" She sat down on the sofa.

"The night John was killed on the Mount of Olives, do you remember, Sebastian?"

"Yes, I remember, What about it?"

"John was shot attacking a woman, maybe he was going to chop of her head like he did to Jonathon Mautner."

"So what?" Seb was becoming agitated.

"I was that woman, Sebastian, the nameless woman attacked on the Mount of Olives." Seb stared at her disbelievingly.

"How can that be?"

"Simple, I knew him. I was on his Pilgrimage." There was a silence in the room. "Don't you want to hear about it, how it came to be, how he talked of saving the sinner Sebastian Carrington at the Jaffa gate, how he tried to decapitate me?" Seb looked around the room, at Laura, at Jack, oblivious and at the sleeping Martha.

"No, I don't want to hear about it. I want you to go." Alice smiled to herself.

"Well if that's what you really want. Though I don't think you're telling me the truth."

"Just leave. Let us be." Laura snapped. Alice smiled again and slowly rose from the sofa. Seb followed her to the open door where she briefly turned towards him.

"I expect we'll be seeing each other fairly soon," she whispered, "In fact I expect to see quite a bit of you." And then she was out the door and gone.

Seb shivered in the cold of the early afternoon and closed the door behind him.

Chapter 12
January 1999
Jerusalem

The pilgrims spewed into the lobby of 'The New Jerusalem Hotel' opposite the Jaffa Gate of the Old City. Around their necks binoculars and cameras dangled, banging against each other roughly and out of their green 'Shepherd Christian Tours' shoulder bags poked half drunk bottles of still mineral water. The day had been unusually warm for the time of year and the struggle up the Via Dolorosa had left most of them exhausted though exhilarated at experiencing the site of Christ's crucifixion.

Alice Hunt slumped into one of the large leather sofas that were systematically scattered around the lobby and turned to the man next to her.

"Well, John, I'm quite interested to know how you found it all. The site of Christ's death. You don't get to see that everyday. Not exactly Hemel is it." She paused and smiled at him, brushed the dandruff off the collar of his Fred Perry shirt and added, "Tell me, what did it do for you, John, seeing the place where he died?" Slowly the man turned his head towards her. He was unshaven and his eyes were fixed and intense.

"It filled me with sadness, Alice. But it wouldn't have done that for you would it? It wouldn't have filled you with sadness. Your cup overflowed a long time ago didn't it Alice? I know. They don't, but I do. You're just a whore, Alice, a whore!" he hissed and turned his head back.

"Oh, John, what are we going to do with you? Still not getting your sunshine out of a bottle? People are talking about you; I've seen them. I know, including the Bishop. They think you're going weird on them. Did you know that, John? Did you know that's what they're thinking," and she leant over and whispered into his ear, "you know, that you're a fucking crackpot." John continued to stare vacantly into space and there was a silence between the two of them. "Listen, John dear," Alice eventually went on. "Dearest John. I don't think you're a crackpot. Quite the opposite, I think you're a great man. And besides, it doesn't matter what they think. But you need me don't you John. This is a strange place, isn't it? You need me to get you home, because this lot," and she swept her arm before her at the pilgrims dotted around the lobby, "they don't give a toss about you. They want rid of you."

"I don't know," he answered continuing to stare into the space in front of him.

"Well I do. Remember I've heard them speaking about you and believe me it isn't good what I've heard. Now this is what you need to do. You need to go and have a shower because you look a mess. Go and have a shave and you'll see that they'll stop talking about you. When you've done that come along to my room for a drink and if you do what I say now I'll give you what you like. But you've got to be nice and clean. Do you understand me?" John didn't react. "John, do you understand me?" Alice repeated. Slowly John rose from the sofa. Some of the pilgrims watched him from behind their papers and paperbacks.

"Oh and John, hide that tattoo, your England tattoo. They don't like it." John cast a brief but wild glance at Alice before marching out of the lobby, knowing that the eyes that burnt into him belonged to a group of people who despised him.

"Do you mind if I join you, Alice, just for a moment?" Alice looked up from that day's edition of Jerusalem Today bought in a small shop near the Basilica of the Holy Sepulchre.

"Oh, Bishop, please do. Have a seat," she answered gesturing to the end of the sofa vacated by John. The Bishop clumsily lowered himself and sank beneath her and as if conscious of this stated,

"I really must lose some weight."

"Oh, Bishop, don't be so absurd. Everybody loves you just the way you are. The Friar Tuck model is much more vogue!" Alice answered. The Bishop chortled to himself.

"You're very sweet Alice, very sweet indeed but clearly no sort of deterrent to my rising cholesterol." He took her hand. "Now I need to talk to you, I need to talk to you about John Gutheridge."

"I thought you might."

"Well what's going on with him? He seems to be acting, well how should I put it, oddly I suppose, yes oddly. I mean I know he's had his problems and of course we're not unsympathetic, but it's upsetting people. Is he, you know, taking his medicine, if he's on any that is, not that it's any of my business?"

"Bishop, Bishop, slow down. One thing at a time." Alice put her hands up to the Bishop as if to say 'stop'. "Ok, there's no doubt that he's a bit overawed by it all. We all are I suppose but I guess he's not coping as well as the rest of us. He's a very devout man and this has a lot of meaning for him."

"I have absolutely no doubts about that, my dear. He's a very devout man indeed. To devout perhaps." Alice's mouth broke into a wide grin.

"Perhaps, Bishop, perhaps. Look I'm keeping an eye on him. He's just gone to clean up before supper. If I think we have a difficulty I'll let you or Tom know. But at the moment I think he'll be fine."

"That's so typical of you my dear. Always putting others first. A real Good Samaritan if ever I knew one."

"I don't know about that, Bishop. You haven't seen my naughty side." Alice continued to grin.

"I don't believe for a moment such a thing exists and if it does I'm a little to old and long in the tooth to start exploring it now." The pair of them started to laugh. When the laughter had subsided the Bishop took Alice's hand again.

"And how are you, Alice?"

"I'm fine, Bishop, honestly, I'm fine."

"We all miss him, you know."

"I know." Alice whispered. The Bishop looked out over his flock.

"He was a good man and a good servant of the church." Alice was quiet. The Bishop pushed himself up awkwardly. "Mind you I expect he's watching all of this and having a right old laugh."

"I expect so Bishop. My father seemed to find most things funny." Up on his feet the Bishop turned back towards Alice.

"Take care Alice. If you need anything let me know."

"I'm fine, Bishop, really. By the way, between you and me, he is taking his medication. I've made sure of that." The Bishop nodded his acknowledgement, turned again and waddled towards reception to collect his key.

Alice returned to her edition of Jerusalem Today and read about the genocide in Kosovo. On page four, in a section called 'Other News from around the World', she came to a headline that read:

'Philadelphia Cult plan Israel entry.'

Alice read the brief article.

"A Christian Cult operating out of Philadelphia are planning to enter Israel according to national intelligence. The leader of the Caring Christians, Joshua Fisher III, plans to be killed in Jerusalem in December and 'resurrected' three days later as one of the witnesses of the Revelation and so provoke the Second Coming of Christ and the end of the world. A source reports that the authorities are currently unconcerned by the possible threat that the cult poses to national security."

Beneath the article was an unremarkable picture of Fisher with a thick, bushy moustache and large, tinted glasses. Alice stared at it briefly and then turned to the next page.

"Anything good in you paper, Alice?" Alice looked up at a balding, ruddy man sat on a nearby sofa.

"Not really, Donald," she answered, "here, take the paper. I'm off for a shower." She got up from the sofa, flattened down her tartan skirt and popped the paper onto Donald's admiring lap.

Up in her room Alice Hunt started to undress. Naked, she admired her long, elegant body in the mirror of a wardrobe that had seen better times. For a while she particularly admired the cleanly shaven area above her genitals with a tattoo of a Bishop's mitre where most would have hair and in red the word 'cock' fiercely displayed across the centre of the hat - *men are always surprised by that.* Quickly, with her index finger, she rubbed at her clitoris and smiled at herself in the mirror. Still smiling, she lifted her leg onto the end of her low, single bed and with her other hand inserted two of its fingers into a moistening vagina whilst maintaining the rhythmic stimulation at the top of her genitalia. Her breathing became louder and more rapid so synchronising with the movements of her fingers. Then, in a second, she stopped, pulled her arms to her side and marched into the small en-suite bathroom. In the shower she repeated the process, one leg resting on the side of the small, brown bath. This time she allowed herself to go a little further, almost to the point of orgasm. But just at that point she again stopped. Alice was getting ready for the manic, John Gutheridge.

After her shower Alice put on her hooded bathrobe and went back into her bedroom where she poured two large gin and tonics from the litre of gin she had bought duty free at Heathrow. Out of the pocket of her bathrobe Alice took a small folded piece of blue paper which she carefully unfolded and poured its contents of white powder into one of the drinks. She licked the blue paper then squashed it and threw it into the wicker bin stood next to her wardrobe. Then she sat down on one of the bland, high backed chairs next to her bed and started flicking through a magazine. After a couple of minutes there was a knock at her door. Alice put down her magazine, walked over to the door and opened it.

"That's better, John. You look a lot better. Now come in and sit down on the chair at the bottom of my bed." John Gutheridge cast a glance at her, the muscles around his nose and mouth were visibly tense, before he squeezed past her into the dim room. Alice went over to the bedside cabinet, picked up the drink she new to be laced with amphetamines and took it over to John who was sat on the chair at the bottom of her bed.

"Here," she said softly, "this will help relax you. Loosen you up a little bit." She turned and walked back towards her own chair where, before sitting down, she removed her bathrobe from over her shoulders and then sat with one of her legs raised on her bed exposing her genitals to Gutheridge. Casually she picked up her drink, took a sip without breaking her gaze at the tortured man sat opposite before delicately putting the glass back on its coaster.

"Tell me something, John," she said as she began to stimulate her nipples, "What do you think of my tits?" and she lifted her breasts towards him. Gutheridge continued to stare towards the door. "Come on, John, don't be coy, what do you think of them? They're only a pair of tits. Though I say it myself I think they're rather fine. Not too big, not too small, heh, John. Nice suckable nipples, don't you think?" Gutheridge slowly turned his head towards her.

"For Christ's sake, Alice. What are you doing?" Quickly then he raised his glass to his mouth and drained its contents. Alice got up from her chair, undid the rest of her bathrobe and casually walked towards Gutheridge, their eyes fixed on each other. When she reached him she knelt down in front of him. His breathing was rapid and loud enough to fill the room.

"I've just read something in the paper, John. I should have kept it for you but I gave it to Donald. There's a man coming called Fisher, Joshua Fisher. He may already be here." Alice slowly started rubbing at Gutheridge's crutch through his blue chinos and felt his penis start to swell. "Now listen to me, John. Are you listening?" Gutheridge stared at her. "That's a good boy. Now this man Fisher he is coming to die here, I don't know how he is going to die, it doesn't really matter, all that's important is that he is just going to die." Slowly Alice began to unzip the zip of the chinos and took hold of Gutheridge's erection bringing it out into the open. Carefully she pulled back his foreskin revealing deep red swollen glands.

"That's a good boy, John," she repeated, "you've had a very good clean." Rhythmically she started pulling up and down on the shaft of his penis. "Now Fisher thinks he is one of God's Witnesses, you know, John, one of the Witnesses of the Revelation. So he believes that after his death he will be resurrected and do you know what that means, John. Well let me tell you. It means John, the Second Coming, Christ's magnificent return!" Slowly she lowered her head and took his glands into her mouth whilst continuing to masturbate the shaft. Gutheridge looked down at the back of her head, his mouth open and his breathing somehow synchronised with Alice Hunt's rhythmic strokes. If he hadn't been so confused he may have made note of the faded lacerations that ran up and down her inner arm from her elbow to her wrist. Then quickly she looked back up at him. "But you know what else that will mean, John, do you? It will mean the end of the world. That's right, the end of the world. Imagine that. Now if Fisher is who he claims to be that would be fine because as good Christians we would be saved. But Fisher isn't who he says he is, so that must mean he's coming to cause destruction. You see, John, Fisher must be the Anti-Christ." Slowly she lowered her head again and started masturbating him with more ferocity. Gutheridge's breathing became more and more forced and quickly he ejaculated into Alice's mouth. Gradually she slowed down her movements feeling him softening though conscious of his rapid heartbeat brought about by a cocktail of ejaculation and amphetamine. She looked back up at him.

"You've really got a very little cock, John. Shall I tell you something but it has to be a secret. Daddy use to like that." The comment took time to register with Gutheridge but all he could muster was a feeble,

"What?"

"I said, John, that daddy used to like me to suck his cock. His was much bigger than yours. He used to fuck me as well. That's shocked you hasn't it? Your friend, the priest, was a bit of a perv." There was a silence between them. Gutheridge continued to stare at her whilst she zipped him up.

"You're the Anti-Christ, Alice." The words came quietly, "You're a monster, a beast. I should kill you now Alice before you hurt anyone else." The tone in his voice began to rise. "You're a whore beast, Alice, a monster, whore beast. You're evil! I hate you!" and with that the manic John Gutheridge had his madness confirmed as he pushed his tormentor to the floor and fled from the room.

Chapter 13
January 4th, 2000

At precisely 10.20 Sebastian Carrington entered the conference room for the 10.15 meeting.

"Morning," he greeted the hospital's management team, "Happy Millennium and all that," he added as he took his chair at the head of the impressive mahogany table. The group nodded their response.

"Well I trust you've all had a good break. Now back to business. Simone, clinical position."

"Pretty good, Seb. 100% occupancy. Referrals have been strong over the New Year, better than last year. Currently we've got four on the waiting list but one of them's Harry's so that probably won't come to much."

"Fuck Harry. Let's give him a message and drop his referral. We don't need him or his attitude anymore."

"OK, Seb, that's fine."

"How's the business looking, Martin."

"It's looking good, Seb. With this occupancy we're way ahead but there remains a lot of observation around the place."

"Simone, we need to bring down these observations in time for budget planning in the summer."

"We're working on it, Seb. A couple are on the waiting list for Broadmoor but we don't know exactly where on the list. They're not high enough profile to go to the top."

"I know, Simone, it's difficult but keep at it. Roger, HR?"

"A New Year, new staff. We've got twelve new starters. Two in catering, two in maintenance, a couple of staff nurses and the six support workers from the Guardian add. They're being screened by occupational health at the moment. Your due to see them at eleven to kick off the induction."

"Where?"

"In here."

"Usual sort of spiel?"

"That would be fine, Seb."

At eleven on the dot Seb entered the conference room for the second time that morning. Sat around the table were the new employees that were representative of many of the great cultures of the world. Seb walked up to Roger.

"Everyone here?"

"Not quite, one of the support workers isn't here. She's coming from Hemel Hampstead and there's a problem with the trains."

"That's a long way to come."

"She's planning to move, it just hasn't happened yet. Anyway she's not far off, she just rang in."

"Well I can't wait, I've a meeting with the Health Authority at 11.30 who wait, as you know, for no man."

"No, you go ahead, Seb. I'll wait for her at reception and bring her around when she arrives."

"OK, Roger, that's great." Roger left the room and closed the door behind him. Seb turned to the employees.

"Morning." There was a mumbled response. "What's the matter, cat got your tongue. I said morning!"

"Morning," the room echoed.

"That's better," Seb smiled, "much better. Ok, well I'm Sebastian Carrington and I'm the General Manager for the hospital. Well what exactly does that mean? Essentially it means that I facilitate the other Senior Managers in the hospital to do their jobs and those are Simone Carlisle who heads up the Clinical Services Directorate," Seb flicked on an overhead projector and up onto the screen appeared an organisational chart. Beneath Clinical Services read Psychology, Social Work, Nursing and Occupational Therapy. "And then there is Roger who you've just met who heads up the HR team. Any work related difficulties you have such as paid the wrong salary, training issues or if you want to take out a grievance against another member of staff or, dare I say it, the company head for HR. Now who else is there," Seb turned back to the overhead. " Martin, he's the money man, our accountant who makes sure the Health Authorities are up to speed with paying for the wonderful services we provide, because ladies and gentlemen, even though this is a hospital, this is also a business. And as we're a business our primary aim, sordid as it might sound is to make money for our shareholders and if we do that successfully at the end of the day more money goes into our pockets also. When I first came here I tried to keep the clinical and the business issues separate, kind of protect people to focus on their clinical skills. But I quickly found out that you can't do that, it just doesn't work like that. So what I would ask you to embrace today is the concept that you are joining a business and to make that business successful we need to provide the highest quality service, better than any of our competitors. Because if we don't provide that level of service soon we might not have a business and that means you don't have a job. But if you succeed in your job then I can assure you, you will reap the reward. Any questions?" The room remained silent - *it always does after that.* "Ok, a couple of others you should no about. Doctor Tom Bowman is our Consultant Forensic Psychiatrist and Sheila Jones is our facilities manager which includes catering, housekeeping, maintenance, health and safety and anything else you can think of. Right finally I want to talk a little about attitude and behaviour at work...."

Sebastian was interrupted by a knock at the door and Roger popped his head around the side of it.

"She's here, Seb."

"Thanks, Roger, show her in." The door opened wider and a tall figure with her back to Sebastian, squeezed past Roger and into the room.

"Thank you, Roger." The woman's voice was deliberate and elegant. Slowly the figure turned, first to face the other new employees and then through another 90 degrees so that the high cheek - boned face of Alice Hunt starred directly into the face of a stunned Sebastian Carrington.

"I'm sorry, Mr Carrington. What a terrible first impression to have made. You see the trains were up the poll and I have to come a long way. I'm really sorry."

"Seb," Roger intervened, "this is Alice Hunt. You know, the woman from Hemel that I told you about." Carrington didn't answer but instead rested his hand on the edge of the conference room table to give his shaking legs support.

"Seb, are you alright." Again he didn't answer but continued to stare at the bemused expression on Alice's face.

"Sebastian, are you ok," Roger repeated, "You look like you've seen a ghost." Carrington's stare flicked from Alice to Roger. The other employees began to shuffle nervously in their chairs. Sebastian caught his breath and composed himself.

"Yes I'm fine, Roger, thanks. Now take a seat with the others please, Alice."

"It's like I said, Mr Carrington, I'm really sorry." Alice's face lit up into a grin.

"Don't worry about it, Alice and as I said go and find yourself a seat." Alice walked slowly around the table and found an empty chair.

"Thanks, Roger, I'll catch up with you shortly."

"Sorry, Seb, but there is one other thing. The Health Authority are here."

"They're early. Give them coffee and keep them cosy, will you Roger? I'll be with them as soon as I can."

"Sure, Seb," Roger replied and turned and left the room.

"Well I'm sorry about that," a composed Sebastian turned back to his new employees whose numbers now included the psychopath, Alice Hunt. "Now where was I?"

"You were talking about something to do with attitude and behaviour," a man's voice said from the back of the room.

"Ah, that's right, attitude and behaviour. Now we are a small hospital, just a couple of units. But we're high profile. And why are we high profile. Two reasons mainly. The first is that we're an urban site and secondly our patient population. They are all detained. They've all offended because of their mental health needs. Most have been through the Crown Prosecution Service. Some are very newsworthy. Now we have what we call a duty of care to these people which essentially means we are responsible for their well being. And that's why you have been recruited, to deliver that duty of care. I should make it clear that any staff that compromise that duty of care also compromises this business and that won't be tolerated. You see, I view such compromising as a risk and my job is to minimise such risks, is that clear?" The new employees, including Alice, nodded their heads.

"Excellent, well I've got to finish now. No doubt we'll bump into each other from time to time. I hope you have a good time with us and that you learn a lot." Seb picked up the induction programme from the table. "It looks like John our training manager and Pearl our equality manager are next up. They should be here shortly." Casually Carrington tossed the programme back onto the table and marched out of the conference room well aware of the smile on Alice Hunt's face.

The meeting with the Health Authority that registered Grenton lasted a couple of hours and had not gone well. They had come to review statistics for the previous year such as complaints, untoward events, amount of seclusion, escapes and abscondings, use of control and restraint and anti-psychotic medications and a number of other areas related to such an establishment as Grenton.

By one thirty they seemed satisfied that all was in order, refused any lunch on the grounds of conflict of interest and left. Sebastian Carrington picked up the phone and spoke to the catering manager,

"Jean, sorry it's short notice but could you arrange for a sandwich to be sent to my office with a bottle of sparkling water." There was a brief silence as Seb listened to Jean before he selected Tuna, apologised again for the lateness of the order and hung up. Without too much thought he picked up the phone again.

"Roger, we may have a problem. Can you come around to my office and bring Alice Hunt's file with you."

"There isn't much in it at the moment."

"Well bring what you've got, application, references, occupational health clearance. Anything, ok, Roger."

"I'll be with you in a minute." True to his word there was a knock at Sebastian Carrington's door within the minute and Roger came in and sat down, placing the blue file of Alice Hunt on Seb's desk.

"How did you get on with the Health Authority?"

"Slow start but pulled through. Fuck knows why they have to come so early. Right, Roger, tell me about Alice Hunt."

"What's this all about, Seb? What happened to you at induction when I brought her in? You looked terrible. Do you know her or something?"

"Don't worry about that, Roger for the moment, just tell me about Alice." Roger sighed and picked up the file.

"Alice Jane Hunt," he began, "Caucasian, born 1960, single and lives in Hemel Hempstead. Academically very bright, 10 'O' levels, 3 'A' levels at two 'A's and a 'B'.

"What were they in?"

"English, Psychology and Religious Studies. When she left school she went to work as an assistant to a local business man."

"She didn't go to university?"

"No. It seems that she stayed with this guy for ten years or so."
"What kind of business was it?"
"According to her CV, exports."
"What sort of exports?"
"I don't know, it doesn't say."
"Don't you find this strange, Roger?"
"No, Seb, I don't and I'm not quite sure why you do."
"Ok, carry on."

"Ten years ago she left the business to do a degree in Psychology at King's College, London for which she got a 2.1 and then she went to work as an administrator at St Paul's. Finally she did her Masters in Criminology and received a distinction for a thesis into the psychology of sexually abused children." Roger looked up from the file. "This is her first job since her Masters."

"Where's the pathway in all of this, Roger, I simply can't see it."

"Well there is something in all of this."

"And what's that?"

"She's very devout. In her spare time she runs a Sunday school in Hemel Hempstead, has done for twenty years. She does a lot of fund raising. For goodness sake her second reference is from a Bishop, headed paper, the lot." Roger pulled the letter out the file and waved it in the air.

"Read it." Roger sighed again and began to read.

'Thank you for asking me to supply a reference for the above named woman.

I have known Alice since she was a little girl. She is the daughter of one of my priests, Paul Hunt, who was the vicar of Saint John the Baptist at Hemel Hempstead. Sadly Paul died last year. For the last twenty years Alice has led the Sunday School at St John's which means that she has had responsibilities for the spiritual direction for the youth in that area. Her successes have included helping youngsters in trouble manage to learn ways to stay out of trouble sometimes through the use of church facilities.

Alice is a very caring, warm and loving person and whilst I don't really claim to be any kind of expert in your field, I have read the job description and would say that it is this fine temperament, and her academic background that make her most suitable for this post.

An example of this is that earlier in the year I led a pilgrimage to the Holy Land. Unfortunately one of the pilgrims who had past psychiatric problems became ill. Alice did everything to look after him and to reassure all the other pilgrims and though sadly the man died in dramatic circumstances, the well being of the other pilgrims was primarily the result of Alice's ability to contain the conflict in that most intense of places.

Without doubt I would recommend her for the post.

There was a silence between them as Sebastian absorbed what he had heard. Then he remembered John Gutheridge at the Jaffa Gate and in the thicket at the baptism site and then his passport picture on the television in the bar at Tiberias confirming his death on the Mount of Olives.

"Are you all right, Seb?"

"I'm fine. Who's the first reference from?"

"The tutor at King's. There's also another from a clinical tutor at Broadmoor where Alice did a placement. Do you want me to read them?"

"No, don't bother. I already know what they say. Let's look at the recruitment process."

"Nothing remarkable. Add out in the Guardian in October, shortlisting and interviews in November, references and offers in December."

"How many applications?"

"I'm not sure exactly but in excess of 70, maybe 80."

"And who shortlisted and interviewed." Roger checked the file.

"Jane and Michael."

"The heads of nursing and psychology."

"That's right, Seb. Come on Seb, what's this all about?"

"I thought we were going to introduce attitude testing as part of the recruitment process, Roger, you know, after that fucking psycho doctor which cost us a fortune!" There was a knock at the door and into the office came one of the kitchen assistants with Seb's tuna sandwich and the bottle of sparkling water. Sebastian calmed himself.

"Thanks, Shirley, put it on the desk." Shirley did as she was instructed and left.

"Sorry, Roger, I just think we've got a problem."

"The attitude testing is part of this years strategy. We're working at it."

"Don't worry about it. Like I said sorry. She's too good though, isn't she? Too good."

"Are you going to tell me about it, Seb." Seb unwrapped the sandwich, took a small bite and walked over to the office window. The day was grey and a faint drizzle peppered the window frame. Seb swallowed the Tuna and turned back towards Roger leaning his back on the window so that he was silhouetted against the greyness outside.

"Remember last year I went to Israel with my old man?"

"How could I not remember, they're was all that trouble wasn't there. I remember thinking when you told me that you could have written a book about it."

"Let me give you a quick recap, a reminder, Roger. There was this cult, the Caring Christians and their leader Joshua Fisher III. Fisher was going to evoke chaos in December last year. He thought he was a witness of the Revelation and that if he died he would be resurrected and so provoke the Second Coming of Christ and the Apocalypse." Seb paused. "It all sounds so fantastic now. Absurd." In silence Sebastian Carrington walked to his desk and poured himself a glass of water before returning back to the window. "On about the third day in Jerusalem at the Jaffa Gate of the Old Walled City I met an Englishman who claimed to be John the Baptist who thought Fisher was the Anti-Christ. The day after a man who looked like Fisher, called Jonathon Mautner had his head chopped off on the Mount of Olives and when I met the English John the Baptist at a baptism site he told me he had killed Fisher. When I told him he had killed Mautner and not Fisher he tried to kill me and I started losing the plot, Roger. A day later I saw on the news in a bar in Tiberias that John the Baptist was in fact John Gutheridge. The reason I knew was because John Gutheridge had been killed by Israeli Intelligence whilst trying to strangle a woman. A bloke called Fred helped me stay on track. Then of course we spotted Fisher at Tel Aviv airport and had him arrested somehow. I remember speaking to a man called Andrew, one of Fisher's disciples or whatever they were called in the departure lounge who said he would be back to fulfil Fisher's ambitions. Is that how you remember it, Roger?"

"Well it's been eleven months, Seb but that is how I remember it."

"There's been developments, Roger."

"What do you mean developments? What possibly else could have happened."

"Well firstly that Andrew went back to Jerusalem in December and on the 28th attempted to incite a riot on Temple Mount and managed to get himself killed. Things didn't go to plan for him though because we're all still here."

"My God, that's incredible."

"Not as incredible as this. When we got back after Christmas from Laura's parents a woman came to see me claiming to be the woman that Gutheridge was strangling when the Israelis shot him dead."

"That's extraordinary."

"What's extraordinary about it, Roger is that the woman was Alice Hunt." Roger was speechless.

"It can't be, Seb," he whispered, "it can't be."

"No, you wouldn't think so, but unfortunately it is. We've recruited a psycho, right out of the top drawer."

"How do you know she is a psycho?"

"It's the way she talked to us. It was really disturbing, chilling. We got rid of her but she said to me that we would be seeing a lot of each other. I didn't know what she meant," Sebastian smiled to himself. "I do now. Look at the reference from the Bishop, Roger. That man he refers to with psychiatric problems, that's Gutheridge."

"How did she know about you, Seb? How did she know where to find you?"

"I don't know. She wanted to tell us but as I said Laura and myself got rid of her. I told Gutheridge my name and where I lived at the Jaffa Gate, at least I think I did, 'My names Sebastian Carrington, Seb to my friends and I live in London' or something like that. He must have told her. That's all I can think of."

"Right we've got to get rid of her."

"And how are we supposed to do that, Roger. She has a contract, so on what grounds? We believe you to be a psychopath so we're dismissing you. She's plausible and that what makes her so dangerous. If we get rid of her she'll drag us through the courts and we'll lose and we'll be stumping up to 50 grand for someone who's been in our employment for less than a day. That will go down well at head office.

And the police can't help us anymore with the new legislation. We've got nothing on her."

"What do we do then?"

"Do the new recruits know about the thirteen week probation period?"

"Yes, it was covered at interview and then again this morning by John and Pearl."

"Good, that's how we'll get her. She'll do something in that time. When she does it we'll get her in here and I'll sack her. She's got me in her sights so she'll come after me. I just need to be patient and if she can't damage me she'll damage something close to me like my reputation…"

"Or your family."

Sebastian's silhouette looked down at Roger.

"No, families aren't her thing. She saves children. Remember the Sunday School and the thesis. She saves children, but what from. No, this is about men isn't it? The business man, the Bishop, that's one smokescreen and a half, and then John Gutheridge."

"And now you perhaps, Seb."

"Perhaps, perhaps not. Leave her file with me, I want to go through it again. And Roger, not a word to anyone."

Chapter 14
Valentines Day, 2000

Sebastian Carrington picked up his post from reception and went through to his office. Once a week he left home early to walk 5 miles to Grenton from Winsmoor Hill in a superficial attempt to fight the beginnings of middle age and its waistline. Today he had been caught out by a freak shower and though the sun was shining Sebastian Carrington arrived at work wet.

In his office he took off his great coat and jacket and from a drawer in his desk he retrieved a towel and started drying his receding hair. It always struck Sebastian that a towel was a strange thing to keep in a general manager's drawer, but he still always kept it there for such an occasion. Then he sat at his desk and started to go through his mail. There wasn't much; minutes of the last executive meeting, a letter from a large South London Trust wondering how long they were going to be charged for special observations for a patient at Grenton on the Broadmoor waiting list, and a thank you letter from the Director of one of the company's northern operations who had been entertained by Sebastian the previous week.

At the bottom of the pile was a card in a pink envelope. In capital letters it was addressed to Sebastian Carrington c/o Grenton. Sebastian eyed it briefly before running his paper knife from one corner to the next, and pulled it out. It was home-made on expensive green cardboard. On the front was stuck a picture of the Dome of the Rock and the Old City of Jerusalem clearly cut out of a newspaper. From where the picture was taken Sebastian could see that there had been a strong snow fall and this was endorsed by the caption beneath that said 'Jerusalem Experiences Worst Snow Fall for 50 years.' Sebastian could also tell from the picture that it had been taken from Dominus Flevit, the point where both Jesus and Jonathon Mautner had wept over the Old City, one with a real tear for the incompetence of man, the other an ash tear and a victim of a psychotic homicide. Sebastian could sense his heart beating harder within the cavity of his chest.

Slowly he opened the card and a newspaper clipping fell out onto his desk. In the card was printed on a piece of white paper stuck onto the green card;

'Behold the Lamb of God which taketh away the sin of the world.'

Happy Valentines
Love A'

Seb unlocked the drawer of his desk and took out the file on Alice Hunt. From out of the file he took Alice's application and turned to the section marked Education/Training. Then he picked up the envelope and placed the 'C' of Carrington above the 'C' of Criminology and immediately realised them to be the same. He closed the application with the envelope still in it and returned it to its file.

He picked up the clipping that had fallen out and opened it out. It was a picture of a lamb with its legs tied lying on a black background. The text underneath said;

'Bound Lamb, Francisco De Zurbaran C1635-1640'

Seb looked at the picture. The lamb seemed to be lying on a table but the blackness made it impossible to see. From its white fleece grew yellowing horns that merged eventually with the blackness. Sebastian read the text.

'This might appear to be an example of animal art, a subject more suited to Landseer. It could even be a grisly bit of still life from those vast assemblages of animal and vegetable eatables which were popular in the 17th century. But for all its stark and meticulous realism, this lamb, lying bound with string on a stone shelf is of course nothing of the kind. It is a concrete visualisation of the Agnus Dei, the Lamb of God.

Zurbaran was a Master of the still life in the bare and uncompromising Spanish idiom. Here however to has put to explicitly devotional use his gift for making the simple and everyday sharply vivid. This is Christ the lamb or Codero, which, according to the Spanish mystic Fray Luis de Leon, indicated his meekness and purity. The metaphor of Christ the lamb is common in the Bible, a text rich in the language of herding. 'Behold the Lamb of God which taketh away the sin of the world', announced St John the Baptist. St Peter compared Christ to a 'lamb without blemish or spot'. Christ the lamb was one of Zurbaran's most popular subjects – five other versions are known. A 17th century owner of a similar painting was said to value it more than 100 real sheep.'

Sebastian folded the clipping and put it back into the card. Then he picked up the phone and thumped in a four-digit number. He heard it ring a couple of times before it was answered.

"Good morning, Bradshaw Unit, Charge Nurse speaking."

"Susan, hi, it's Seb."

"Hello, Seb, how are you?"

"Ok, yourself?"

"Fine thanks."

"How's things on the unit?"

"Pretty quiet at the moment, touch wood."

"That's good Sue. Listen is Alice Hunt with you this morning?"

"Yeah, she is."

"You couldn't spare her for an hour could you?"

"She's in the community group at the moment. I'll send her round when it's finished."

"What time will that be?"

"Ten."

"That's fine." Seb hung up and dialled his secretary.

"Morning Seb," she answered cheerfully

"Hi Rose, everything ok?"

"So far, Seb, so far."

"Good. Listen Rose cancel the 10.15 will you. No on second thoughts let them go ahead just without me."

"Anything else?"

"Yes coffee for two at ten and divert all my calls from that point."

"No worries, Seb."

Sebastian sat back in his chair and contemplated that Alice had now made contact.

The coffee arrived at precisely ten o clock. Five minutes later Rose rang through that Alice Hunt had arrived for her appointment.

"Send her through, Rose will you. Remember to divert my calls, no interruptions."

"It's done, Seb."

Seconds later there was a knock at my door. Seb got out of his chair and walked up to it. There he took a deep breath, put his hand on

203

the handle and in one swift motion pulled the door open. Alice jumped, surprised at being faced by the General Manager in this way.

"Hello Alice, sorry if I startled you. Come on in." He turned, gestured for Alice to take a seat and walked around to his chair behind his desk.

"Coffee?" he asked as Alice closed the door and sat in her chair.

"Thanks, Mr Carrington, or can I call you Sebastian now we're behind closed doors." Sebastian poured two coffees and pushed one towards Alice with a small milk jug and matching sugar bowl.

"Alice, everybody here calls me Sebastian, or Seb if you like. Now why the Valentine's Card?"

"Why not? I though you may like it."

"That's not really the point is it, Alice? Whether I like it or not."

"No I suppose not. I though it might have reminded you of Jerusalem and you know events."

"I don't need reminding of Jerusalem and events, Alice, especially in a Valentine's Card."

"I didn't mean any offence, Seb" Alice replied dryly, "That's what he called you though."

"That's what who called me, Alice?"

"John"

"Gutheridge? Don't start that, Alice."

"Yes, John Gutheridge." There was a pause, *should I, shouldn't I*.

"He called me what?"

"He called you what was in the card." Sebastian starred at her. "He called you, Seb, the Lamb of God."

"Why on earth, Alice, would he do that? You're making this up."

"Why should I make it up. He thought he was John the Baptist and remember the clipping, remember what John the Baptist said, 'Behold the Lamb of God that taketh away the sins of the world.'"

"You're making it up Alice," Sebastian repeated.

"Why should I make it up, Seb?"

"Because that's the kind of person you are." The two of them stared at each other and then almost simultaneously picked up their coffee cups and took a sip. Delicately Alice put her cup down on her saucer.

"I've seen you before Seb."

"You've been to my house, Alice."

"No, I don't mean then, I mean last year, in Jerusalem. Our pilgrimage went in the middle of January for six weeks. John was ok when we arrived, well he seemed ok but the place got to him, like it did to you, Seb, but a little more. I kept an eye on him but I think he had stopped his Lithium or whatever he was on. He started to go grandiose. He started to think he was John the Baptist, but of course you know that."

"When did you see me Alice?"

"I suppose it must have been some time in February, a couple of days after John absconded from our group. We were staying in a hotel close to the Jaffa Gate just outside the Old City. One evening I nipped into the Old Jaffa Gate to a small shop to buy some tonic water. When I came out of the shop I saw John reading from his Bible next to the Citadel of David. Nobody was paying him a blind bit of notice. I watched for a while trying to work out what the best thing I could do for him, try and get him to come back to the hotel, I don't know if that was an option because the other pilgrims were pleased to be rid of him. Perhaps try and get him deported." Alice paused and took another sip of coffee

"Go on, Alice."

"Well then you came along with some older bloke. I suppose he was your father, Seb."

"Maybe."

"Well the two of you had a quick chat and your dad, because it was your dad, he went and walked one side of the Jaffa Gate whilst you went to listen to John. To me it looked like you had gone hunting for psychosis and now of course, now I know what you do, I know that I was right. Anyway I saw you become agitated. It was a strange moment, as you became more agitated, John appeared to relax. I couldn't hear what you were saying or anything but I saw you pull out a paper and show something in the paper to John. You chatted on for a while and then suddenly you just turned and marched out of the gate. You were so pre-occupied you forgot about your dad who had to run after you. That's when I saw you, Seb. So now maybe you might start believing me." Again there was a silence in the office, broken only by the ticking of the second hand of a clock above Sebastian's head.

"Ok Alice, maybe you should return to your duties now." Alice looked shocked.

"But don't you want to hear the rest, Seb, now that Laura isn't around to interfere. Don't you want to find out what happened to John after you left."

Sebastian stood up and walked towards the windows. The sun was high in the sky surrounded by a clear blue sky – it was a perfect spring day. He turned and perched himself against the window and said,

"Go on then Alice, tell me."

Alice drained the dregs of her coffee cup. and went around the desk and sat in Sebastian's chair, swivelling it to face him.

"This is what happened, then Seb. When you went out of the gate he shouted something after you like save yourself, I couldn't really hear for the noise. Then he slumped down and sat there almost like he was meditating. It was strange to see him so peaceful when he was so unwell. I decided to go up to him and when I reached him I knelt next to him. He seemed to stare right through me. I asked him if he was ok but he didn't answer. So I asked him who you were and he answered that you were a Sebastian Carrington from London, but he knew better."

"What did he mean by that?"

"We'll hang on, I'll get to that. He said you had shown him an article on Joshua Fisher III the leader of the Caring Christians Cult planning the Apocalypse for December. Somehow his mind made a link with you showing him the article and your interest in what he had been reading to you, Revelations 11 wasn't it Sebastian?"

"Just go on Alice."

"Well I had also told him about Fisher from a brief article I had read a couple of days earlier, in fact the day he absconded. I was really worried because he believed Fisher to be the Anti-Christ. At the Jaffa Gate just after you left he told me that when he absconded he bought a magazine with a profile on Fisher in a big colour supplement. He said that he had seen Fisher in Jerusalem near the Mount of Olives."

"But Alice what he did mean, ' he knew better'?"

"He thought you had brought him a message. The fact that you cared about Revelations 11 and showed him the article with its picture of Fisher. He thought you gave him a sign."

"A sign. That's ridiculous. What do you mean Alice, what do you mean?" Seb whilst trying to stay calm was becoming more and more agitated.

"You confirmed for him Seb that he had to kill the Anti-Christ. Destroy it. When he said to me that's Sebastian Carrington from London but I know better, I also asked what he meant. He answered;

'Behold the Lamb of God which taketh away the sin of the World.'

For him you were God's messenger and for his psychosis you were Christ."

"Never, that can't be Alice."

"It's the truth, Seb. Had you not had that little interaction Jonathon Mautner may still be happy at home with his wife and darling children. Bit silly of you really, wasn't it?"

"You're making it up, Alice."

"I can't make that up, Seb and you know it. It happened."

"But what about you?"

"What about me?" Alice replied swivelling her chair towards the desk and refilling her cup with lukewarm coffee.

"What did you say to him, at the Jaffa Gate, about Fisher?" Alice swivelled her chair back round and placing her coffee cup to her lip sweetly answered,

"You better go and do what your messenger wants you to do." Alice took a sip.

"You said what?"

"You heard me, Seb."

"What the fuck did you say that for?" Alice shrugged her shoulders. "Mautner's dead because of that."

"No, Seb, Mautner's dead because you went fucking around Jerusalem trying to find nutters, that's why Mautner's dead. You'll have that all your life now, Seb. Talk to us about behaviour and fucking attitude." Seb gasped for breath as Alice rose from her seat.

"Anyway I better get back, things to do. I'm a busy girl," and she headed for the door. But as she reached it she heard,

"Alice, I haven't finished yet."

"Maybe I have," she replied, her hand on the door knob

"Alice, I said I haven't finished. Come back and take your seat." Alice turned around and was surprised to see Sebastian composed and back in his seat. She smiled, raised her eyebrows and headed back for her original chair.

"Well," she said flattening her skirt, "What else?" Sebastian tapped his fingers onto the desk.

"How come you were on the Mount of Olives at 2am being strangled by him?"

"I arranged it at the Jaffa Gate."

"How did you arrange it?"

"I said I would meet him 24 hours after Fisher was dead. When he said he had seen Fisher I didn't know if it was the real Fisher or not. To him whoever it was it would be the real Fisher and after your little message, Seb, well somebody was going to cop it pretty quick. Mind you I didn't expect him to chop of his head and the tear and all that, very symbolic. So Seb, it was simple. I just said I would see him 24 hours after at a point at Gethsemane that we both knew close to the Church of the Agony."

"But you knew he would get killed. Its only two hundred yards from Dominus Flevit, he was bound to get killed. And you, you knew he would attack you. I saw him that afternoon, he talked of half killing Satan. He must have thought of you as the other half."

"Yeah I got that a bit wrong. I knew they would kill him, but since he had decapitated Mautner he had really lost it, he came for me quicker than I thought."

"You set the whole thing up."

"That's right Seb, the whole thing." Strangely for a moment Seb found himself admiring the woman opposite but quickly realised where such admiration might lead.

"What about Israeli Intelligence. What did they say?"

"Oh, come now, Seb. I was the victim remember and it's easy when you've got the old Bishop on your side vouching your integrity. Very plausible."

He picked up Alice's file and looked at her CV.

"This man you worked with in export for ten years, what happened? Why did you leave?"

"Let's put it this way Seb, he had a little accident."

"He died?"

"Unfortunately, yes."

"Were you in a relationship with him?"

"That's a little personal isn't it, Seb?"

"Come on Alice."

"Yes I was."

"And your dad, the Priest of St John the Baptist, he died last year." He paused and added, "Were you in a relationship with him too?"

Alice looked away from Seb and out of the window.

"How perceptive of you Mr Carrington," she shrugged.

"And John Gutheridge, how did you lure him to the Church of the Agony?"

"With an offer of what he likes best Sebastian."

"I thought as much, Alice. What now?"

"Now that would be telling, but I'll think I'll hang around for a little while longer. You can't touch me at the moment Seb because your story would sound ridiculous. So don't try firing me, otherwise you've got a very loseable and embarrassing court case."

Alice got up from her chair.

"Back to my duties then," she nodded at Seb and left the office.

Sebastian sat in his chair, fingers on lips and contemplated whether Alice was going to kill him.

Chapter 15
Sunday 20th February, 2000

9.15am: Sebastian Carrington sat on the terrace in his small garden with his wife Laura. It was unusually warm, almost strangely warm, and they had decided to have breakfast outside. Their son Jack was playing "Donkey Kong" on his Nintendo 64 in the front door and their three month old daughter Martha was fast asleep upstairs. Seb picked up a piece of toast, chewed on it and looked out at the garden that his brother in law had landscaped a couple of years before.

"You're quiet." Laura broke the silence.

"I know, sorry. I was just thinking."

"What were you thinking about?"

Sebastian picked up his coffee and took a sip.

"It was a year ago we went to Israel. Well, just over. It's the twentieth today, we went on the 18th. Strange looking at those flowers," and he pointed to a bed of crocus. "This time last year there was only one up. The whole bed's up this year. It must be warmer." Laura looked at the colourful flowerbed.

"Seb, something's troubling you. I can tell."

"It's nothing. Just something to do with work and like you know I try not to bring it home."

"But Seb you are bringing it home. You've become really quiet in the evening. You're so absorbed in your thoughts that Jack has to ask you a question three times before you answer him. I have to ask you three times, Seb."

"I know, I'm sorry."

"Well look, come on, talk to me. What's going on?"

"Really, it doesn't matter, Laura. I'll sort it out."

"This isn't fair, Seb, this isn't fair." Seb turned and looked at his wife. He stared at her for a good five seconds, took a deep breath and said,

"Ok, I'll tell you," then he turned his gaze away from her and looked down to the bottom of the garden. "You know when we got back from your parents after Christmas, and that woman was waiting for me?"

"I could hardly forget, Seb."

"Remember I told you when she left she said to me I'll be seeing rather a lot of you or something like that."

"Yes, I remember. What about it?" Laura was starting to sound anxious.

"When I returned to work on January 4th, after the holidays, we had a number of new employees start." Sebastian paused and looked back at Laura, then added, "She was one of them."

"She was on of them!" Laura exclaimed, "How could that be?"

"We've employed her as a support worker. She responded to an ad in the *Guardian* in October. She's well qualified. Masters in Criminology, a distinction in a thesis on the Psychology of Sexually Abused Children. She runs a Sunday School in Hemel Hempstead, has done since her teens. She even had a fucking reference from a Bishop – you see it's all very plausible, Laura."

"What's that suppose to mean?"

"Exactly what I said, all very plausible."

"Well that's fine isn't it? You know you've recruited the right person if it's plausible."

Seb turned to look back down the garden.

"Not really," he answered.

"Why not?" Laura asked.

"Because, Laura, darling, she's a psychopath."

There was silence between them.

"How can she be a psychopath, you know with all that credibility".

"Lots of reasons, abuse, accidents I don't know. All I know is she's a psychopath and she's killed people."

"She's killed people? Seb, what are you saying?"

"She killed Gutheridge."

"Seb, the Israeli Intelligence killed Gutheridge." Seb didn't answer.

"Seb, the Israeli Intelligence killed Gutheridge." Laura repeated.

"Well that's how it kind of looks. But she set it up."

"How did she set it up?"

"Look, Laura, I can't tell you now. It was very clever, real clever. But I will tell you when I've sorted it out, when I can get it right in my own mind."

"If that's what you want, Seb. Who else did she kill?"

"Some exporter that she worked for ten years ago. I don't know what happened but they were in some sort of relationship. I don't know if it was abusive, but anyway something happened and she did away with him."

"Are you sure?"

"Pretty much. She kind of told me, though it was seen by those investigating as an accident."

"That's terrible."

"It gets worse, Laura, she also killed her father." Laura looked blankly at him. "He was a priest in Hemel Hempstead where she runs the Sunday School. The church is called St John the Baptist."

"Why did she do that?" Seb appeared to be staring into space, focused on nothing.

"Because, Laura," his head appeared to briefly wobble from side to side as if he was drunk and his eyes looked dazed, "because he was fucking her. He had been since she was a kid, for years. So in the end she killed him and now it would seem she has a taste for it."

"What are you going to do?"

"I don't know, Laura, I don't know," he sighed. "She sent me a Valentine's card."

"A Valentine's card?"

"Yes, a Valentine's card."

"Why didn't you tell me?"

"I don't know, Laura," he repeated.

"What did it say?"

"It said:
The Lamb of God that taketh away the sins of the world.
Happy Valentines
Love A

Or something like that. There was a clipping in it of a picture of a lamb by some obscure 17th century Spanish painter – I can't remember his name. The lamb was bound. According to the text it represented the meekness and purity of Christ. I don't think it meant that to her, though."

"What do you think it meant to her?"

"The bound lamb. I think it meant vulnerability, bondage, things she's had to endure."

"But why did she send it to you, Seb?"

"She said Gutheridge perceived me as the Lamb of God."

"How could that be?"

"When I showed him the profile of Joshua Fisher III, Gutheridge's Anti Christ. She said I gave him a message to kill Fisher."

"Oh Seb that's absurd. You don't believe her do you?" Seb didn't answer. "How does she know you spoke to Gutheridge?"

"She saw us the day at the Jaffa Gate. When I had left she spoke to him. Gutheridge had spoken to her about me being the Lamb of God stuff. You know what she did then? She told him to carry out God's work. And that's how Mautner died." Seb rubbed his eyes and took a deep breath. After a moment Laura took hold of his hand and leant towards him.

"Seb listen to me. She's playing games with you. You realise that don't you?"

"I don't know, maybe she is, maybe she isn't."

"Seb, she is. She is playing games. Games that she can't help. You need to go to the police." Seb thought back to the day when he had left the Essene, John the Baptist at the Jaffa Gate, when himself and Derek couldn't go to the authorities because it all sounded so fantastic.

"I can't got to the police. They'll think I'm mad. I need to sort it out myself."

"But Seb you can't. How can you possibly do that? Think of me for God's sake and Jack and Martha. You've got to go to the police."

"I can't do that. She's too plausible. She'll destroy me, don't you see?"

"No, Seb, I don't see. Are you saying she's going to kill you?"

"No, I'm not saying that."

"How can you be so sure?"

"Because, Laura, it's simple. I never slept with her."

"I'm sorry, Seb, but that doesn't convince me. What do you mean that she'll destroy you?"

"Exactly that. She isn't going to kill, but she knows if I go to the police then that's it. I can't prove anything and my reputation...." He never finished the sentence.

From the kitchen door their conversation was interrupted.

"Dad, dad, phone for you." Seb got up from his chair, rubbing Laura's shoulder as he passer her. Quickly she grabbed his hand and squeezed it, though she never looked up at him.

"Who is it, Jack?" Seb asked his son.

"I don't know, work I think."

Seb walked through the kitchen to the front room and picked up the handset.

"Sebastian Carrington."

"Sebastian," came the reply, "It's Simone. We've got a problem."

"Hi Simone, what is it?"

"It's on Bradshaw Unit. The patients last night, they all went berserk."

"What do you mean went berserk?"

"Exactly that, Seb. They were all as high as kites, hallucinating all over the place, paranoid as hell. We've had to use all 6 seclusion rooms because of the levels of violence."

"What's it all about, Simone?"

"I think you should come down here, Seb. I really think you should come down."

"I'm on my way." Seb went back out to the garden.

"There's a problem at the hospital. I've got to do down there."

"Oh Seb it's the weekend. Let them sort it out."

"I can't. I'll be back shortly," and with that he turned and went back into the house.

At 10 'o' clock he met up with Simone in his office.

"All right, Simone, what's happening?"

"Well, the night shift reports that when they came on everything was ok. Handover was nothing out of the usual. Than about ten they all seemed to becoming more and more aroused, more paranoid, threatening towards staff. None of them would take any medication. They refused to go to bed. There was a big concern about a riot and a hostage taking so the staff sought support from the other units and the police. The police came in full riot gear. Things weren't really settled until 4am."

"Christ, Simone, why wasn't I called earlier?"

"I'm sorry Seb, the Night Co-ordinator seems to have panicked and forgotten procedure."

"Who the hell was it?"

"Paul Wilcox."

"Right, well that needs sorting out Simone. I'm really fucked off with that sort of thing. If he can't do the fucking job get rid of him."

"Ok Seb, I'll start the investigation first thing tomorrow."

"So what caused it?"

"Well, Seb, we've been screening the patients urine this morning"

"And"

"They've all tested positive."

"Positive to what?" Simone took a deep breath.

"Cocaine, Amphetamine and PCP. Some had cKatybis but that's not unlike what we would have expected." Sebastian stared at Simone, disbelief registering across his face.

"Are you saying, Simone that the whole fucking unit was high on Coke, Amphetamines and Angel Dust. Angel Dust! How the hell can this be."

"I'm not sure Seb but I've got a few ideas. Only 25% of the patient group on the unit have histories of using class 'A' drugs. Over half at the moment don't have any drug history. That means,"

"That means, Simone, " interrupted Seb, "that somebody's done a spiking job."

"Precisely."

"Where? How?"

"Again I'm not sure, but it could have been through the water vendors, the tea or coffee machine, put in the evening sandwiches." Sebastian buried his face in his hands; *she'll destroy me.*

"My view is also, Seb, that because of the quantity and where it probably will be found that it can't have been a patient or a visitor. It must have been a member of staff."

Sebastian looked up at her.

"Who was on duty, yesterday afternoon, the p.m. shift?" Simone opened her filofax and pulled out a scruffy piece of paper.

"Pauline Jones was in charge, then there was Robin, Maguba, Joan and Darren as staff nurses and James, Alice and George as support workers"

"Alice Hunt, Simone."

"Yes, Alice Hunt."

Seb got up from his seat and walked to the door.

"There may be media on this, Simone. Alert the units, ensure the policy is followed. If they want any comment they come to me and me only. Ok, I've got my mobile keep in touch."

"Where are you going now Seb?" Sebastian turned at the door and looking at Simone, answered simply.

"Sunday School."

Sebastian received the first phone call as he drove down the slip road of the M25. It was a reporter from a local newspaper called Jennet Whittington.

"Mr Carrington I'm led to understand that a significant amount of illicit drugs was made available to a large number of patients during the course of yesterday which resulted in riot police having to access your hospital," she opened up with.

"Just a second Jennet who did you say you work for?"

"The Southgate Herald," she answered.

"Ok. Jennet and what are you looking for?"

"Well that's quite clear Mr Carrington. I'm investigating an allegation that a significant amount of illicit drugs was made available to a large number of patients at your hospital yesterday which meant the police had to be called," Jennet repeated.

"Who made the allegation?"

"Come on, Mr Carrington, you can't expect me to reveal my sources, though a police spokesman has said that some of their guys were called to your place at 11pm last night."

"Ok Jennet this is what I'm going to say. There was an incident within the hospital last night that required us to ask the police for support. This is not necessarily unusual. It is normal procedure for hospitals such as ours, that is secure hospitals, to request assistance to pre-empt possible adverse situations and maintain the safety of our patients who we have a duty of care to. So what I'm saying is that the hospital followed a written policy to seek the support of the police in line with expectation of the services we provide."

"And were their drugs involved?"

"Jennet, our own investigation into what happened last night has only just begun. You can't expect me to be specific until I'm clear of the facts."

"So why were they called?"

"They were called in line with policy to ensure the safety and wellbeing of our patients who we have a duty of care to."

"Ok, Mr Carrington. I'll be in touch."

"Ok Jennett, talk to you again."

Seb broke the line but within seconds it was ringing again. This time it was a cable news channel prepared to go off the record concerning the drug issues but Seb maintained the line he had taken with the Southgate Herald. Eventually they informed him they were sending a crew up to Grenton.

"Well I'm afraid it won't be very exciting for you. If you want to give up prime time to show your viewers a picture of a medium secure unit that's up to you. There's no story here."

Seb hung up and then searched through the phone book item. He called up the Company's Managing Director who was satisfied with Seb to carry on with the line he had taken but to get in touch with the PR people to prepare a press statement and put some spin on the story. Immediately he rang through to the hospital where Simone answered the phone.

"How's things, Simone?"

"Christ, Seb, there's journalists calling from all over the place. What the hell's happened?"

"Don't worry about it Simone, just put them through to me. Have you got yesterday's reports?"

"Yep, they're in front of me."

"Ok, how many visitors to the unit yesterday?"

"Let me see," she paused, "three Seb, only three."

"Anyone of interest, drug dealing sibling anything like that?"

"No Seb, nothing here I'm afraid."

"Ok, Simone I'm going to get onto our PR people and I'll phone you with a number shortly. You need to deflect any more media attention towards them from that point."

"Ok Seb, I'll talk to you soon."

"Simone, keep a cool head."

"Will do, bye."

Again Sebastian Carrington hung up. Then he pulled into the lay by and brought the car to a halt. Again he searched his phone book item and soon found what he was looking for.

He dialled the number of the Agency and was greeted to 'Firstline Media PR' by an answer phone that gave the number of the on call PR consultant, Caroline James. Having written it down he dialled it and on the third ring a voice cracked down the line.

"Caroline James. Can I help you?"

"Caroline, hi my name's Sebastian Carrington. I'm the General Manager at Grenton."

"One of the PGH group?" She replied.

"Yeah, that's right, Caroline. We've got a slight problem and it's attracting bundles of media attention."

"Ok tell me about it."

"Last night our patients were doped with Amphetamine, Cocaine and PCP and we had a near riot. The police had to be called in."

"What's PCP?"

"Angel Dust."

"Christ, I thought that went out with the Hippies."

"So did I but we're both wrong. Anyway everybody's got hold of this it seems."

"What Angel Dust or the story?" she quipped. "Sorry, Sebastian, I'm sure you don't want to hear comments like that now. Big leak, wonder why?"

"I don't know."

"Ok Sebastian, what's your view?"

"I think it's a member of staff."

"Oh shit, that's not very helpful."

"No I know, but I think there's another option."

"What's that?"

"Visitors."

"Ok were their visitors yesterday?"

"A few but unlikely to have been any of them."

"So?"

"Well I think the line we take is that there were plenty of visitors and of course it is illegal for us to body search visitors, only their bags, you see."

"Yes I see. It would have been easy for someone to have carried that quantity of powder in on there body."

"Exactly and as you probably know, Caroline we have some very colourful characters up here. My fear is people breaking in not out."

"Ok I like that visitor angle and I think what we also do is talk about how well managed this attack, because that's what it is essentially an attack, how well managed it was."

"Yeah that's it."

"You'll need to talk to the Health Authorities tomorrow, Sebastian. You'll have to reassure them. Not good for brand or product at the end of the day, is it?"

"No it's not, but you know, this is survivable."

"Course it is. It's not like you've removed the wrong kidney or taken somebody's tubes out."

"No." Seb answered.

"Tell me Sebastian, what about the member of staff?"

"I don't know. No idea really. There were a lot of people on duty, conscientious people. But there's also cleaners, porters, maintenance people, caterers."

"Yes I see what you mean. Could be the person who leaked also did the deed. Pretty likely I should think."

"Maybe. We'll have our own investigation. See what it throws up. Anyway Caroline thanks, can I get the hospital to divert through to you now?"

"Sure, Seb. What's your number in case we need to talk?" Seb gave Caroline James his mobile number, phoned Simone at the hospital, then restarted the engine and headed west.

At 11am on the outskirts of Hemel Hempstead he stopped outside a newsagent. Inside he bought a copy of the Independent on Sunday and an A to Z fold out map of Hemel Hempstead and St Albans. He tossed the paper into the back seat and unfolded the map. When it was completely open he turned it round and looked for the list of local amenities. Having located the list he went down it with his index finger: Leisure Centres, Hospitals, Cinemas and Theatres, Churches. Then in the same way he went down the list of Churches: St Paul's, All Saint's, St Andrew's, St Mary's, The Parish Church of St Peter and St Paul, *St John the Baptist;*

    St John the Baptist
    Glebe Street
    Hemel Hempstead
    Reference: E4

Sebastian turned the map back round and located the grid reference E4. He found Glebe street with ease and then in the middle of the square he saw † and written next to it *St John the Baptist*. He put the map face up on the passenger's seat next to him and restarted the engine.

Ten minutes later he entered Glebe Street from its southern end. Slowly he drove up the quiet road. The housing was modern, no more than twenty years old, suggested affluence and was ugly, though the aesthetics of the street were improved significantly by the line of birches that guarded the pavements on each side. About half way up, to Sebastian's right there was a break in the trees and he saw for the first time a modern, circular one-storey building. From its roof a twenty-foot wooden cross had been erected.

Sebastian pulled the car up, turned off the engine and held the steering wheel. He felt sweat in his hands, on his forehead and around his eyes. He opened the door, swung himself out and walked towards what he thought was a monstrosity of a building. At the front of the church was a large blue sign that read;

The Parish Church of St John the Baptist
Glebe Street, Hemel Hempstead

Sunday Services: Mass   9.00 am
                    Holy Communion   11am
                    Evensong   6.00pm

Presided by Reverend Paul Hunt

"These are the two olive trees and the two candlesticks standing before the God of the Earth." Revelation 11

Sebastian stared at the sign.

They haven't changed the sign. The Reverent Hunt is dead, killed by his daughter for fucking her when she was a child. These are the olive trees and the two candlesticks standing before the God of the

Earth. What was the line before? What did John Gutheridge say at the Jaffa Gate? What did the Essene, John, say at the Jaffa Gate:

Sebastian found himself talking out loud,
   "*And I will give power unto my two witnesses, and they shall prophesy a thousand two hundred and three score days, clothed in sackcloth. These are the two Olive trees, and the two candlesticks standing before the God of the Earth.*
That's why Gutheridge was reading Revelation 11.

Seb pulled himself away from the sign. The sun was high in the sky and caused a shadow from the cross on the roof to dissect the Church car park and into Glebe Street itself. Slowly he walked towards the Church entrance and opened the door to the foyer. For a Church so new it smelt so old; the decay of hymnbooks mingled with the reek of incense. Slowly he opened the second door went through and stood at the back.

The congregation was receiving communion, the Priest offering them the sacrament of body and blood. Seb watched them a little awkwardly as they shuffled up to the Alter to receive a rip of wafer and a sip of wine. Seb looked around the Church. It was well lit from the sky lights in the roof. The chairs for the communicants were set out in a crescent shape fanned around the Alter and Pulpit. To the left of the Alter was a door. On it was a sign that said 'Access to Official Personnel only'. To the right, in symmetrically the same place, was another door on which was another sign that read 'Sunday School'. Gradually Sebastian followed the curve of the Church to the door to the right. He ignored the quizzical looks he was getting from some of the congregation and went quietly through the door which its sign that said 'Sunday School'. Immediately he found himself in a small hall. At the far end was a stage with a piano on it and around the periphery of the hall were uncomfortable looking gray chairs ready to be called into action for a play or a musical or whatever else took place in this Church. Sat on the stage were perhaps twenty children arranged in a fan like the chairs around the Alter in the main Church. In the middle, on one of the uncomfortable gray chairs, sat the psychopath, Alice Hunt.

Alice looked up from the book and smiled at Sebastian over her horned rim glasses and tweed jacket and skirt.

"Hello, Mr Carrington" her voice echoed in the hall.

"I've been expecting you. Isn't that so children? I said we were going to have a special visitor today, didn't I children?"

"Yes Miss Hunt," the children cried out in unison.

"And isn't that smashing. Here he is. This is Sebastian Carrington, somebody I work with and like me children he went to where Jesus lived last year and today he's come to tell us all about it. Now say hello children."

The children turned towards Sebastian and cried out, "Hello Mr Carrington."

"That's right, children. Now Mr Carrington would you care to come and join us on the stage." Seb felt his mouth going dry under the gaze of the children and found himself rooted to where he stood.

"Mr Carrington, could you please come and join us on stage, the children are waiting."

"I'm sorry," he spluttered, "I'll be there in a second." Slowly he turned towards the stage, walked up the three wooden steps at the front and walked around the fan of children. When he reached Alice Hunt's side, she put down her book at the place she had reached and said,

"I'll go and sit on the piano stool. You can sit here," and with that vacated the gray chair and took up position next to the piano. Sebastian sat down and without thinking picked up the book and closed it. The book was called 'The life of John the Baptist'. Seb smiled to himself and put it back down on the wooden boards of the stage.

"When you're ready then, Mr Carrington." Sebastian cleared his throat and looked at the children.

"Well Alice is right. I went to what we called the Holy Land last year. It was a very interesting place. I visited where Jesus was born, can anybody tell me where that is?" Immediately twenty hands went into the air and the hall echoed to the sound of "me, me, me." Sebastian pointed at a boy in a gray sweater at the back.

"Bethlehem."

"That's right Bethlehem. Well done."

"Tell him what happened to all the children in Bethlehem, Seb, you know what Herod did," interrupted Alice.

"Please, please tell us, tell us," echoed around the hall.

"Well," Sebastian swallowed, "you see there was this very nasty king and he though that Jesus would replace him as king so at the time Jesus was born he had," he paused.

"Had what, Mr Carrington?" Sebastian took a deep breath.

" He had all the children killed." The fan of children stared at him quietly. One of the younger girls in the front row started to cry.

"He's frightening me."

"I'm sorry. I didn't mean to."

Alice got up from the piano and took the crying girl into her arms.

"Really, Seb," she said quietly, "You didn't have to put it like that. I've never heard the slaughter described so insensitively to children."

Alice returned to the piano.

"Carry on Mr Carrington," Sebastian composed himself,

"Well we also visited Jerusalem where Jesus was..." Sebastian stopped himself.

"Where Jesus was what?" asked Alice. Sebastian looked at her and struggled.

"Don't you know?" the boy in the gray sweater, "Crucified, that's what happened at Jerusalem. Jesus was crucified."

The door at the back of the hall opened and a man in a dark suit came through.

"Ready, Alice."

"Ok, thanks, John. Well Children the service is over so you need to go and join your mums and dads. We'll see if Mr Carrington can come back next week." As one the children got up, dashed down the stairs of the stage and exited into the main church to be reunited with their parents

Seb sat silently on his chair staring after them, even after the door was closed. Then he turned to Alice and asked,

"Alice, did you dope up my patients last night?"

Alice laughed.

"Who, moi? Would I do a thing like that?"

"Yes, Alice you would. In fact I don't even know why I asked the question."

"Channel 4 thinks it will make a good story Sebastian, you know drug induced riot at a secure hospital. I expect they'll be getting in touch soon. You're going to look pretty silly."

"I'm going to the police, Alice."

"On what account?"

"That you doped the patients."

"That'll make an even better story. Staff induces riot. Bit like the old nurse who did the babies, isn't it?"

"No, not really Alice,"

"What was that called, what that nurse had, remind me?"

"You know full well, Alice."

"Oh Sebastian, you're such a sad character. I don't know how Laura, Jack and Martha put up with you." She paused. "Maybe they shouldn't have to."

"Oh Alice, are you threatening me?"

"No," she replied getting up from the piano stool, "I'm not threatening you Seb." Slowly she walked over to him and stood in front of him. "Why should I?" Then in what seemed one movement she pulled up her tartan tweed skirt, revealing to Seb her shaved pubic area and the tattoo of the Bishop's Mitre with the word 'Cock' emblazoned over it.

"Fancy some of that, Seb?" she starred down at him. Seb looked up and caught her gaze.

"Like I said Alice. I'm going to the police." Alice dropped her skirt, laughed and began walking around the stage.

"Oh, Seb, when are you going to learn. What the hell are the police going to say? You can't prove anything. They'll think you, the creditable General Manager of some poxy hospital, has gone bonkers. I say Seb there's a thought, maybe you already have. Maybe you have gone bonkers." Sebastian starred into space as Alice returned to her piano stool.

"Well, let's face it, Seb, this has been fun but maybe enough is enough. I'm going to let you off the hook." Seb turned to he.

"What do you mean?" He was barely audible.

"Well you strike me as ok, Seb. Not like that creep Gutheridge or that pervert father of mine or the exporter. I don't need to destroy you when I know I can already. This thing with the drugs, it'll blow over. I think that's enough."

"What do you mean?" Sebastian repeated.

Next to your chair on the left is my bag. Pick it up." Sebastian picked up the bag.

"Now feel inside for an envelope and take it out." Again Seb did as he was instructed and pulled out a plain white envelope. It was addressed to Sebastian Carrington at Grenton Hospital.

"I was going to post it tomorrow, but I thought you would be along and there's not time like the present. Go on open it." Sebastian ripped open the envelope. Inside was a white sheet of paper and a pink one.

On the white one Sebastian read:

Dear Mr Carrington

*It is with deep regret that I have to resign my post as support worker at the hospital. This is for personnel reasons and no reflection on the hospital itself which clearly is an institution that practices to an exceptional standard. As I have not been employed for the full thirteen week probationary period I am only required to work one weeks notice. However sadly I am also **unwell** at the moment and so I am happy to forfeit that weeks salary. I would like to thank you and your staff for the experience.*

God Bless
Alice Hunt

The letter on pink said:

Dear Seb

Well you never quite turned out to be the Lamb of God. I can't say how sad I am to be losing your acquaintance but from your point of view it is for the best. Things may happen from time to time. I would invite you to follow them, but from a distance. St Albans isn't all that he makes out.

Well done for not fucking me. That could have been fatal.

Love
Alice

Seb folded the letters and put them back in the envelope.

"Is that it then?" he said to Alice

"I suppose so, Seb. Unless you don't want it to be."

Seb got up from his chair and walked to the end of the hall.

"Sebastian," Alice called after him. "Goodbye, Sebastian Carrington, goodbye." She smiled sweetly at him.

"Goodbye, Alice Hunt," and with that he opened the door back into the Church and was gone.

Chapter 16
Stowton

"Dad, hi, it's Seb."

"Hello Seb, I've been reading about your Angel Dust."

"Who hasn't. It's a nightmare. I've got Health Authorities wanting to sue, relatives, patients, the whole lot."

"Hmm, a bit of a mess then," Derek went on.

"Yes it is, but the lawyers don't seem bothered. They view it as sabotage so I'll just let them get on with it. Anyway how are you and mum?"

"We're ok. We had some sad news though today."

"Oh dad, I am sorry. What was that?"

"You remember, Jan, from the pilgrimage?"

"Of course I remember her. She had her credit card stolen at Mary's tomb and she had to go to the police with Robin on the coach when they left us at Gallicantu."

"Well, Seb I'm sorry to say she died yesterday."

"She died?" There was a brief silence. "How did she die?"

"We're not sure, she was just found dead at home. She has a cleaner who goes in on a Monday. Found her in bed, couldn't raise her. It looks like she just passed away in her sleep. There's going to be a post mortem."

"But she wasn't very old."

"I suppose she was in her sixties."

"Gosh, that's terrible I am sorry."

"Well these things happen, Seb. Anyway what can I do for you?"

"We were wondering if we could come up this weekend. I'm desperate to get out of London. There seems to be press everywhere I turn."

"I don't see why not. I'll get Mary to have a word."

Sebastian heard Derek calling for Mary and then the words, 'wanting to come up'. There was a cackle as Mary took the handset,

"Hello Seb, sweetheart. Dad says your wanting to come up."

"If that's all right. Don't want to be a bother."

"Of course it's alright. When will you come, Friday?"

"Probably, we'll see how things go. It was terrible about Jan."

"Yes terrible. Mind you, she was a stupid woman." Seb was taken aback by the comment.

"That's hardly the point, mum."

"Didn't she have her credit card stolen when you were away with dad?"

"Yes, she did. It was a shame."

"Ok, then Seb, keep your head down, you're not very photogenic. See you at the weekend."

Sebastian hung up and turned to Laura.

"Do you remember me telling you about Jan on the pilgrimage, the one who had her credit card stolen and who washed her hair at the Church of the Holy Sepulchre, you know, where Christ was crucified?"

"Yes of course I remember."

"She died, Laura."

"That's terrible. How?" Laura echoed Sebastian's reaction.

"She was found in her bed by her cleaner. She wasn't very old. I suppose it happens from time to time."

"What did they say about the weekend?"

"That's fine. No problem. Why don't we try to hitch up with Paul and Rebecca on Saturday night for my birthday? Mum will look after the kids."

"Ok, give Paul a ring. See if he can book anything."

The post mortem for Jan showed that she had taken a massive amount of arsenic and the case was referred to the Coroners Court with an expected verdict of death by misadventure, which essentially meant that the state believed Jan had killed herself.

"That doesn't make sense," Sebastian Carrington said to his wife Laura when Derek had informed him, "She wasn't a depressive."

"How do you know?" Laura responded

"How do I know what?" Sebastian snapped back

"How do you know she wasn't a depressive? Lots of people kill themselves. Lonely, ageing woman. Maybe she had had enough, Seb."

"But what about her faith?"

"Seb, listen to yourself, get real."

"There was no note."

"There doesn't have to be. Who would she leave a note to?"

"I don't know, the Church, perhaps."

"Don't be absurd, Seb. People don't leave suicide notes to the Church."

"No I suppose not. It's just been a strange few days. I just can't see it. She wasn't a depressive," he repeated.

Seb went to the fridge in the kitchen and poured himself a 1664, then returned to the lounge and sat down with Laura.

"Did you get hold of Paul?" she asked.

"Yeah. He's booked us into some up market Italian somewhere between Stowton and Birmingham.

"What time for?"

"Nine on Saturday night."

"Is your mum ok about the kids?"

"She's fine." Laura snuggled up to Seb.

"That's good," she said, "you can have a nice relaxing birthday."

After Laura picked up Seb from work the drive to Stowton took hours, the Friday night traffic out of London being predictably appalling. It was almost eight 'o' clock, with Jack and Martha fast asleep, when they drove past the sign welcoming them to Stowton, the historic Minster town. Slowly the car weaved through the narrow medieval streets of the town which, over time, had been converted into an elaborate one way system to deal with the industrialisation and technology of the modern world. At the Minster itself Seb pulled over. Floodlit, it looked spectacular with the North Porch, Transept and the octagonal Chapter House radiant in the artificial light.

"Amazing," Seb was speaking to himself. "How come this beauty is here in the middle of nowhere?"

Laura and Sebastian sat in silence and admired the Norman Cathedral.

"How did they build these things?" Laura eventually asked herself.

"It's the power of the Church, Laura," Sebastian found himself answering. "This is the symbol of God's rule. It must have scared the shit out of them. It still does with some people. You just don't mess with it." He started the engine of the car. Five minutes later they arrived at Derek and Mary's, a modest semi detached on the outskirts of this quaint English town. Both children woke up, Jack particularly excited to see his doting grandparents, Martha oblivious but as always hungry. Eventually the two children settled and the rest of the evening passed uneventfully. Nobody mentioned Jan and her dramatic use of poison that she used to help her leave this world and the power of the church behind.

Seb was last to arrive at the breakfast table. The events of the last week had left him shattered and he had slept for ten hours. He still felt tired.

"Happy Birthday," Laura greeted him and Jack handed over a card and an attractively wrapped gift. Quickly he ripped the paper off. It was a golf game for Jack's Nintendo.

"That's great Jack, love it," he leant over and gave a kiss to Jack and then another to Laura.

"You ask for the weirdest things."

"No, love, this is perfect. You just don't understand."

"Well I'm glad I don't," she smiled and squeezed his hand. Derek then handed him a card.

"From me and your mum. A little something inside."

"Thanks Dad," replied Seb knowing what the little something was, "It always helps."

Mary came into the room clutching the morning's post.

"Happy Birthday, Seb," and she gave him a kiss on the cheek before turning to Derek to give him the small bundle of letters.

"What are you doing today then?" Mary asked

"I thought I'd give Laura a good look round the town, a little tour, have a bit of lunch at the Saracen's Head. Then tonight remember we're going out with Paul and Rebecca for a meal. You said you would baby sit the kids."

"That's fine. Sounds like you're planning an awful lot of eating today," Mary answered.

"Seb there's a card for you here," Derek interrupted. Seb turned and looked at him blankly.

"Are you sure?" He eventually asked.

"Of course I'm sure. Sebastian Carrington c/o 17 Barrowell Gardens, Stowton, Warwickshire." Derek handed him the pink envelope. It was franked as a special edition from Warwick Castle. Seb examined the envelope and immediately recognised the capital

'C' of Carrington to be the same as the capital 'C' of Criminology on the application form of Alice Hunt that was filed at Grenton Hospital. Sebastian looked at Laura uneasily and shook his head.

"It's from Alice."

"It can't be," Laura replied. "How would she know you're here? How would she know you're coming here?"

"I don't know?" he answered, still shaking his head.

"And who may I ask is Alice?" Mary asked.

"It's an employee of Seb's," Laura answered.

"Ex-employee," Seb corrected her.

"Ex-employee. She's kind of been stalking him."

"What do you mean stalking?"

"You know, sends him cards, letters, follows him around."

"Have you told the police?"

"No, not yet," Seb answered.

"Why not?" asked Mary.

"Because I thought it was sorted."

"Open the card, Seb. See what she has to say." Seb's hand trembled as he took a knife from the table and ran it along the top of the envelope. On the front of the home-made card was a large picture of a hollow tear. Inside the tear was Christ crucified on the cross. Underneath the tear were the words Happy Birthday. Seb opened the card. As with the Valentine's card a newspaper clipping fell onto the dining room table. On the inside cover of the card was written;

"We philosophers and free spirits feel as if a new dawn were shining on us when we receive the tidings that old God is dead. Our heart overflows with gratitude, amazement, anticipation, expectation. At last the horizon appears free again to us, even granted that it is not bright. At last, our ships may venture out again, venture out to face any danger. All the daring of the lover of knowledge is permitted again. The sea, our sea, has opened again, perhaps there has never been such an open sea."

Nietzsche.

Sebastian's gaze wondered to the other side of the card which read;

231

"The problem for people like me, dearest Sebastian, is that we just can't let things lie. I'll be waiting for you later in my ship. Don't make me come and find you, 'Birthday Boy'.
Love A"

"Well what does it say?" Mary asked.

"Nothing much," answered Seb quickly picking up the paper clipping and returning it and the card to its envelope, "Just Happy Birthday". Laura looked at Seb knowingly.

Upstairs in their bedroom Sebastian Carrington showed Laura his birthday card from the psychopath, Alice Hunt. Whilst she read it Sebastian opened the clipping. The heading said:

Stowton Woman's Death Thought to be Suicide

The death of Stowton woman, Jan Wheelan, is now thought to be suicide as opposed to natural causes. Tuesday's Post Mortem revealed lethal quantities of arsenic in Ms Wheelan's blood stream.

Ms Wheelan, 55, of 35 Johnson Drive, was a regular worshipper at the Minster where she also acted as a volunteer at particularly busy periods of the Church calendar. Those close to Ms Wheelan are deeply confused and distressed by her death. The Bishop of Stowton, the Right Reverend Alec Dunwoody informed the Independent, that Ms Wheelen 'was a charming woman, a keen and supportive member of the Cathedral. Last year she had participated in a trip to the Holy Land under my leadership and was a deeply valued member of the party. All at the Minster are deeply shocked by her untimely death'. When asked whether in the eyes of the Church the alleged death of Jan Wheelan by her own hand constituted a sin the Bishop answered, "We are all sinners."

Ms Wheelan lived on her own with no known surviving relatives. The case has been referred to the Coroner's Court in Warwick.

"What does all this mean, Seb, 'I'll be waiting for you later in my ship'?"

"I don't know, Laura. Its like you said in the garden last Sunday, she's playing games."

"I thought you said all this was finished with last week?"

"I did. I thought it was. How stupid of me. People like Alice don't end things like that. She's toying with me."

"Look, Seb this is getting really frightening. I think she's going to hurt you. Maybe she's going to hurt us?" Sebastian was quiet. Slowly he sat down on the bed.

"I didn't think she would hurt you or the kids It's men she loathes. I didn't think she would harm me either but now I'm not so sure. The point is that what she does is meaningless so its impossible to predict. She is unpredictable, predictably unpredictable almost. Though of course not quite." Laura sat down next to him, "and what makes it worse," he continued, "is that she's here."

"Here? What do you mean here?"

"Here, Laura. She's here in Stowton."

"How do you know?' Seb handed the clipping to Laura. Laura read it slowly.

"Why has she sent you this?"

"Look at the bottom of the clipping. It's obviously the right hand column of a page. Can you see what it says at the bottom?" Laura looked at the bottom of the clipping and read:

23 FEBRUARY 2000 STOWTON INDEPENDENT 3

"It's the local paper. She must have brought it here. And the postmark on the envelope, pretty isn't it. It's Warwick Castle. So, Laura, she's here." Sebastian allowed himself to fall back on the bed.

"You never answered my question, Seb. Why did she send the clipping to you?"

"Well I suppose it's some kind of trophy." He sat back up again. "She's telling me that she killed Jan. Not suicide or natural causes. Simply good old murder. So that means I'm wrong. She kills women as well."

"Ok well, Seb that's it. We've got to go to the police."

"What and tell them a Sunday School Teacher from Hemel Hempstead killed some sad aging spinster. The first thing they'll say is what's the motive. So what is the motive, Laura?" Laura didn't answer.

"Come on Laura, tell me, what's the motive?"

"I don't know Seb. Why don't you tell me?"

"Ok I will. The motive is to fuck with my brains. That will sound good at the police station won't it? Would sir care to tell me why Mrs Sunday School poisoned Mrs Religious spinster? Well actually officer it's perfectly clear, it's to fuck with my brains. Obvious!"

"All right Seb, that's enough! It's no good getting angry with each other." Sebastian put his head in his hands.

"I'm sorry, Laura. Maybe you're right. I'll go and see our solicitors on Monday. See what they think."

"I think you're right Seb. I think she is fucking with your mind. Go and see Sarah. She'll be able to give you her view and she'll be able to articulate it." She paused "Mind you, she'll probably think your off your head but you can cross that bridge when it happens."

Seb looked up at his wife and they both laughed.

For the rest of the morning the Carringtons walked around the old Minster Town. It was busy with tourists coming to see the Archbishop's Palace, the old cobbled Medieval streets and the Minster itself before boarding their coaches for an afternoon visit to Warwick and its famous castle. Jack however was most interested in the eighteenth century workhouse that was being renovated on the edge of town. The stories from the guide of the poverty and anguish of the past appealed to his sense of security in the present. At one 'o' clock they stopped and had lunch at the Saracen's Head, a pub where in the past various royalty and other aristocrats had taken refuge when life in the capital became a little heated. It was busy and their order of sandwiches and chips took almost an hour to arrive by which time Sebastian had drunk two pints of local beer and was feeling decidedly less anxious about his unusual birthday card. When they eventually left the Saracen's Head the weather had changed. Large dark clouds threatened rain.

"We'll go back via the Minster. I want Jack to see it". The walk to the workhouse that morning had not taken them past the Cathedral.

"Ok, you take Jack. I'm going back with Martha now. She needs to go down properly for an hour or two."

"Fine we'll be back in an hour or so." Seb and Jack crossed the road as the first spots of rain hit the ground. "Come on Jack quick, otherwise we'll get soaked." They took the second turning on the left and the Minster, hidden by the narrowness of the old town's streets, was immediately upon them.

"What do you think of that, Jack?"

"It's ok. Not as good as St Paul's," he answered as they ran through God's Acre to the entrance at the North Porch. Inside it was quiet, surprisingly empty and the two of them, father and son, walked with purpose up the Nave towards the Transept.

"Look at that, Dad," and Jack pointed to the arched roof above the Transept. There a magnificent ceramic Christ on the Cross ejaculated out across the Nave, nails bashed through his hands and feet and blood pouring down his face from the crown of thorns he wore on his head. A green cloth covered his genitals. He looked at the point of death - *the moment of true redemption.*

"How does it stay up?" asked Jack

"I don't know. It's very clever."

"He seems to be watching us, Dad"

"I think he's meant to be."

"He looks so sad." They walked on past the Transept Alter where most services took place through the choir screen and into the choir itself, carved magnificently to celebrate the glory of God in the highest. To their left was a number of chapels dedicated to the saints of Stowton; St Thomas, St Oswald, St Paul and St John and a cloister that led through to the octagonal Chapter House that seated the influential clergy of the Diocese. In front of them was the High Alter, the holiest of holy sites within the Minster.

Seb and Jack went into the Cloister. On display was a line of fourteen sculptures that depicted each of the stations of the Via Dolorosa. Each station up until the crucifixion was higher than the next so that standing behind the first of Christ's progress you viewed all the way up to Calvary. Then the step formation reversed and the final three sections of Christ being cut down and entombed reduced in height. Jack looked at each of the sculptures but lingered longest at the crucifixion.

"You saw where this happened, didn't you, dad?"

"I'm not sure Jack."

"But I thought you went to see it?"

"I may have seen it Jack, I can't be sure."

"Don't you believe then dad?" Sebastian was taken aback by the question.

"I believe there was a man called Jesus who may have been important. I'm not sure that he did what the Bible says he did." Sebastian, feeling both uncomfortable and guilty, chose his words carefully and thought of the Sunday School in Hemel Hempstead.

"Come on, let's get back to see Derek and Mary."

"Ok," Jack replied, "Let's get back." He was keen to see his grandparents.

Outside, the rain had stopped but the clouds were still dark and travelling swiftly from west to east. At the bottom of the path that took them back to the road Seb and his son, Jack, looked once more at the Minster.

"Do you want to come with Daddy and Granddad to the service tomorrow, Jack?"

"No, I'll stay with Granny," he answered authoritatively. " It looks like a boat, doesn't it, Dad?"

"What did you say?" Sebastian looked at his son.

"The Church. It looks like a boat."

Seb looked at the silhouette of the Cathedral against the bleak background of the day. The Transept towered high in the sky, with the Nave on one side and the Choir the other.

"How does it look like a boat, Jack?"

"There, where the choir sing, that's the front. It juts out like the front of a boat. Then in the middle where it goes high into the sky, it's like a funnel and the clouds look like smoke coming out of it. And then the rest at the back, it's long and narrow just like a boat would be."

Seb hunched down on his legs and put his arm around his son. With his finger he traced the outline of the silhouette and realised the shape he was making was indeed the shape of a boat.

"A ship," he whispered under his breath. *I'll be waiting for you later in my ship. Don't make me come and find you birthday boy.*

"A ship!" he repeated.

"That's right, dad," Jack said. "A great big ship."

"Come with me Jack." Seb took the boy's hand and walked over to the nearby board that showed the times of the services. At the bottom it read.

"The Minster will be locked at 6.30 every evening and unlocked at 8.00 every morning."

Back at the house Seb excused himself that he was tired and went up to the bedroom. Out of his briefcase he took some notepaper and a black pen. On the first sheet of paper he wrote;

In the event of my Death.
This is the last will and testimony of
Sebastian Carrington
of Winsmoor Hill, North London
d.o.b 26.02.1965
In the event of my death everything I own goes to my wife Laura Carrington.

He put the will into an envelope and wrote on the front "The Last Will and Testimony of Sebastian Carrington – 26.02.1965", and put it into his briefcase.

Then he took out an A4 pad and after a quick thought he started to write. He wrote of Joshua Fisher and the Caring Christians, their disciple, Andrew, killed on Temple Mount, the headless Jonathon Mautner, a psychotic called John Gutheridge and the psychopath, Alice Hunt. He wrote of the Priest Paul Hunt, who sexually abused his daughter, and the death of an exporter and finally he wrote of Jan Wheelan and who had killed her. By the time he had finished it was growing dark. Again he folded what he had written and put it in a larger brown envelope and wrote on it: *"The reason why I've written my wil.l"*

At six o' clock he went downstairs into the front room and put on his coat that was hanging up on a coat peg in the hallway. Then he went through Derek's coat until he came across his bunch of keys which he quickly concealed in his own pocket.

"Gosh, I didn't realise I had slept so long," he said as he went into the front room. "It must have been the beer at the Saracen's Head. You should have woken me Laura." Laura smiled up at him.

"Why have you got your coat on Seb?" she asked

"I thought I would wake myself up with some fresh air before we meet Paul and Rebecca. Clear my head."

"Want any company Seb?" Derek inquired.

"No, I don't think so. I won't be long."

"Ok, son."

"Keep to your word, Seb. We need to get the kids down as well as get ready."

"I will, darling," and he walked over to her and gave her a kiss. Patting Jack on the head he went through into the kitchen, took a carving knife out of the cutlery drawer and went out the back door.

He went into the garage, and after a quick search found the durable torch that had been sat in various Carrington garages for years. He tested it and it flicked instantly into life, its strong beam piercing the darkness of the night outside of the garage. Then Sebastian Carrington made the fifteen-minute walk to Stowton Minster.

It was nearly 6.30 when he arrived. He stood in the car park and watched the North Porch until the last of the visitors had cleared out and one of the Vergers had locked up for the night. Sebastian was bothered by the floodlighting. He took out the bunch of keys and eliminated them one by one, quickly identifying Derek's front and back door key and also his car key. Only two keys remained. One was a Yale key, the second a much larger heavy, iron one that looked like it had been designed to open a Norman Cathedral. In his pocket he held onto these two keys. Quickly he crossed the road from the car park and strolled up the path that he and Jack had run up earlier in the afternoon towards the North Porch. There he inserted the large key into one of two locks, turned it and immediately felt the mechanism spring open. Then he took the Yale key, inserted it into its lock and pushed the door open. Without hesitating he passed through and shut the door behind him.

The Cathedral was lighter than Sebastian had anticipated from the floodlights filtering through the stain glass of the windows. However the light was inconsistent provoking flickering shadows and pockets of deep blackness. Seb took out the torch and switched it on. Slowly he moved into the middle of the Nave. Once there he turned up the central isle towards the Transept and its Alter where the Minster's regular services took place. Despite the fact he was wearing trainers his steps echoed unsympathetically throughout the mighty Cathedral.

About half way up the Nave he made out the back of a shadowy figure sitting on the first chair of the front row. He focused his torch on the figure, dressed in black and wearing a trilby hat. The figure grew, like Masada had, with each step but never moved or flinched. When he stood along side the figure and with the Alter magnificent in the beam of the torch, he said,

"Hello, Alice." There was no answer from the figure next to him. "What's the matter Alice. Not like you to have nothing to say, cat got your tongue? Didn't you think I would work it out?" He turned slowly towards the figure and shone his torch directly into the face of the figure. Sebastian caught his breath.

"Oh my God," he whispered. "This can't be," and he found himself staring at the side of Robin, the tour organiser's, cyanosed head.

"Robin, Robin, are you ok?" His blue lips seemed to be extended, almost pouting. There was no response from the motionless man.

"Robin," Seb snapped "What is it?" Again there was no answer. Sebastian stretched out his index finger and lightly touched the side of Robin's head. Immediately he pulled it back, shocked by the coldness of its skin. The jerk however was all the momentum that was needed for Robin's head to start to slide, slowly at first, off his shoulders, bounce of the next chair in the row and land face up on the stone slabs of the Cathedral floor. The body, headless, sat still, looking at the Alter. Shaking, Sebastian shone the beam into the face of the tour organiser. Under his right eye a tear had been painted in black ash. Seb recoiled and dropped the torch, the front of which smashed on the stone surface plunging the Cathedral into its eerie light produced by the floodlighting and the stain glass windows. Still moving backwards, Sebastian tripped on the row of chairs opposite and fell crashing into the gap between the kneelers and the row itself. He turned over on his face and vomited, vaguely conscious of a light going on above him. When he had finished retching he turned again and looked into the face of the ceramic Christ crucified high into the ceiling and spotted, which he hadn't earlier in the day, a tear of blood, a different shade to the blood produced by the Crown of Thorns, meandering down the face of the dying Christ. And then Christ was blocked out by the face of Alice Hunt, smiling a welcoming smile and saying,

"Hello Sebastian, thanks for coming. I knew you wouldn't let me down, Birthday Boy," and with that she produced a syringe and lunged it into his left thigh. "It's all about speed, Seb."

"Jesus Christ, Alice what are..." but before Sebastian Carrington could finish his sentence he was asleep.

When he came round he still felt nauseous and his vision was blurred. His legs had been tied – trussed to his arms. Though his body felt well supported only the bottom half of his head was. He lay still and waited, feeling the coldness of the February evening as he no longer wore his coat.

Shortly, from his right he heard footsteps. The footsteps grew louder and louder. It was the sound of heels that echoed menacingly and bounced round the walls of the Cathedral, getting louder and louder all the time. So when Alice Hunt peered down into Sebastian's face, he was rigid with terror.

"Like I said, Seb, thanks for coming." Sebastian tried to swallow.

"Why did you do that to Robin? What's he done?"

"Nothing, Seb. Don't get so upset about it. Tell me how are you with heights?" Carrington didn't answer. "Someone at your poxy hospital told me you weren't too good with them. Apparently your phobias are heights and dentists, Sebastian. Let me show you something." She bent down and literally rolled Sebastian over on to his front. Sebastian looked ahead of him and saw the side view of the ceramic enamel crucified Christ, blood tear and nails.

"I think he looks better from up here. Don't you agree?" Seb looked down and far below he could make out the headless torso of Robin still sat erect at the Altar. It was at this point that Sebastian Carrington simultaneously lost control of bladder and bowels.

"You really don't like heights do you, Seb. You really don't!" She mocked him.

"For goodness sake Alice, stop this."

"Stop this. Stop this. Well I suppose I am being a little cruel," and she took hold of Carrington's legs and arms and pulled him further onto the stone gallery that ran along both sides of the Cathedral. "Now calm yourself down, Seb. Stop shitting yourself. What would your employees think?" Alice sat down with her back to the wall so that she faced Sebastian.

"Don't you find this exciting, Sebastian. Tell me why did you have that knife in your coat?" Sebastian didn't answer. "Oh well doesn't really matter. I stuck it in Robin's head and put it on the High Alter up the top there. I wonder how Mary's going to explain that one, you know, Seb, her best Sunday carver stuck in poor Robin's head. That should help communion tomorrow." She quietly laughed to herself.

"How did you know? About Stowton, all of this."

"Easy Seb. Loving Dove Christian Tours told me everything. I organised our next tour through them, got to know them well and it didn't take much for them to, now how would you say it, completely breach confidentiality. That's how I found out about you and your tour and where you came from."

"But why Robin?"

"Why not Robin. Unlucky really A case of being in the wrong place at the wrong time as much as anything."

"He's got a wife!"

"Wrong, Seb, he had a wife. He had a wife! She's now a widow and probably better off for it."

"Why did you chop his head off?"

"I like chopping heads off people. Poor John, he should have had his head chopped off just like the Baptist. I chopped the exporter's head off. Truth be known I've chopped off lots of heads. Question is, do I chop yours off and if I decide to, should I kill you first?"

"Christ, Alice."

"Shut up, Sebastian," Alice interrupted. " Look at you all trussed up like the Lamb of God, Seb. Just like my valentines. Are you suffering, Sebastian? Are you suffering. John would be upset with you. You've turned out to be a bit of a false prophet haven't you, just like the others."

"I never claimed to be any prophet. This is madness, Alice."

"Madness is it, Seb? I don't think so. The problem for you, Seb, your problem is that nobody understands me. Me, Seb. Nobody can understand me and nobody can define me. You know why that is? I'll tell you why, Seb. What sets me apart from crap like you is that I have unmasked Christian Morality."

"I don't understand what you mean, Alice."

"You see, you don't understand."

"Understand what?"

"Understand me. Understand who I am."

"Well who are you then, Alice?" She giggled to herself again.

"Why Sebastian, I'm him," and she pointed over his trussed up body to Christ crucified.

"You're Christ!" Seb exclaimed. "Stop messing me around Alice will you. You sound as mad as Gutheridge or Fisher. But you're not mad, Alice are you? You know exactly what you're doing. You know exactly what you're saying." Alice slowly started clapping.

"Well done, Seb, very clever. Very clever indeed. You really are a bit more with it than the others."

"Look, Alice, perhaps I can help you. I know a lot of people."

Alice stopped clapping.

"Oh no, Seb, big mistake. And you were doing so well. Seb, you've forgotten something. Remember, I don't like offers from men. It brings out the worst in me. You should know that."

"Alice, not all men are your father. I'm not your father. You got him, isn't that enough?" Alice starred at him.

"Seb, you're boring me. Tell me, what do you think will happen tomorrow when they find Robin's head?" Again there was silence as Alice casually looked around the Cathedral.

"Who cut off Mautner's head, Alice?"

"Who do you think did, Seb?"

"You."

"Maybe, maybe not. You'll never know. Seb, who cut off Jonathon's head up there on the good old Mount? Me or Gutheridge? It doesn't really matter, does it? But let's face it, didn't it strike you odd that old John boy was running around with a Polaroid. Can you really imagine him putting the head on the bench, putting a little ash tear on it and then taking its picture? For fuck sake, Seb, he was all over the shop at the time." Seb stared at her. "Anyway I've had enough. It's time for us to part company." Alice pushed herself up and took hold of the rope that bound Seb's arms and legs.

"Alice, for Christ sake. Please," he pleaded as his bowels opened for a second time.

"I'm sorry, Seb. For a man you're ok. But I can't let you go. Can't you see that? I simple can't. I'm sure if you think about it you'll see my point of view." Slowly she started to drag Sebastian Carrington towards the edge of the gallery.

"Alice," his eyes bulged and a tear fell from his eye and rolled down his cheek just like the blood tear of Christ at the moment of redemption.

"Alice, please don't kill me. I don't want to die."

"I'm sorry my little Lamb of God. Pass over quietly, sweetheart. I don't…"

In the space of a second, if not less, blood spurted from the hole in Alice Hunt's head onto the face of Sebastian Carrington, followed by the sound of the crack of a gun firing its load. Through the crimson shower Sebastian saw Alice's expression change to one of surprise. Briefly she gazed at him and smiled.

"Well done, Seb. You win. Sweet Lamb of God." Her knees trembling, she let go of the rope, lurched forward and fell over the edge of the gallery. Sebastian heard the heavy thump of her landing and immediately wondered why she didn't take him with her and instinctively knew that she could have. Her last action was to let him live. The psychopath Alice Hunt was redeemed through her death.

"Sebastian, Sebastian!" It was the voice of his father, Derek.

"Its ok we're coming, stay still. We're coming," and this time it was his wife, Laura's voice that bounced around the walls of the thousand year old building.

Sebastian lay trussed up like the Lamb of God and felt the blood of Alice Hunt roll over his lips and up his nostrils. Again instinctively, he licked the blood with his tongue and tasted it. When Laura and Derek arrived at his side he still couldn't work out what it tasted of. Laura cut at the rope with a knife. His wrists and ankles were bruised and he found it difficult to get to his feet. Laura and Derek helped him up and he noticed Derek's gun by his side.

"Where the hell did you get that from?"

"National Service. I've had it for thirty years."

"And it worked."

"Luckily for you it would seem it did".

"You shot her, dad. You shot her!"

"I didn't have much choice. I had to shoot her. She was going to kill you." Derek looked at his son and asked. " Whose is the torso down there?" Sebastian took a breath.

"Robin," Sebastian answered.

"Oh no. Robin. Are you sure?"

"Alice put his head on the High Altar. God what am I saying," and he put his head into Derek's chest and started to cry "Dad, I've messed myself. I'm filthy." Derek cuddled his son.

"That doesn't matter because you're alive. Do you hear me, Seb? You're alive. Come on now, let's get down. We phoned the police before we came. They should be here any minute now." Laura put her arms around both of them. Sebastian turned to her. She smiled but there was nothing to say. The three of them started walking along the gallery, footsteps echoing and then down through the steep stairwell of the tower."

She must have carried me up here.

At the bottom of the stairs Sebastian asked, "How did you know where I was?"

"Jack," answered Laura. "He talked about how you both thought the Minster looked liked a ship after you left us today. I went upstairs to get the birthday card she sent you. *I'll be waiting for you later in my ship.* I saw the bed hadn't been slept in and that the briefcase was open. I found your will, Sebastian, and we read the reason why you made it. It had no legal standing. You never had it witnessed."

By now they had reached the body of Alice Hunt. She lay in a pool of blood and the back of her head was missing. Her mouth was open and her teeth were barred.

"Goodbye, Alice Hunt." Sebastian looked at her and admired her grotesque smile. Then he looked at Laura and Derek.

"Let's wait outside, in the fresh air."

Slowly they walked down the Nave of the Cathedral and out through the North Porch. The agnostic Sebastian Carrington took a deep breath, looked to the skies, and thanked God for his life.